The plane went down…and took their love with it.

All Brandon Barlow-Barrett wants is a week away from his family's newspaper empire, time on the slopes to relax and refocus. What he gets is Lucy Cameron, the most extraordinary woman he's ever met.

Lucy Cameron doesn't take vacations. Not until now. Her very first vacation is full of highs--falling in love with Brandon Barrett--and lows--realizing she has to tell him she earns her living as a stripper.

But there's no time to reveal her secret. On the way back from a day trip to a neighboring Colorado town, their plane's engine sputters and stops. All they have left is the dangerous peaks of the mountains, a nearby lake for a crash-landing, and Brandon's last-minute declaration of love.

Books by Laura Browning

Winning Heart

The Barlow-Barretts: An American Dynasty
Bittersweet, Book One
Balancing Act, Book Two
Remember Me, Book Three
Broken Heart, Book Four

Published by Kensington Publishing Corporation

Remember Me

The Barlow-Barretts: An American Dynasty, Book Three

Laura Browning

LYRICAL PRESS
Kensington Publishing Corp.
www.kensingtonbooks.com

Lyrical Press books are published by
Kensington Publishing Corp. 119 West 40th Street New York, NY 10018

All Kensington titles, imprints, and distributed lines are available at special quantity discounts for bulk purchases for sales promotion, premiums, fund-raising, and educational or institutional use.

Special book excerpts or customized printings can also be created to fit specific needs. For details, write or phone the office of the Kensington Special Sales Manager:
Kensington Publishing Corp.
119 West 40th Street
New York, NY 10018
Attn. Special Sales Department. Phone: 1-800-221-2647.

First Electronic Edition: January 2013
eISBN-13: 978-1-61650-437-3
eISBN-10: 1-61650-437-4

First Print Edition: January 2013
ISBN-13: 978-1-61650-848-7
ISBN-10: 1-61650-848-5

Printed in the United States of America

To the men in my life who keep me grounded and give me the space I need to work. Thanks guys!

Chapter 1

"I didn't dump the proposal on your desk and take off. Jesus, Dad," Brandon Barlow-Barrett growled into his Droid as he waited to check his luggage. His gaze wandered to the check-in line next to him while he continued to listen to his father's biting tones on the opposite end. "I'd like to remind you I've had this vacation scheduled for more than two months. On top of that, I gave you the proposal two weeks early, so you would have time *at your leisure* to go over it in its entirety."

A curtain of long, blond hair several people ahead in the row next to him caught his eye. The owner towered above the people surrounding her. His gaze traveled from the hair to the ass, outlined in a pair of snug, faded jeans, and he smiled in appreciation. Long, long legs ended in high-heeled cowboy boots that just added to the woman's already considerable height.

"I won't listen to your response right now. You've had the proposal on your desk for all of one hour, and it's three hundred pages. I don't want you to flip through it. I want you to read it. You aren't Congress, and this isn't health reform."

Brandon ground his teeth as his father continued to insist he'd already seen what he needed to.

"Dad! Times are changing. If we don't change with them, there will be no Barrett Newspapers to pass along to anyone." He reached the counter and slapped his suitcase in the space next to the ticket agent. "Look, gotta go. I'll be back in a week. We can talk about the proposal then—once you've had the chance to *read* it."

Brandon clipped the phone to his belt. He knew better than to allow Alexander Barlow-Barrett time to respond. He handed the suitcase to the airline agent, got his baggage claim receipt and his boarding pass, then glanced around in a casual way to see if he could locate "Legs" anywhere, but she was already gone. Damn. Flirting with her could have made for

an interesting flight. After locating his gate, he discovered the plane was
on time and already boarding. Great. If there was one thing he hated, it
was spending any more time than he had to aboard a commercial flight.
Even in first class, he found the seats didn't have the leg room he needed.
But, since stepping into his elder brother's role, he'd become a lot more
conservative with the company's cash, so no taking the private jet for
vacation.

A gate agent and a flight steward stood at the open door to the boarding
ramp. When he approached he caught the tail-end of their conversation.

"God, what I wouldn't give for one night with a woman like her."

"You got that right, dude. Can you imagine those legs wrapped around
you?"

"Shit, yeah!"

Brandon arched a brow. The two men grinned at him. After checking
his boarding pass, the steward's demeanor became deferential. "Thank
you for flying National, Mr. Barrett. Linda will be your flight attendant.
Just let her know what you need."

Brandon nodded. Laid would be nice. Sex hadn't happened in months,
but he doubted it was one of the choices on Linda's menu. It turned out
she was younger than his mother by only a few years, so he settled for a
shot of bourbon on the rocks.

* * * *

Lucy looked out the window, watching with interest the luggage being
loaded aboard the jet. It might have been mundane to most travelers, but
then she wasn't most travelers. In fact, this was the first flight she'd ever
been on. Little Lucy Cameron was getting a vacation at long last. For a
week, she would be able to leave behind Jasmine LeFleur, the name she
used as one of the top dancers at Flamingo Road. The high-end strip club
catered to well-heeled clients around the Washington, DC area. It also
paid extremely well.

Reflected in the glass next to her, her smile gleamed. She'd earned
enough dancing at the club to pay off her college loans—even the ones for
her masters—in less than five years. So traveling to Colorado to go skiing
was a treat she was giving herself. Sure, she would have to stick to the
easiest slopes since she didn't have experience, but her primary purpose
in flying there was to see the Rockies.

The baggage handlers had finished their task and were moving the
ramp away from the body of the jet. The engines picked up RPMs, and
Lucy looked around at her fellow passengers. Most of them looked
bored or were already plugged into laptops, iPods or whatever was their

technology drug of choice. No one seemed to share the excitement she experienced just being onboard. Okay, maybe she needed to dial down her enthusiasm a couple of notches so she wouldn't come off like an unsophisticated goofball.

Nevertheless, she paid close attention while the flight attendant went through all the pre-flight instructions about fastening seatbelts, getting emergency oxygen and using her seat cushion as a floatation device. Since they were going from DC to Denver, Lucy had serious doubts a floatation device would be necessary. At least she hoped not.

They roared down the runway, engines whining, and the pressure of take-off weighed on her. The whole time, she watched everything grow smaller and smaller on the ground below until it resembled the patchwork quilt at the foot of her bed, one of the few things she could say had belonged to her real family.

Once they landed in Denver, Lucy checked her schedule. She would be taking a commuter flight from there. The itinerary said it was a propjet, whatever that was. As she made her way to the correct gate, she began to suspect *propjet* was simply a synonym for *small*. Her musings about the plane ended when she reached the gate area and saw the other passengers, one in particular.

He stood out from the skiers and vacationers, his expensive suit making him look like he'd just stepped out of a boardroom, and had in all likelihood. Lucy glanced at him from the corner of her eye. In general, she avoided staring at men because they were usually staring at her. It made her uncomfortable—and wouldn't that make everyone laugh. Who'd ever heard of an exotic dancer who didn't want people watching her?

The man's gaze swung her way, so Lucy averted her eyes, studying the resort poster hanging on the wall to his left. Not very smooth, but the best she could come up with, short of spinning away from him. She'd gotten enough of a glimpse of his face to know he wasn't the type to have any trouble getting women to fall at his feet. Hazel eyes, more a combination of topaz and green, sun-streaked hair that glinted gold in the light, and a wide mouth with a full lower lip—yeah, he would make most girls' hearts throb.

"Flight 780 to Falcon's Head is now ready for boarding. Please use the door for gate 74A and follow the steps." The disembodied voice came through the public address system. This time there was no ramp. They exited the building straight onto the tarmac, then climbed the short flight of steps into the commuter plane. Propjet not only meant small—it didn't even mean a jet.

Lucy felt someone's gaze on her, so when she reached the top step and ducked through the door, she glanced over her shoulder. Mr. Boardroom was right behind her. He smiled. Lucy swallowed and turned away, almost bonking her head as she straightened. Wow! His smile was devastating. Forget other women falling at his feet, she was about to join them.

* * * *

Brandon kept his expression neutral when Legs, as he'd come to think of her, sat in the window seat next to him. The flight from Denver to Falcon's Head wasn't long, but he began to wish it was a little longer. He had every intention of leaving with Legs's name, phone and where she was staying, especially since her finger was bare of rings.

After securing his briefcase beneath his seat, he took off his suitcoat.

"Would you like me to hang your coat?" the young flight attendant asked.

"Thanks." Brandon settled his big frame into the cramped seat. There was no first class here. His long legs almost bumped the wall in front of him.

"You can angle your legs this way, if you'd like."

Brandon shifted at his seatmate's invitation, stretched and then allowed himself to meet Legs's gaze. *Beautiful* was all he could think, looking into a face with the most arresting dark gray eyes dominating it. Gazing into their depths was like staring into the ocean on a storm-tossed day.

"Thanks."

One corner of her mouth curved upward and a dimple appeared. "That seems to be a favorite word of yours."

Brandon blinked. Was she cracking on him? He held out his hand and grinned. "I have others. I'm Brandon Barrett."

When she slipped her hand in his, he sensed several things at once. First and foremost, he felt like he'd just received an electric shock. From the slight widening of her eyes, he guessed the feeling was mutual. The second thing that struck him was the strength of her grip. So many women shook hands like they were holding out a limp rag, but this woman's hands held power.

She smiled. Her hands weren't the only power she possessed. Her smile must have belonged to a model, but damned if he could place her anywhere—and he knew plenty of models, some in the biblical sense.

"I'm Lucy Cameron."

"Well, Lucy. Are you here to work or play?"

She chuckled. It was a rich, seductive sound that sent a shiver of pleasure along his spine. "I'm going to play." She eyed his attire. "Business?"

Now he grinned. "No. Vacation too. But I had a breakfast meeting and then had to race to make the flight out of Dulles." He wanted to keep her talking. "I noticed you in line there. Are you from DC?"

"I work there."

"Modeling?"

She shook her head with a smile, but didn't enlighten him. There were definite keep-out vibes coming off her now, increasing his curiosity, but he held it in and changed the subject.

"Have you been to Falcon's Head before?"

"No. In fact, this is the first time I've been to Colorado."

"Are you here for the skiing, or just sightseeing?"

"I'm going to ski, which is another thing I've never done. What about you?"

"Major vice, I'm afraid. Most of the time I ski back East because it's easier to get away for a weekend." No need to tell her he'd once been shortlisted for the Olympics, but maybe this could work to his advantage. "Have you set up lessons?"

She shook her head. "I figured I would handle instruction when I did the whole ski rental."

"I can walk you through it all. Even get you started, if you'd like."

She tucked a strand of her shiny golden hair behind her ear. It was straight, but not thin and wispy like so many blondes. "I don't know. I don't want to impose…"

Hell, maybe she was here with someone, or meeting someone. "No problem. No doubt you and your friends already have plans, and here I am trying to barge in on them."

"Oh, I'm not…" She faltered to a stop, before appearing to come to a decision. "I'm on my own."

"Then let me show you around, get you skiing."

Her smile showed gratitude, but still a little caution. "I can't imagine it would be much fun for you. You must be pretty good."

Yeah. He was, but if he could arrange to spend a day with her, he'd ski backward down the bunny slopes the entire time and grin like a kid in a candy store while he did it. However, looking at her, he didn't think it would take all day. She looked like an athlete.

"I am, but I'm also here on my own to relax. Look, I taught two of my younger siblings to ski. Up to you."

She smiled, glancing at him from the corner of those long-lashed gray peepers of hers. "I'd like that."

"Great." The tenor of the engines shifted. "We must be getting ready to descend." Brandon pulled out his phone. "What's your cell number?"

She blushed. It was just a faint rose tint to her golden skin. "I don't have a cell."

He couldn't keep the surprise from his face. Even if they didn't use it, he wasn't sure he knew anyone anymore who didn't at least carry a prepaid phone for emergencies. "No big deal. Sometimes I'd like to be a little less plugged in. Where are you staying?"

"At the lodge at Falcon Summit Resort."

He grinned. "Me too." He leaned across her a bit to peer out the window. "If you look, you'll be able to see some of the slopes from here."

He was rewarded when she laughed in that husky voice of hers. "Oh look, Brandon! It's like looking at a line of ants."

His laughter joined hers. "It is. Never thought of it that way. Tomorrow and Sunday will be even busier, but if we get out there early, we can get ahead of the crowds. Can you stand getting up at dawn on your vacation?" And, boy, wouldn't he love to see what she looked like when she woke up in the mornings.

"Sure. I'm an early riser most of the time."

Their conversation was interrupted by the captain coming over the speaker with details of their arrival and the weather forecast. Though it was late in the season, it sounded like conditions for the upcoming week would be ideal. Brandon glanced at Lucy's profile. Since she'd returned to looking out the window, her face was averted a bit. Damn, but it was almost like she'd never seen the world from this view. On first acquaintance, she appeared to be an odd mixture of sophistication and naivete. Whichever was real, it was damned intriguing.

* * * *

Lucy accepted the ride Brandon offered in his rental car. It would save her from squeezing into the resort's hospitality car—at least she kept telling herself that was the reason she'd accepted his offer. The truth was, she wasn't sure she'd ever met a man as handsome as him. If he was hitting on her, it was with a whole lot more class than the usual crowd of men who patronized Flamingo Road. And for the last couple years, those were the only men she had encountered.

When they reached the lodge, he turned to her before they got out. "Would you like to have dinner with me tonight?"

Lucy's natural caution reared up. Maybe the invitation was him looking for company, but she wanted to keep things casual as a precaution because of the way her body responded to him. She shook her head. "No. I don't think I'd be very good company tonight. Can we meet in the morning?"

He nodded. "Six thirty in the front lobby."

"I thought they didn't open 'til nine?"

"They don't, but I figured we could get some breakfast first, and I have an in with the owner." His grin was so disarming, all Lucy could do was nod.

"Let's get our bags in, and you can take it easy." When he cupped her elbow with his palm, Lucy discovered she liked the casual touch. It was a courtesy he didn't have to think about, he simply did it.

While she checked in, another clerk was helping him a few feet away. Lucy handled the registration and credit card information, overhearing the way the clerk said *Mr. Barrett*, as if he were a valued guest. He probably was. From years of counting on tips to help her make her living, Lucy had come to recognize the difference between off-the-rack clothing and clothing that was hand-tailored. There was nothing even resembling department store about anything touching Brandon's skin.

"Are you set?" He waited for her to get her bag on her shoulder. When she nodded, he took her free hand and held it for a moment. Once again, a shock of heat and awareness zinged through her at the touch of his hand. "Have a good evening, Lucy. I'll see you here. Six thirty. Be ready to ski, okay?"

"I will." He started to turn away, and she added, "Thanks for the invitation, Brandon."

His grin was lopsided. "We'll see if you still feel the same way tomorrow afternoon."

* * * *

At loose ends, Brandon called Matt Petersohn, Falcon Summit's owner, right after he'd settled in his suite.

"Hey, Matt."

"Bran!" His friend's voice was warm over the phone line. "They told me you'd checked in. Everything good, dude?"

"Perfect, as always. You free for dinner?"

"Yeah. Why don't I have it delivered to your suite around seven? We can chow down then sit and scratch while we talk about why you don't come out here to ski much."

Brandon laughed, agreed and hung up. At last, some of the tension from his work at Barrett Newspapers drained out of him. God only knew, he'd wanted to take over Seth's position, had been overjoyed when his elder brother had put his foot down and walked out the door. But in the last few months, he'd also come to realize how much of a buffer Seth had been between Alexander Barlow-Barrett and the rest of them.

Now Brandon was the one juggling his father's rigid personality against what he knew was the best interest of the company. The industry was changing at a pace far beyond what anyone could have predicted when Brandon had graduated from business school ten years ago. Seth had been quiet and dogged, but he'd been making changes during that whole time.

The problem was everything had to be ramped up big time if they were going to keep their flagship national daily a household fixture. And, damn it, he needed his father to realize the only way it would happen was without the smell of ink or the feel of newsprint. Those days were gone, but they could still compete. There was another market out there between fancy phones and e-readers, but they needed to tap into it now. The whole world was plugged in. It was time Barrett Newspapers lived the same way.

By the time Matt showed up at his door with a couple waiters pushing carts with covered trays trailing him, Brandon had showered and exchanged the suit for a pair of well-worn jeans and a thick Nationals sweatshirt. His feet were bare and he had a bourbon in his hand. He set the glass aside so he and Matt could do the back-slapping guy hug thing.

"Damn, Matt," Brandon said, eyeing his friend's thick black braid and close-cropped beard, "you're taking this mountain man thing to heart."

Matt flicked a finger at Brandon's conservative haircut. "You're the one to talk, Mr. Powerbroker. How's it feel to be heir to the throne?"

Brandon shook his head. "Some days, not a whole lot different than stepping into a pile of horse shit."

"Papa Barrett snarling again?"

"It's not the snarling. It's the rigid immobility." Brandon stared around him. "You've made changes here."

Matt laughed. "Had to. Too much competition from other places. We've added some glitz and enough luxury to make *Grossvater* Petersohn flip over in his grave, but the bookings are up—and not just during ski season. We've added guided hiking and fishing trips during the summer." Matt uncovered a couple plates and Brandon smelled the rich aromas of wine sauce and butter.

"Damn. Let's eat. I am freaking starved."

They were almost finished when Matt looked across the table with a grin. "So my concierge tells me you came in with a drop-dead-gorgeous blonde. Keeping her all to yourself?"

Brandon stiffened for a moment, then laughed. "Not sure yet. I met her on the plane. She's here on vacation. Turned me down flat for dinner tonight, but I'm hooked up with her to teach her how to ski."

"Good work."

"Can you get one of your guys to outfit us around seven thirty? I'll pay them extra."

"No problem. Scott's been looking for some OT. You sure you want to teach her yourself? I could have him give her an hour private lesson, then you could hold her hand down a couple of beginner slopes before you hit the expert runs."

Brandon leaned back in his chair, feeling full and mellow after the meal. "You know, in most circumstances I would take you up on your offer, but I have the feeling teaching Lucy Cameron to ski might be fun. She's built like an athlete."

"You going to teach her anything else?"

Brandon sipped his brandy and stared into the fire. "We're not at that point yet, but I will tell you, my cylinders start firing whenever I see her."

Matt laughed. "Well, she's safe from me, buddy. You know I have a hands-off policy on guests to begin with, but it's definitely hands off of any territory you're marking. We've been tight for too long to compete over a woman."

Brandon smiled. "'Preciate that, Matt."

"I'll say no sweat for now, but I reserve the right to change my response to an *aw shit* if she turns out to be worth the glazed look in the eyes of the front desk clerks."

Chapter 2

Lucy smoothed the thin, high-tech long underwear along her legs and over her hips. After shimmying into the top, she finished layering on the new clothing. She grinned at her reflection. Ski Bunny Lucy. She stared into the mirror in her room, and her smile faded. Somehow, she doubted a man like Brandon would be quite so interested if he knew her real title was Stripper Lucy. She stared at her hands, turning them over to examine them. It would be nice to be able to tell him she was an artist for a living, but so far her work in clay hadn't earned her any money. Taking off her clothes and dancing earned her living, and a damned good one. But not one she wanted to share with everyone.

Hell, who was she kidding? She didn't want to share it with *Brandon*. For a little while, she wanted to be able to live the fantasy she really was sophisticated and classy like him. It was just one week. What could it hurt? She would never see him again. Somehow, the thought made her throat tight.

When she saw him in the lobby, saw the welcoming smile lighting his face, she couldn't help but laugh and return it. "Good morning, I'm not late, am I?"

"No." He took her hand and tucked it through his arm. "Come on. We'll grab breakfast first, then we'll get you set with equipment." He ushered her into a small private dining room off the main one. There was a veritable feast on the table. "I didn't know what you might like, so I asked them to bring in a sampling of several items."

Lucy gaped. "I—I only have coffee and a bagel most mornings. Sometimes I splurge following a workout and have a latte." She put a hand to her throat. "I can't believe you did all this."

Brandon laughed. "Dig in. You'll be glad of the calories after I get you out on the ski slopes."

Once she buckled on the ski boots the first time, she decided this might be a whole lot harder than she had anticipated. Accustomed to being able to move fluidly, she felt like Frankenstein's little sister, and could only marvel at how natural Brandon was, even with the boots on. They practiced putting on and taking off the skis. He set their poles aside for the time being, explaining he wanted her to understand how to maneuver the skis first and learn to balance without depending on poles.

"We'll pick them up once we get you going on the intermediate slopes. For now, you can hold on to me." He grinned at her, his cheeks flushed from the cold. He was more patient than she had imagined. Lucy couldn't help thinking he could be doing so much more if she'd just had the courage to turn him down.

When she had graduated to the point where she was snowplowing her way downhill with him skiing backward in front of her but not touching her, she couldn't hold it in any longer.

"Brandon, it's obvious you're a very experienced skier. Why are you hanging here with me? You must be so bored."

He turned from picking up their poles, handing them to her. "Don't you worry about me, Lucy. I'm where I want to be, and I'm not at all bored." He turned so he was next to her. "Come on, baby, we're taking the lift this time."

Lucy had watched the chairs circling and the handful of early skiers hopping on and off the lifts as if it was no big deal. "I don't know…"

"You can handle it. You've got amazing balance. Remember when you exit the lift to keep your weight a little forward. I'll teach you the right moment so the lift gives you some momentum to ski away without any problem."

He was right. It turned out to be a lot less complicated than she'd thought it would be. Now, standing at the top of her first intermediate run, all Lucy could do was grin. She had pretty much figured to be on the bunny slopes the whole day. While she was sure this was nothing to a skier like Brandon, it was a big accomplishment for her, and one she wouldn't have achieved without his help. Going with the impulse, she leaned over and hugged him.

"Thanks, Brandon."

He looked surprised. "What for?"

"For getting me here in just a couple of hours. Skiing an intermediate trail was my goal for the week."

"Given the athlete you appear to be, I'll have you going down some of the easier advanced runs in a day or two. Now, let's practice using your poles before we head down. You'll find them more useful on these longer runs."

Lucy wasn't sure when she'd had such a good time or laughed so much. After landing on her butt the first time, she soon mastered controlling her speed and making the wide turns along the intermediate trails they explored. When Brandon suggested getting lunch, she agreed with reluctance.

"Trust me, baby, you'll be glad for some rest once your body gets around to telling you you've been engaged in something new to it." They put their skis in storage and headed to the lodge. Brandon took her hand in his. "I hope you don't mind, I asked the staff to have lunch ready for us in my suite."

Warning bells went off. Lucy pulled her hand from his. "I think you're making some assumptions…"

Brandon stopped her with a touch on her arm. "No. I'm not. It's a suite, Lucy, not a bedroom. We'll be eating in a dining area off a great room with its own fireplace. I think you'll understand why I made those arrangements when you step inside the main lodge."

She'd pissed him off. It was there in the hard set of his jaw, but she couldn't help it. Starting with puberty, she'd become a target. Boys and men had gone out of their way to take advantage of her, so she'd learned to be cautious. But Brandon was right about one thing. When she walked inside the lodge, she was greeted by a wall of sound almost as loud as a full crowd at Flamingo Road with the music pumping.

Brandon stopped her just inside the door. "So, which will it be? Lunch here or in my suite?"

"Your suite. And…I'm sorry."

He wrapped an arm around her shoulders. "Don't worry about it."

* * * *

They walked from the main lodge to a smaller building which housed Falcon Summit's luxury suites, and Brandon was beating himself up. *Don't worry about it.* The problem was she did need to worry. He would like nothing better than to strip off all those layers of clothing and get her on her back in his bed. He unlocked the door and opened it before allowing Lucy to precede him. From long habit, his gaze dropped to her bottom, outlined in the tight, figure-hugging material of her ski pants. *Oh yeah.* Being a gentleman was going to get harder and harder.

"Wow, Brandon." Lucy looked around her, eyes wide. "This is amazing. I thought I had a wonderful room, but this is unbelievable. The view of the mountains from your great room is incredible."

The view from where I am is incredible. "Like I said, I'm friends with the owner, so I get some perks." Which wasn't the complete truth. Matt made sure Brandon could get a suite anytime he wanted one, but Brandon paid fair market value for it too. He watched Lucy wander around the room, her fingers lingering over a sculpture on a side table and brushing over a copy of *National News*. He was reluctant for her to find out his connection to Barrett Newspapers. As wary as she was, he was afraid she might pull back completely.

"Oh, look, lunch is set here on the table right by the window." She turned to grin at him. "I am so starving. I guess it must be all the fresh air."

Brandon unzipped his jacket and tossed it aside. "No doubt. Let me have your jacket and we'll tuck in."

She slid out of the pink and gray coat to reveal a form-fitting turtleneck beneath it. Brandon's body temperature shot up several degrees. Lord help him, but she had an amazing body. When she handed him the jacket, their fingers brushed, their eyes met and the heat level jacked up another notch.

"Lucy." Her name hung in the air. He saw her swallow and blink before she took a step back. Brandon sighed. Whatever there was between them, she wasn't ready to let her guard down, which made him wonder why she was so cautious. Someone with her beauty and generosity shouldn't live life through a filter of mistrust. Brandon took a deep breath, smiled and gestured toward the table. "Let's eat."

Even as hungry as she was, she ate with delicacy and care. She avoided anything high fat, and limited the starches. Curiosity once again getting the better of him, he said, "You know, you don't seem like a person who needs to watch what they eat, yet you do. You say you don't model, but you eat like someone who does."

Lucy paused with a bite of salad on the way to her lips. "I just like being in good shape." A vague sense of disappointment filled him. She'd lied. There was more to it, but he didn't feel like he knew her well enough to pursue the truth. Hell, admit it. He didn't want to scare her off.

"Matt's invited me out on the resort's newest expert run this afternoon," Brandon told her as he finished his sandwich. "It's been a couple of years since we've been able to hit the slopes together."

Lucy sipped from a mug of tea and set it aside. "I was going to hit the pool. They've got lap swimming time this afternoon, and I need to get in a workout."

Brandon nodded, wondering again what made her such a fanatic about keeping physically fit. She sure didn't seem like one of those obsessed women on the verge of a serious eating disorder. "You swim every day?"

She shrugged, her gray eyes once again a little wary. "Swim or run. I—uh—I lift a couple of times a week too."

"Sounds almost like the training schedule Matt and I had to adhere to while we were on the ski team in college." He hoped the comment might get her talking about why she spent so much time working out.

"You competed?" she asked instead, turning the conversation around to him. Not what he'd wanted, but he couldn't very well ignore her question.

"Yes. Matt and I also competed outside of school. We were both shortlisted for the Olympics. I didn't make the cut. Matt did."

"So why isn't he still competing?" Lucy asked. "I've heard of plenty of skiers who compete into their thirties. Why would he stop?"

"Injury. I'm sure you've seen the video in the opening of some of those sports shows. It was a pretty nasty accident over in Switzerland. Matt was lucky. He had some great surgeons who were able to not only repair the damage to his leg and back, but even got him to the point where he could ski again."

"Just not to the point where he could be competitive, right?"

Brandon nodded. "The difference between being a great skier and being a world-class athlete isn't measured in much more than tenths of seconds. Matt tried to come back, but he was never able to break into the top ten in any of the World Cup competitions. He didn't even finish one season following his recovery before he decided to hang it up. His dad was ready to retire, so Matt came here and took over Falcon's Summit. He's made improvements and turned it into a first class resort."

He didn't add he had been a major investor in the resort, much to Alexander Barlow-Barrett's frowning disapproval. But the money had been his, from the trust fund that had come into his control when he'd turned twenty-five. And it had paid off. Matt had not only succeeded, he'd already paid back Brandon's investment with interest.

"Do you miss the competition?"

Brandon shook his head. "No. It was never that serious for me. I guess my family would tell you I'm the same about many things in my life. I enjoy sailing too, even competed in a couple of international races, but it wasn't my life. What about you? What do you enjoy?"

Lucy laughed. "I've sailed. I grew up along the Maryland shore. I worked a couple of summers at a resort where I taught people how to sail little skiffs. I've never been on anything big."

He caught her hand in his, the energy sizzling between them again. "Maybe I could take you out some time."

She slipped her hand from his, and smoothed her hair from her face. "Maybe."

"What else do you enjoy?"

"I'm a potter. I've got a small studio I work in from home."

"So is that what you do? You're an artist?" He could now understand the strength in her hands if she spent a good part of her day manipulating clay.

She shrugged. "It's a hobby, I guess. It's not like I've earned any real money from it. What about you? I know you ski. I know you wear suits and have breakfast meetings."

Brandon shifted. "I work for my father's company. We're in communications." It wasn't a lie. And unless she examined *National News* in great detail, she would never notice the *Barrett Newspapers, Inc.* at the bottom of the logo. He didn't get the feeling she'd tied the name Barrett to communications, but something sure as hell was bothering her. She'd set her napkin aside and pasted a cool, polite smile on her face.

"You must be busy. Look, I should get going. Thanks for the ski lesson and the lunch."

She stood and Brandon followed suit. "That sounds a whole lot like a goodbye."

She evaded his eyes. "You have plans. I have plans." She shrugged.

"Can I take you out to dinner tonight?" He saw her hesitation. "Friends, Lucy. I won't deny I'm attracted to you, but if you're not… I get that, okay? No pressure. Just two people on vacation trying to enjoy some time together."

"All right."

He grinned. "Put on some dancing shoes. There's a great dinner and dance club. Quiet. Plenty of jazz."

He held her jacket for her while she slipped it on. The flowery scent of her hair and skin teased his nostrils. His hands lingered for an instant while he fought the urge to lift her hair to the side so he could nuzzle her neck. He only hoped his ski pants would hide the hard-on he now had. So simple, yet the scent of her was enough to turn him on. She glanced over her shoulder at him with those expressive eyes of hers.

"What time?"

"Seven." Brandon couldn't resist. He stroked a finger along her cheek. "I'll see you this evening."

* * * *

Back and forth. Lucy hoped the repetition of her swimming workout would make her forget how much she wanted to touch Brandon, and how little she trusted those feelings. He worked in his father's business. It reminded her too much of all those years ago, of the one man who had broken through her wariness. Edward had been everything she'd thought she wanted. He had known right from the start what she was. In fact, he had seen her dancing. That was how they'd met, but he had been different from the other men. There hadn't been any catcalls or suggestive remarks. Instead, he'd shown up several nights in a row. After the fourth night, he had invited her out for a late dinner. From there, it had turned into flowers, dinner dates, picnics in the park. Eventually it led to bed. She'd given him her innocence, and he'd given her an education.

Lucy executed a perfect flip-turn and continued to swim, her stroke fluid and efficient. She had gone out for the swim team at her first high school. The early morning practices got her out of the house. She'd been good too. Then her foster father had tried to invite himself into her bed. There'd been no swim team at the second high school. By the time she'd reached the fourth school, Lucy had seen little point in joining anything. Instead, she kept to herself and made sure she got her school work done. If she couldn't get a scholarship, then she would at least make sure her grades were high enough she would be eligible for loans to pay her way to college. That was one goal she would not give up.

An hour of swimming, then Lucy vaulted from the pool. She ignored the looks from the men coming out of the locker room and wrapped her towel around her body. She ducked into the Jacuzzi in the women's locker room and laid her head against the back, letting the bubbles from the jets soothe her tired muscles. She closed her eyes and Brandon's face came to mind. He was so gorgeous that every time she was around him, she wanted to touch him. Would it be so wrong? Could she just enjoy what they had for this week? This vacation was like a slice out of time. It wasn't the reality of her life. This was her reward, and wouldn't Brandon be one more facet?

By the time he knocked on her door, Lucy had come to a decision. She would grab onto everything she could during this week, including Brandon, but she would do it with her eyes wide open this time. She smoothed her hands over the black silk dress she'd donned and opened the door. Her reward was the widening of his eyes and the smile curving his mouth. He was in a dark dinner suit, once again looking like a powerful businessman rather than an ex-skier on vacation.

"You look beautiful," he murmured. "Do you have a coat?"

"A jacket."

He helped her on with the short white wool jacket, then kept a hand at the small of her back while they made their way out to the parking lot. The club was everything he'd promised, tasteful and understated with music that added to the atmosphere without overwhelming it.

She ate with gusto, even consuming an extra roll. Brandon raised a brow. "Splurging?"

Lucy laughed. "I've decided to get into the spirit of things. It's my vacation, after all, so I'm going to enjoy it."

Brandon reached across the table and captured her free hand. "Does enjoying it include spending more time with me?"

"I would like that, but I don't want to hold you back from skiing like you should."

His thumb stroked across the back of her hand. "I can ski the expert slopes while you swim or run. I want to spend time with you, Lucy." God knew, she wanted to spend time with him. Looking into those green-gold eyes of his right now was making her stomach flutter and her breasts tingle. "Why don't we dance? Then I'll have an excuse to hold you close."

"Yes." She was definitely onboard with dancing. As they walked toward the polished wood floor, she wondered if it was her imagination or had his hand slipped from the small of her back just a little lower? The music was jazzy but slow, so he turned her into his arms and held her close to the length of his body. His hardness pressed against her hip.

When she glanced at him, he leaned down to whisper in her ear. "That's what you do to me. I won't deny it, but nothing happens unless you say so."

Their gazes locked. Lucy laid her head on his shoulder. Was she ready to take the next step? Ready to take him as her lover? She'd told herself she wanted to grab onto everything this vacation had to offer. It seemed Brandon in bed was on the menu.

* * * *

Something was different about her tonight. She had come to some sort of decision during the afternoon, and Brandon hoped her decision included spending time with him. It seemed, as they danced, that it did. He closed his eyes, her body rubbing along him. Any brush of her against him was exquisite torture. He brought her closer, struggling to resist the urge to cup her bottom with his hands. Remembering they were out in public wasn't easy when all he could think about was getting her naked and burying himself inside her.

The dance ended, and he tilted her chin, brushing her lips with his. "Thank you. Would you like some coffee or an after-dinner drink?"

"Both."

By their third dance, he'd found a darker corner of the dance floor where he could allow his hands to roam a little more. Her arms were twined around his neck, her fingers teasing the short hair on the back. His nerves thrummed like an alarm, telling him this woman was different. She was the one.

"Lucy," he growled. "I want you." Her cheek rested on his shoulder. When he finished speaking, she turned to him. In the dim light, the gray of her eyes was as deep and unfathomable as the sea. Her lips parted. Brandon took one hand from her hips to raise her chin and they kissed. The heat of it made him stifle a groan. God, he had to have her. "Let's go."

He kept her hand in his through the parking lot and into the car. When they reached the lodge, he turned to his suite and she never hesitated to come with him. Once inside, he took her coat and turned on the gas logs in the fireplace. He shed his suitcoat and loosened his tie. He'd like nothing better than to just get naked, but didn't want to come off as too much of a guy.

"Would you like something to drink?" He had to clear his throat. Smooth.

She nibbled her lower lip and his cock twitched. "No."

He took her in his arms, needing to get his hands on her. The feel of her pressed to his aroused body made his pulse beat faster. "My God, Lucy. Do you have any idea what you do to me?"

Her fingers grasped at the cotton of his dress shirt. "If it's anything like what you do to me…" She lifted her gaze and now what he saw was a blaze of passion so intense, he growled.

"I want you naked. I want me naked, and all I can think about is touching you skin to skin." He slipped his index finger beneath the neckline of her dress and watched her tongue poke out to moisten her lips. Christ. He was going to explode before he even got her clothes off. She was sex personified. After pulling her close, his fingers found the zip and eased it down with a snick that sounded loud in the quiet of the room. His hands brushed over her shoulders, taking the dress with him. With a slither, it pooled at her ankles and she stood in front of him in a strapless, black bra and a lacy excuse for panties. "Holy shit."

Her glance slid down over him. He knew he was tenting his trousers, and had to fight the urge to adjust himself. God, he felt like a teenager.

When she met his gaze again, she reached for his tie, pulling it loose at the same time she pulled him closer.

"Kiss me, Brandon. Like you mean it."

Like he meant it? My God. He wrapped her in his arms and crushed her mouth beneath his. With one hand grasping her ass and the other on the back of her head, he plundered her mouth with his tongue. His body went even more rigid and he groaned. He was burning up, and shaking as if he'd never had a woman before.

"Oh, Lucy," he whispered into her hair when they both came up for air. "Touch me. Please. Let me feel your fingers on me." He jerked the front of his dress shirt, not caring when several buttons snapped off. Then her hands glided inside and his tension eased at the same time his arousal burned out of control. When her fingers rubbed his nipples, he closed his eyes and moaned.

"You like when I touch you there?"

"Yes."

She pulled his shirt from his pants. He wriggled out of it and let it fall to the floor.

"More," he muttered.

She bent her head and leaned in, her mouth and tongue closing over the tight little bud. "What about this?"

Beyond words, he growled and tugged her down to the fur rug in front of the fireplace. She lay on her back, hands behind her head and her lacy bra barely concealing her breasts.

"I've gotta have you, Lucy. Now. We can come back for all the niceties later, but if I don't get inside you, I'm going to lose it like some high school kid."

"We need—"

"A condom. I have one." He reached into his back pocket to get his wallet while Lucy rose to her knees and began unfastening his trousers. God Almighty, he wasn't even sure he could wait long enough to cover up. When her hand brushed his shaft, he hissed. "Stop. I can't take any more."

With the foil-wrapped packet in one hand, he toed off his shoes, yanked down his trousers and boxers and stepped out of them. His eyes never left the sight of her in her lacy lingerie and thigh-high stockings. In less than a minute, he'd covered his cock and was kneeling between her legs. Too impatient to even finish undressing her, he moved her panties aside and thrust forward with his hips. To his amazement and pleasure, she climaxed on his second thrust, showing him just how turned on she was.

He grasped her hips and flew in and out, crying out as his balls tightened and he spilled his seed.

Brandon rolled to his side, panting and embarrassed. Not exactly a testament to his ability as a lover. "I'm sorry," he grunted.

"It was good." Her breath came in little gasps. When he met her gaze, one brow arched, she touched his cheek. "It was."

He leaned over her and brushed her lips with his. "Thank you for saying that. I'll make it better next time."

He stood and went to the bathroom to strip off the condom.

Chapter 3

Lucy watched him retreat. Drooled, more like it. He might have been a businessman, but there wasn't an ounce of fat on him. Broad, muscular shoulders tapered to a tight ass that made her want to grab it with both hands. Below were long, very muscular thighs and calves, due no doubt to the competitive skiing. She realized she was still wearing her bra and panties—well, sort of. Both were twisted to one side so they no longer served their intended purpose. With that in mind, she stripped them off. She stood, kicked off her high heels and put one foot on the arm of the couch so she could take off her stockings.

Hearing Brandon behind her, Lucy glanced over her shoulder. His eyes were wide and focused on her ass. He held a blanket in front of him, but from what she could see, he was still as naked as when he'd left.

"I brought you a blanket." His voice sounded strained.

Lucy removed the other stocking and turned to face him. She was not self-conscious about her looks. How could she be when she spent three to four nights a week taking her clothes off in front of a crowd? His discomfort made her uneasy.

"Is everything all right?" she asked, hearing the slight hesitation in her voice.

Maybe she had been too aggressive. Men like him wanted to be in charge, but she had been so hot for him, she'd scared him off. Her lower lip started to tremble, so she clamped down on it with her teeth, but there was nothing she could do to hide the tears welling in her eyes, and she wasn't used to them. She never cried, so why now?

Swallowing around the tightness in her throat, she ventured, "Did... did I do something wrong?"

And the first tear fell. Even through the blur she could see the horrified expression now on Brandon's face. She should have known better. My God, Edward had always been so stiff-upper-lip and concerned about what would keep up appearances. Now here she was in this classy guy's suite, crying like a baby after jumping his bones like some cheap hooker. Lucy spun and grabbed her dress. Without bothering to put on either bra or panties, she started to pull it over head.

"What are you doing?" Brandon growled.

"Leaving."

"Why?" He tossed the blanket on the couch and grabbed her shoulders. "I know it wasn't very good for you, but I promise…"

Lucy wiped her eyes and stared at him. "Not good? I jumped all over you, and then before you even got started I came and you came…and it's my fault."

Brandon pulled her to him, crushing her hands between them and smashing her cheek against his chest. "It was me. I rushed you. I've never felt this tied in knots. It's been like this from the moment I first saw you. Please, Lucy. Don't leave like this."

"You want me to stay?"

He pressed her hips into his heavy erection. "Does this feel like I don't? Come on, baby. Sit on the couch with me. Talk to me. Okay?"

She nodded.

* * * *

Brandon grabbed his boxers and pulled them on. They did little to hide his aching dick, but at least he wouldn't be all out there in front of her. God almighty. He'd been so bad, he'd made her cry. So now he felt like complete and total shit. And he'd had the nerve not so long ago to shake his head at the way his older brother had fucked things up with his woman. *His woman.* Was that how he already thought of Lucy?

A sidelong glance showed Lucy dabbing at her eyes with the corner of the blanket. He stroked her cheek and her hair.

"You look fine," he reassured her. "Look, what's a little mascara between us? I've got sisters, so I'm used to it, though I have to admit, I don't think I've ever made a woman cry with my ineptitude as a lover. Tonight's just full of firsts for me." Yeah, like beginning to think he was in love with a woman he hadn't even known forty-eight hours. And how crazy was that?

"I don't normally cry," she admitted in a near whisper. "I'm sorry."

Brandon rubbed his cheek, still smooth since he'd shaved again before picking her up for dinner. "Look, Lucy. Can we start this again? I think we both got off on the wrong foot. I don't know about you, but I was so damn hot for you, I couldn't think of anything other than being inside you, getting skin to skin as close as I could."

"I felt the same way. I'm sorry I was all over you."

A weight lifted off him. "You all over me was great," he admitted with a rueful chuckle. "When you touched me… Wow. You set me on fire."

She let the blanket drop. "You're not upset because I practically attacked you?"

"No. In fact, if you'd like to try it again… Shit. Scratch that." Brandon hadn't felt this awkward since high school. "I mean, I'd like us to try again, but slower. Damn it, Lucy, I feel like I just took a fine wine and chugged the bottle instead of savoring the bouquet. I want to savor you because you're worth it." Oh hell, her eyes were welling again. "Don't cry on me again. Please!"

Between hiccups she smiled a watery smile at him. "These are happy tears. I thought you didn't want to see me anymore, that I'd come on too strong."

He took his thumbs and wiped off the moisture beneath her eyes. "No way, baby. It was hot. Look, why don't we put some clothes on and get a snack."

"I've got my dress…"

"I don't mean time-for-you-to-leave clothes. I'll let you borrow a shirt. We'll raid the mini-fridge Matt stocked and we can talk while we eat."

A few minutes later, he was sure he'd never seen anything lovelier than Lucy wearing his Nationals sweatshirt and a pair of his boxers. With her long, golden hair hanging loose and the makeup scrubbed off her face, she looked as yummy as an ice cream cone on a hot summer day. And, damn, wouldn't he just like to lick her all over. Instead, he was scrounging around in a fridge, pulling out cheese, Cokes, and then finding crackers in a cabinet over the mini-bar.

"Mind sitting on the rug in front of the fireplace?"

She grinned at him. "Not if you don't mind me toasting my toes on the hearth."

He glanced at the toes in question. Hell, even her feet were sexy, slender and fine-boned, her toes painted a bright coral. They lounged in front of the fire, nibbling on cheese and crackers and sipping soft drinks. If anyone of his acquaintance had seen him right now, they would have laughed their asses off. Brandon Barlow-Barrett, known for his reputation as a flashy dresser and host, was entertaining a beautiful woman—admittedly, one dressed in his boxers and sweatshirt—while he lounged in a pair of flannel sleep pants and a t-shirt. After stroking a finger down her nose, he laughed, feeling freer than he had in a while.

"What's so funny?"

"The fact I have a beautiful woman sitting in my suite while I'm on vacation, and we're camped out in front of the fire eating cheese and crackers and drinking Cokes."

Lucy raised her brows. "You mean instead of being in your bed having wild monkey sex?"

He laughed. "Well, yeah. And, you know, I think I like you in my clothes."

She picked at the sweatshirt with her thumb and forefinger. "This old thing?"

He liked how she had relaxed. It made him feel better about being such an idiot earlier. "I like you having something against your skin that I've had against mine." Her smile faded, and he continued in a soft tone, "That doesn't freak you out, does it?"

"No." She touched his cheek. "It makes me feel...I don't know...like I matter."

It was an odd comment because he got the feeling she wasn't just talking about mattering to him. She meant mattering to anyone. As if there might be no one in the world who cared whether she existed or not. Brandon tucked her hair behind her ear. "You matter."

The atmosphere had gotten thick again, and he needed to ease the tension. Neither one of them were quite ready for the heat level between them. It was too much, too soon, and he needed to know her better—that is, if she would even talk to him tomorrow after the way he'd fucked up tonight. Picking up a piece of cheese, he slipped it between her lips. "Here. Eat more. In my official capacity as head of the Lucy Matters Club, I must make sure you eat enough."

She chewed and swallowed. "You're different."

"My family says the same thing, most often with a great deal of exasperation."

Lucy shook her head. "No, I mean from other men who ask me out. You see me."

He arched a brow. "See you? What do you mean?"

She shifted so she was sitting staring into the fire with her back half-turned toward him. "I mean, see more than the hair and the body. You see a person."

Brandon blinked, his chest aching at her tone. "I'm glad you feel that way because you would have every right to look at me like I'm just another shallow prick."

She angled her head so she could look at him over her shoulder. Her eyes were dark, assessing. "You are so far from that." She grinned at him, crossing her legs Indian-style. "Tell me about your family. Are you from around the capital?"

"Northern Virginia." He didn't want to go into detail about the estate, complete with butler. "My parents live out in the country. Only my youngest sister, Morgan, is at home anymore. She's in college."

"You have more sisters?"

"Two others, both younger. Also two brothers—one older, one younger. Six kids total. What about you?"

Lucy shook her head. "I don't have any family left. My parents died when I was very young and my grandmother raised me."

"And she died?"

Lucy nodded, her gaze focused on the flames in the fireplace. "When I was twelve. She had a massive stroke. Although she didn't die right away, it felt like it to me. She was gone from the house. And with her gone, I had to go too."

"Go where?" Brandon asked, but he already had some idea.

"Foster homes. I was already in my second by the time Gram did die."

He wanted to offer comfort, something not in his nature, or it hadn't been until now. Feeling a little off balance, Brandon stroked her hair away from the side of her neck, traced his finger from there to her shoulder and squeezed. "How many were there?"

She glanced over her shoulder. "Too many. I learned to make myself almost invisible."

And he could read between the lines. Disappearing had been impossible. Brandon could imagine what she must have been like as a teenager. Beautiful and no doubt sheltered if she'd been raised by a grandmother, a perfect victim for any unscrupulous male. He cleared his throat. "Were you hurt?"

She shook her head. "Not really. There were some who tried, but I managed to evade them. I spent all the time I could at school or the library studying. I wanted to go to college because the academics were the only thing I had going for me. I had to get loans, but I did it."

Brandon thought of his Ivy League education, paid for from the Barlow-Barrett coffers. "What did you major in?" Maybe he'd get an inkling of what she did for a living.

"Art history. In fact, I have a masters degree. I guess it's about as useful as a philosophy degree. But I've managed to make a living." She sat without saying anything for a moment, staring into the flames. "This has been nice, Brandon, but I should probably go."

He scooted behind her and rubbed some of the tension from her shoulders. "You know, I'd love to have you stay, to give you a better idea of how it could be between the two of us. But I also want you to know that's not the only thing I want, so, yeah. Why don't we get dressed and I'll walk you to your room."

"You don't have to. I'm a big girl."

He arched a brow. "My mother would disown me if I allowed a date to go home without an escort." He helped her to her feet. "Will you ski with me again in the morning?"

Lucy looked surprised. "You don't have to do that either. Now I have an idea of what I'm doing, I can go on my own and not hold you back."

He brushed her cheek with his knuckles. "I want to ski with you. Part of the fun is sharing it. We'll make a day of it. Lunch here again and then we'll head into town tomorrow afternoon and look around some of the shops. Come on. It'll be fun."

"All right, but if you change your mind and decide you don't want to ski with a newbie, my feelings won't be hurt."

The skiing wasn't what it was about, but he couldn't tell her. He wanted to spend time with her, whenever and however he could, because he was determined this would be more than just a vacation flirtation. "I won't change my mind." He handed her clothing to her. "The bathroom's the first door on the left if you'd like some privacy."

"Thank you, Brandon." She grinned at him. "Your mother would be proud of your manners."

He laughed. "Right."

* * * *

Lucy stared at herself in the bathroom mirror. Her hair was a mess, her makeup a wreck, and she felt better than she had in ages. Maybe it was the faded Nationals sweatshirt, or the boxers hanging on her hips. She picked up the sweatshirt and brought it to her nose. She smelled his aftershave and the warm, male scent that was his alone. Would he laugh if she asked to keep it?

Get over it, Lucy. What was she doing? Brandon was out of her league, an older, more mature version of Edward Montgomery. But damn it, he wanted to be with her, so at least for this week, she would enjoy every minute of it. There would be plenty of time to disappear into her own world.

Attitude in place, she stripped off her borrowed clothes and put hers on with the speed of someone accustomed to making quick costume changes. She did that very thing several times a night when she was working. After wiping the dark circles from beneath her eyes and attempting to tidy her hair, Lucy returned to the great room to find Brandon standing near the gas logs. He was in his slacks, dress shirt and suit coat. He looked rumpled and sexy enough that she wanted to strip him naked again.

"You're missing a few buttons," she murmured.

One golden brow arched. "I'm not planning on letting anyone else close enough to figure that out." He smiled. "Come on, baby, let me walk you to your room. I'll even be a gentleman and just give you a kiss good night—the way our first date probably should have ended."

"First date. So there will be a second?"

He picked up her wool jacket from the back of the couch and slipped it around her shoulders. "As many as we can fit in, and more if you'll let me."

Lucy had to ignore that. She couldn't think beyond this week right now. She'd been down the same road and knew disappointment lay at its end. So she smiled at him instead. "Walk me to my room."

He took her arm and tucked it through his. They had to walk outside for a few yards, but then they were inside the main lodge. The night clerk gave them a nod, but otherwise the halls were empty. Lucy wasn't sure how late it was. She didn't feel tired, no doubt because of the company and the attraction. When they reached her door, she dug in her pocket for her key card. Brandon took it from her and slipped it into the lock. Once the door was open, he scanned the room.

"You take this escorting me home with more seriousness than I've ever encountered."

He leaned against the door jamb. "No sense being careless." He put his hands on her shoulders and drew her close. "Come here. Let me give you a good night kiss."

It felt right, being pressed close, feeling his arms surround her. The kiss started off a gentle brushing of lips, but the heat was there, and building. When his tongue touched her lips, she parted them, welcoming him. Her arms twined around his neck.

"We've been here before," he whispered, his lips brushing her mouth. "I should stop. Tell me to stop."

"You should stop," she whispered back.

He cupped her face with his hands, kissed her forehead. "I'll see you in the morning. We'll get some breakfast first, 'kay?"

She nodded. He tucked her inside the room and closed the door. Lucy leaned against the wall and stared at it. God. She knew better. She really did. So why was she letting herself fall for him?

* * * *

Brandon stared at the closed door, his body aching. He was not where he wanted to be. Right now, all he wanted was to be on the other side of the door, taking Lucy's clothes off, laying her on the wide bed he'd glimpsed and covering her body with his. He would ease the ache between her thighs, worship her body with his and show her what it could be like between them. There would be no rush, no hurried, desperate coupling like he'd subjected her to earlier.

He was amazed she was still speaking to him, let alone that she'd agreed to ski with him again, to see him again. He closed his eyes. She'd felt so wonderful wrapped around him… Brandon pushed away from the wall, forcing himself to go to his suite before he did something foolish, like break down her damn door.

Chapter 4

Lucy couldn't believe how much she looked forward to seeing him the following morning. She took extra care with her clothing and makeup, laughing because she would probably fall on her ass in the snow and no doubt sweat off most of her foundation. When she entered the lobby, Brandon was standing next to a tall, muscular man whose dark hair was pulled into a braid at his nape.

Both men turned at her approach, Brandon with a smile, his companion with an assessing gaze that roamed from her feet and ended on her face. Lucy was used to being sized up by men, but in an overtly sexual way she found easy to ignore. This man's regard was wary, as if he were deciding whether she was worthy of Brandon's friendship.

"Lucy, come meet the owner of this place and my good friend, Matt Petersohn. I think I mentioned to you we used to compete together."

Lucy smiled and shook Matt's hand. "You did. It's a pleasure to meet you. I'm afraid I'm new to skiing, so I'm not familiar with any of the sport's athletes."

"Your newness is why I'm here. Bran mentioned wanting to take you to one of the runs higher on the mountain. I rated it advanced because of the length, but the vertical drop is gradual enough that a less experienced skier would be safe—as long as she's in great shape."

Lucy laughed. "So you're here to check me out?"

"That's right. Why don't we grab some breakfast first, and then I'll join you for a couple of trips down the Lodge View trail."

"You don't mind, do you, Lucy?" Brandon asked. She detected just a trace of worry in his voice.

She smiled at them. "Not at all. The fact you would bother makes me feel a lot more secure about even attempting such a thing."

Brandon grinned. "Great."

She watched Matt's easy manner with his employees and his guests and was impressed. There was no doubt he was in charge, but he treated everyone with equal politeness. His employees greeted him by first name. After they finished eating, he stood. "I'll grab my jacket and my gear and meet you at the lift in about fifteen minutes. Good for you?"

"Sure thing, Matt," Bran assured him. As he and Lucy went to get their equipment, Brandon grabbed her arm and pulled her into an alcove near the door. He took his time, kissing her on the lips, then grinned into her face. "Good morning. I've been wanting to do that since I first saw you. Are you sure you're okay with Matt evaluating you?"

"Not a problem." She didn't want to tell him it made her feel cared for, and it had been so long since anyone had looked out for her best interests. But it warmed her, and Lucy held onto the feeling.

Matt was there at the lift and, this early in the morning, just a few hardy skiers were already out. They shared the chair, Lucy sandwiched between the two men. When they reached the top, Matt indicated they should go to the left.

"Lodge View's a pretty quiet run. Did you do it yesterday?"

Brandon shook his head. "I kept her on the other side, on the shorter run to give her more experience getting on and off the lift, that kind of thing."

Matt smiled at her. "This run has a few turns a little tighter than what you did yesterday, but it will give us a chance to see if you can maneuver well enough, plus the length will be a good indication if you've got the stamina for a longer run."

Lucy grinned at them. "I'm game."

In all fairness, she was fit enough from dancing she'd had no soreness whatsoever following skiing yesterday. Matt stepped up the pace a bit, so the run today demanded more concentration, but when they reached the bottom, she now saw a gleam of approval on Brandon's friend's face.

He clapped her on the shoulder. "You might be new to skiing, but it's obvious you keep yourself fit." He looked at Brandon. "Go on. I just wish I could join you, dude, but I've got to go over supply orders with my managers. Stop by my office when you get back and let me know how it goes."

"No problem."

Brandon put an arm around Lucy's shoulders. "Ready, baby?"

She nodded. "If you two think I can do it, I'll give it a try."

By the time they returned to the lodge at lunchtime, Lucy was glowing with exertion and couldn't remember when she'd had so much fun.

Brandon slung his arm around her waist and pulled her close. She fit perfectly along his side, and her smoldering attraction caught fire.

"I ordered lunch in my suite. I've also got a whirlpool tub in the master bath if you'd like to work out a few kinks." He glanced at her with a sly grin. "It's big enough for two."

Heat raced through her. It must have shown because the grin left his face and his green-gold eyes blazed like the sun.

When he spoke again, his voice was a throaty growl. "What would you say to trying the tub first?"

Lucy could be nothing other than honest. "Yes."

He hurried her through the lodge. When he opened the door with his key card, she noticed a slight tremble in his fingers. Apparently they were both turned on. He proved it true as soon as the door shut behind them. His fingers went to the zipper on her jacket, sliding it down at the same time he leaned in to kiss her.

"Damn, baby," he choked, drawing back. "I swore I would go slow with you this time around, but every time I get near you, I feel like an out-of-control teenager. I'm so damn hard right now."

She was feeling the same way, and was already working on his clothing. With his jacket unzipped, she slipped her hands inside and around him until she could pull him into her. When his hips met her stomach, his erection rubbed her. Lucy gulped.

"You know, slow can be for after lunch. Let's just do fast now."

He pulled back a bit and stared into her face for a moment before the hard planes of his softened and he chuckled. "I am so with you."

Laughing together, they stripped off their clothing. Lucy finished first and took a moment to enjoy the pure, masculine beauty of him. Dark gold hair covered his chest and arrowed down to his thick cock. When she saw how hard he was, she gulped and took off down the hall to the bathroom with Brandon right behind her. She had already turned on the taps when he caught her and spun her into his arms.

"I watched your tight little ass swaying in front of me all morning and could barely concentrate on skiing because of the effect you were having on my body. Now, it's a question of if I can wait long enough to get you in the tub, if I bend you over right here or set you on the counter and just spread you open."

Lucy took a step toward him and twined her arms around his neck. She had never felt so comfortable right off the bat with any man, and though she trembled with arousal, there was no hesitation in her. "Let's start with the last and work our way backward."

"I like the way you think, lady."

Brandon's hands slid down her back, cupped her bottom and lifted her. She almost gasped when the contrast of the cold marble vanity touched her overheated skin. Brandon's hands slid along her thighs, flooding her with even more sensation. While one held her hip, the other dipped and cupped her sex. Now she did gasp. Then he slipped a finger inside and she moaned.

"Look at me, Lucy," Brandon ordered, and she glanced up from what he was doing. His gaze burned. "I want you right now. Nice can come later."

His fingers moved and she threw her head back. "Please," she choked. She heard the slide of a drawer, his fingers withdrew for a moment and the sound of a foil packet tearing followed. Then there was another, thicker probing between her legs. Lucy's eyes snapped open, and she met his gaze.

"Now," she hissed.

He thrust into her, filling her until she was positive she would burst with pleasure. When he began to stroke, she moaned. Skin slapped against skin. They panted. Forget gentleness. Brandon's lovemaking was fast, hot and intense, and their releases tumbled one over the other with equal fury. He leaned his forehead on the top of her head, and Lucy held onto his shoulders, afraid she would collapse into a boneless puddle at his feet. She couldn't think, just feel.

Gradually, the sound of running water intruded. Her breathing settled.

"The bath," Lucy gasped.

"Shit!" Brandon withdrew, turned the taps off, then stripped the condom from himself. "In the nick of time, though I suspect we'll overflow it when we get in." He arched a brow at her. "Ready?"

"Absolutely."

* * * *

Brandon tossed the condom in the trash, his heart beating double-time. Last night had surprised him with its intensity, just now had shocked the shit out of him. He'd had his share of lovers, even had a couple of women he'd thought he was serious about. He'd never had anyone like Lucy.

"You getting in?" she asked.

He smiled at her. "Yeah." As he'd suspected, the water overflowed onto the tile. When Lucy cast a worried glance at it, he grinned. "Don't worry. I'll talk to the concierge about getting someone in to clean it."

She nodded and eased back, sinking to her shoulders. "Oh Lord, that feels good. I often indulge myself at home once I've worked out at the Y."

Brandon climbed in facing her, more water sloshing over the sides. Lucy had her eyes closed, her expression peaceful. She looked beautiful. She looked like she fit in his life. He wanted more than this week. He wanted them to become a couple when this vacation was over with. And when had he become tied to a female like his pathetic elder brother? Seth's sole focus these days was Tessa, especially with her getting so close to delivering their child. He'd watched the protectiveness with amusement, but now he understood. Lucy had knocked him sideways, and he wasn't at all sure she was even aware of it.

He caught her foot beneath the water and began to massage it. Her eyes fluttered open and she purred. No other way to describe it and, oh man, did it make him go hard again. Too bad he hadn't brought a condom with him. Her foot brushed his cock. Now her eyes snapped open.

"Brandon?"

He nodded. "Oh yeah, I'm hard again, but I'll live."

"Yes, but I don't want you in pain." She shifted positions until she had somehow scooted between his legs. Her hand wrapped around him.

"Oh man."

He let her caress him until he was afraid he couldn't handle it any longer. When he rose from the tub, he held his hand out to her. "Come on. Grab some towels. We'll continue this in bed."

They took turns drying each other off, and if their efforts became caresses and kisses rather than toweling dry, Brandon had no complaint. Now, with his lips traveling across Lucy's taught belly to the weeping heat of her sex, he doubted she had any complaints either. At last, he would show her the exact way he wanted to pleasure her. She was so responsive, her body moving with him and her cries filling the air, that when he tasted her, his body tightened with the need to come yet again.

Not yet. Not this time. This time was for her and her only. But in the end, Lucy wouldn't let it happen with her as the sole focus. She pleasured him in return. Now at long last, they lay wrapped in each other's arms, the covers drawn up while they dozed in the aftermath of what they'd shared.

Brandon had found the one thing he had doubted he ever would—his woman.

It took a while, but hunger drove them into the living room. Lucy was once again in his Nationals sweatshirt and boxers, while he'd pulled on flannel sleep pants and a t-shirt.

"This is getting to be a habit," Lucy joked.

"Mmm. One I think I like. Eat up, baby. I want to take you into town this afternoon."

They showered together after lunch, though it took some time to finish playing and start washing. Back in their skiwear, with snow boots replacing ski boots, Brandon dropped an arm around her shoulders and guided her out to his rental car. The trip was a winding one, but beautiful, made more so by the woman sitting next to him. Wow, he had gone nuts.

Once they reached Falcon's Head, Brandon had to juggle for a place to park. At the tail end of the ski season, it seemed everyone was trying to get one last trip in. Afraid they would become separated, Brandon took Lucy's hand and laughed when she raised one brow at him. "I don't want to lose you."

Her smile altered, her gaze grew serious. "You won't. Not if you don't want to."

"Lucy…" He brought her hand to his lips. "Come on. Let's go in here." He drew her in off the crowded sidewalk, not even sure what kind of store they were entering.

"Oh!" At her delighted exclamation, Brandon realized they'd entered a small art gallery. And she had a masters in art history. He couldn't have planned it better if he'd tried.

"Would you like to look around?"

She smiled, her gray eyes alight. "You don't mind?"

An unaccustomed feeling of tenderness welled in him at the look of excitement on her face. Her gaze was drawn to a section including pottery and sculpture.

"Oh. Brandon. Look!" She pulled him by the hand over to a sculpture of a cowboy huddled on his horse as if seeking shelter from inclement weather. "I think this is a real Frederic Remington sculpture…not a reproduction."

"How can you tell?" He was curious.

She bent closer to the sculpture. "The base is the first clue. A lot of reproductions are mounted on marble bases. It's very rare to see an original one outside a museum anymore. And I see this one is not for sale. No surprise there. When an original goes up for sale, it's a big deal, like a Sotheby's or Christie's auction."

He could see how much she wanted to put her hands on the artwork, and knew admiring art was not her true love. She looked at it with the desire to create, to be able to feel what the artist had felt beneath her own fingers.

"I see you're admiring the Remington." An older woman, either the owner or manager, approached them. "It is an original, and not for sale, I'm afraid."

"I thought it might be an original, but of course without being able to see the foundry mark and numbering…"

The woman's eyes lit. "You're familiar with authenticating art work?"

Lucy shifted. "I'm an art historian, but not professionally. I also work in clay."

Brandon stepped back and observed, seeing a side to Lucy that was new to him. Her personality was happy and easygoing, so envisioning her being intense about anything was difficult. But when it came to discussing art, she was in her element. He followed the two women from the Remington to a display of Native American pottery.

The owner handed her a pot, which Lucy examined in detail. "This is modern pottery," the owner said, "an olla, done in the traditional style."

"What's an olla?" Brandon inquired.

Lucy answered him. "It's a type of unglazed pot that's been a staple of most Southwestern Native American tribes for more than a thousand years. The jar would be used for soups, stews…any number of things. Ollas exist in every culture, but this style is consistent with this part of the country." She turned to the owner. "It's fantastic there are still potters keeping the tradition alive."

They looked at some more pots, Brandon content to walk behind the two women. "So are you a potter?" the gallery owner inquired.

"Yes. I learned it from my grandmother. I had to give it up for a few years, but I've been working with several designs, some on the wheel, but others using a coil technique like many of the eastern Native American cultures."

"Do you have any of your work on display?"

Lucy shook her head. Brandon saw her blush. "I haven't made a determined effort to market it yet, so I guess it's more of a hobby right now."

"If you're interested in pottery, you should go over to the museum in Coyote Creek. It's a long drive from here, but you can fly it in less than an hour."

Lucy started to shake her head. Brandon spoke. "I have a pilot's license."

The owner brightened. "You can rent a plane at Air Service at the airport. Pilots are available most of the time, but if you have your pilot's license, you could fly it yourself."

Brandon wanted to be able to give the trip to Lucy. He'd seen just how much pleasure being able to look around the gallery and talk to the owner had given her. He could imagine the trip to Coyote Creek would be even better. "We may do that. Thanks for the suggestion."

They chatted for a few more minutes, then said their goodbyes. Lucy was almost bouncing on her toes she was so excited. Brandon grinned. She looked at him and laughed. "I'm having so much fun. Thank you for bringing me into town."

He caught her hand as they started past a coffee shop. "How about some coffee and a snack? We can plan our trip to Coyote Creek."

She stopped. "You don't have to do arrange a trip, Brandon. You came here to ski. I've already taken you from the slopes."

They found a table in a corner. "How do you figure?"

"This trip to town for starters. Admit it. Without me, you wouldn't be here. You'd be on the slopes with Matt. And you for darn sure wouldn't be skiing down even advanced trails. You'd be on the expert slopes."

The waitress stopped by to get their order. After Lucy ordered a skim latte with an extra shot of espresso, Brandon smiled. "Make it two, and bring a couple of those chocolate croissants."

"Brandon!" Lucy protested. "I can't eat that."

He arched a brow at her. "Who said it was for you? And the first thing you should understand about me is I never do anything I don't want to do. Spending time with you? That's something I want. And I would like nothing better than to fly us both over to Coyote Creek tomorrow."

She leaned back and crossed her arms across her chest. "To look at pottery?"

He leaned forward, his arms crossed on the table. "To look at you looking at pottery. A distinction that makes it all worthwhile for me."

She flushed. Another thing he liked about her. Even though she oozed confidence in herself and her body, there were times when he had to wonder if some of it wasn't simply an image she forced herself to project. Now she nibbled her lower lip, worrying it until he wanted to lean forward and kiss her.

"All right," she said at last.

Brandon smiled. "Well, since I have your agreement, let me try something else. Care to spend the night with me? I want to make love to you right in front of the fireplace."

Her lips parted, but she was forestalled from a response when their waitress showed up, setting their lattes and the two chocolate croissants right in front of them. Once she had departed, leaving the check facedown on the table, Brandon raised his brows.

"Well?" Inside, he worried for an instant she might say no. Then she grinned and tilted her head.

"You don't snore, do you?"

"Not that I know of. What about you?"

"My cat will never tell."

* * * *

Lucy had to keep reminding herself what was between Brandon and her was only a little vacation romance. She couldn't consider this as serious because what was happening was a slice out of time. He was like a dream, the fulfillment of a fantasy, but when this week was over, reality would return. She would return to taking her clothes off for money, and he would no doubt be back in the boardroom, his adventures with her no more than a memory.

"So, will you stay with me tonight?"

She should say no. That would be the safe way, but when she looked into his hazel eyes, there was only one answer. "Yes."

Those eyes of his heated, like watching the glow of a fire when a log had been tossed on top. The heat warmed her, made her feel the answer she'd given was the right one. Brandon cut a bite of croissant. "Eat, Lucy." She started to shake her head. "Let me feed you. Just this once."

She took the flaky delicacy from the fork, her eyes closing with bliss at the combination of buttery crust and smooth chocolate filling. She swallowed. "You are a dangerous, dangerous man."

He carried her hand to his lips. "If we were someplace a little less public, I would show you how dangerous."

"Brandon?" A woman interrupted in a drawl of bored sophistication. Lucy caught a trace of a scowl cross Brandon's lean features before his expression assumed a bland social veneer she had never seen.

"Taylor. Slumming? I thought Aspen was a little more your speed."

"Mother wanted someplace quiet and said she needed my support, so here I am."

"Well, I hope you have a marvelous time. We were just leaving."

They were? Lucy kept a pleasant smile on her face. Brandon got to his feet, so she followed suit. The smaller woman eyed Lucy's height as if she were akin to a giraffe in the zoo.

"Aren't you going to introduce me to your friend?"

Brandon eyed the other woman with what appeared to be distaste and then did something Lucy would never have imagined.

"No." Taking Lucy's hand, he tossed a twenty on the table and pulled her out onto the street. She let him march her along the sidewalk in the direction of their parked car for about a hundred yards and then planted her feet.

"Would you like to explain the little scene back there?" Although she tried to ignore it, some of those insecurities from an adolescence spent being bounced from home to home surfaced once more. "Are you embarrassed to be seen with me?"

Brandon spun and stared at her, his brows drawn together in a thunderous frown. "*What?* You think blowing her off was because of *you*?" He grabbed her, holding her for a moment as if he wanted to shake her. Instead, he snatched her to him and buried his face in her hair. "Never, Lucy," he growled. "I didn't want to introduce you to her because she's a first class bitch. My sister Anna went to school with her. Taylor was one of a group of girls who tormented the hell out of her. You are too good for the Taylors of this world." He leaned back and pressed a kiss to her forehead. "Come on, lady. Let's get to Falcon's Summit. I'd like to spend the evening and the night making love to you."

Chapter 5

They decided to eat dinner in the dining room, even if it was at a table tucked away in a secluded corner near the windows. From there they could look out and watch some of the night skiing on the lower slopes closer to the resort.

"Matt added lights a couple of years ago. His father had always fought them, but once he took over, Matt went ahead with it."

"I'm guessing there was some sound business behind his decision."

"Yes. The research he'd done showed they were close enough to Denver to draw in day-trip crowds from there. And there were plenty of folks who wanted to be able to get in a full day of skiing, including some after sunset. Matt says it's paid off."

Of course, he didn't add he was the one who'd pushed for the expansion. He'd seen the potential there for a big return on the investment. He'd been right. That happened a lot when it came to business. His instincts were most often on the money. Looking at Lucy, he hoped his instincts were likewise correct when it came to her. This was no holiday fling, in his book. He planned to ask her to continue seeing him once they returned home. Maybe the trip to Coyote Creek would be the time to do it too.

They took his rental car to the Air Service building at Falcon's Head's airport around mid-morning the following day. A sulky-looking teenager sat behind the counter but did have the grace to stand when they approached.

"Can I help you?"

Brandon's initial thought was this wasn't the image he would have up front advertising his company, but it was a family-run business. "I would like to rent a plane for a one-day turnaround flight to Coyote Creek and back. Do you have anything available?"

"You a pilot?" The kid looked him up and down as if he doubted it could be true.

"I am. I've got almost three hundred hours of flight experience."

The kid's eyes widened, but he started to shake his head. "We don't…"

"Where are you wanting to go?" an older man asked, walking into the room and pulling off his cap so he could finger-comb his gray hair.

"Coyote Creek. For the afternoon."

"I've got to pick up some parts over that way. My rentals are out and I've got one plane down, but if you don't mind being a little cramped, I can get you in the C-182."

Brandon was familiar with the plane. It was one he had flown often. "No problem. I think we can squeeze in."

He didn't want to put off the trip, and he wasn't such an egomaniac he would insist on flying just to prove to Lucy he could. Even cramped in the Cessna would be better than driving. He'd checked out a map early this morning, in case there were no planes available, and discovered how much longer it would take to drive it.

The older man held out his hand. "I'm Tom Hanson."

Brandon shook and finished the introductions. When the paperwork was handled, they followed Hanson out onto the tarmac behind the hangar. The pilot sized them up. "To balance the weight out, why don't you sit in back on the way over, Mr. Barrett. Miss Cameron can be my co-pilot."

Lucy laughed. "I think you'd be better off with Brandon. This will be only the second time I've flown."

Hanson laughed. "This baby just needs one of us to fly, but you will have a better view up front."

"And if I turn sideways," Brandon added, "I might actually be able to stretch my legs out."

He loved the sparkle in her gray eyes as he helped her into the front. He squeezed her hand and she grinned at him. Hanson went through his checks while Brandon watched. The guy seemed not only capable, but accomplished.

"We'll be flying VFR," Hanson said over his shoulder as he powered up the Cessna. "Coyote Creek's unstaffed most of the time. But it so happens there's a friend of mine there with the part I need for the plane I'm working on, so you were in luck today."

The scenery was gorgeous. Lucy pointed out a big buck moving in the pines below. She noticed everything, enjoying the simple pleasure of having a bird's-eye view. Maybe he should get her flying lessons.

"What's that over to the left?" she asked Hanson, pointing out the front window.

"Haven Lake. It's a popular fishing spot for the locals and provides the headwaters for Coyote Creek. It's a hike in, but there are a couple of fishing cabins there. It's about the only flat spot around."

Brandon studied the terrain. Other than the lake, there was a thick coating of pine trees, a few areas that looked like they might be meadows once the snow cover was gone. It would be as picturesque in the summer, he suspected, as it was now. He settled in his seat and closed his eyes. He could hear Lucy continue to pepper Hanson with questions about the area, about flying and about Coyote Creek. Brandon tuned some of it out, thinking back to having her beside him in his bed last night.

They had fit together perfectly. Not just for sex, for sleeping too. During the night, he had awakened to find himself curled around her in a protective embrace, one arm wrapped around her waist. Now all he needed to do was convince her they were good together. Even though she seemed to be open, he still sensed a core of reserve within her. She had revealed a fair amount about her childhood, but he realized he still had no idea what she did for a living. Though she denied modeling, few women were as assiduous about keeping fit and watching their diet. If she weren't so strong and healthy, he'd worry she had an eating disorder.

"We'll be landing in about twenty minutes," Hanson mentioned over his shoulder. "How much time did you want to spend on the ground?"

"There's a museum we want to see. We'll want to grab lunch and maybe look around any local shops."

Hanson glanced at his watch. "I can give you about three hours then we'll need to head back. I'd like to make Falcon's Head well before sundown."

"No problem. What's the situation with ground transportation?"

"No rentals. I'm sure my buddy can either give you a ride into town and pick you up, or he'll let you borrow the Jeep. Once you get into Coyote Creek, everything's within walking distance."

In the end, Hanson gave them a ride into town while his buddy cleaned the engine part and boxed it ready to load in the Cessna. He said he'd refuel the plane so Hanson could grab a bite to eat too.

* * * *

When Brandon took her hand, Lucy glanced at him and smiled. The look in his eyes had changed. Sure, the sexual hunger was still there, but now when he looked at her, warmth tugged at her heart, urging her to open it.

"Let's grab a bite to eat first, then we'll visit the museum." He tucked a strand of hair behind her ear.

"All right." Lucy touched his cheek. "Have I said thank you?"

"More than once, but this is purely pleasure for me."

They found a small diner that looked like the place most of the locals frequented. She liked the fact Brandon didn't put on airs or try to appear superior to them in any way. He was just…Brandon. As friendly and open as he'd always been with her. He'd said he worked in his dad's company, and he had been dressed to the nines when she first met him, but maybe he wasn't quite the powerbroker she'd feared. Maybe it was simply a family-owned company, not an empire.

If that was the case, then it might be possible for them to form a lasting relationship. Lucy swallowed. If they became a couple, she would have to be honest with him. She'd have to reveal how she made her living. It would make a lot of people think twice. Strippers had a reputation. Sure, there were girls who pulled in plenty of money on the side, but Roberto frowned on it, and if he caught a dancer doing more than what the law allowed, she was history. Over the years, Lucy had watched them come and go. It always seemed like the girls willing to sell their bodies for extra cash were doing it for all the wrong reasons…often to get drugs.

Feeding an addiction had never been a motivation for Lucy. She avoided drugs and any more than the occasional alcoholic beverage. Dancing was a career, a way for her to make enough cash to be able to retire and pursue her pottery, making it more than a hobby. She knew what the limits were, and she never went beyond the boundaries.

"What has you so pensive?" Brandon murmured as they finished their meal.

Lucy blinked and shook her head. She wasn't ready to talk about this yet. Certainly not ready to explain her job at Flamingo Road. But when Brandon captured her hands and she gazed into his eyes, she realized time was running out. His look was no longer the look of someone just wanting a little vacation diversion.

"I enjoyed sleeping with you last night," he said. "And I do mean sleeping. While the lovemaking was astounding, waking and finding you in my arms was it for me. That's a repeat. And I'd like to do it more than this week." She must have looked panicked, for he added, "Just think about it. Let yourself absorb the idea and we can talk about it later."

She breathed a sigh of relief. She wanted more with him. She did. But this would give her some room to figure out how to tell him about herself. She didn't consider Brandon to be a prude, but if he worked for a respected family company, then how could he take on a wife with a past…and a present…like hers? That was so not happening. This wasn't some fairytale with an instant happy ending, and to Lucy's knowledge, she had no fairy godmother.

"Brandon…"

"No. Don't say anything now. Let's go tour the museum." He settled the bill at the cash register before sliding an arm around her waist and escorting her out the door. She shouldn't have let it go, but she did. It was less complicated. This day was so wonderful, she didn't want the complexities of their everyday lives to intrude.

The museum was around the corner, just off the main street. From the moment she walked in, Lucy was enthralled. It was a testament to more than the cultural heritage of the area; the owners had also reserved one room to display the wares of current artisans. She studied the techniques in how the pots were constructed and adorned. From vibrant glazes to intricate carving, and even playful additions, such as lizards or jars designed to resemble the budding of a flower.

"This is amazing. The attention to detail is incredible." She ran her fingers over the glossy smoothness of a polished pot with intricate carving covering it. "It's obvious the care and craftsmanship have been handed down through generations."

Brandon peered at the pot, his face close to hers. "You have the same history, don't forget. Didn't your grandmother teach you?"

Lucy started. She had never thought about it in such a way. "Yes. Yes, she did—all she could until her health declined."

When they finished looking at everything, Lucy excused herself to use the restroom. They didn't have much time remaining before Tom Hanson would be there to pick them up. She walked into the front of the gallery and saw Brandon in deep conversation with the owner, then he smiled and shook hands.

As she approached, he smiled at her. "Ready, baby? We're about out of time."

"Yes." She shook hands with the owner. "This was wonderful. I can't tell you what an inspiration it was for me."

Brandon took her hand when they left. "Was it worth the trip?"

She sighed. "Yes! It would have been worth the trip for the scenery flying here. The museum was incredible beyond words. I can't thank you enough."

He stopped in the middle of the street and stroked her cheek. "No thanks are needed. Being able to spend the day with you was enough."

* * * *

As they prepared to board the Cessna for the flight home, Hanson looked at them with a critical eye. "If you don't mind, I'm going to put you up front with me, Mr. Barrett, and have Ms. Cameron ride behind. The parts I'm taking are heavier than I anticipated and I need to distribute the weight so it's even."

Brandon looked at her. "You mind, Lucy?"

She shook her head. "No. I'm getting a little sleepy anyway, so it's a good excuse to take a nap." After Brandon helped her board, she buckled her seatbelt then watched Brandon and Hanson settle in, adjusting and buckling their shoulder harnesses and belts. Brandon turned and winked at her as they taxied onto the runway.

"Don't get too comfy, it's not that long a flight."

"Well, if it's like the flight here was, I'll be able to sleep the whole way."

He grinned. "You need to get more rest at night."

Lucy stuck her tongue out at him as Hanson throttled up and sent the little plane racing down the runway. Brandon laughed. They reached their designated altitude before Lucy wiggled deeper into her seat and closed her eyes. A short nap might pep her up. While she was used to a lot of physical activity, she wasn't accustomed to being awake half the night making love. Of course, she wasn't complaining. Brandon was a beautiful and generous lover. He was just as passionate when receiving attention from her.

Oh, Lord. She longed to find a way to make things work between them once this vacation ended. Her thoughts slowed with the steady drone of the engine lulling her to sleep.

Lucy wasn't sure how much later she awakened, or even what first made her jerk to instant alertness. There were so many things assaulting her senses all at once: the altered tenor of the engine, the clipped tenseness of Hanson's voice and Brandon's deeper tones as he flipped through several radio frequencies with a mayday. Lucy sat straighter, her gut clenching. She didn't need to ask any questions to know something was seriously wrong.

"We're too far to turn back," Hanson stated, "and there's no way in hell we're going to make it to Falcon's Head. The oil pressure is plummeting."

"Mayday. This is November niner-niner-seven-two-three enroute from Coyote Creek to Falcon's Head. We are losing oil pressure…"

Lucy gripped the armrest, desperate to know what was going on but afraid to distract either Hanson or Brandon.

"We're going to lose engine power," Hanson said. "Keep trying to raise someone on the emergency frequency. We won't be making it to any airport. Keep your fingers crossed we've got enough glide to make it to Haven Lake. I'll have to try to put down there."

"Any other alternatives?" From her spot behind Hanson on the rear bench seat, she saw Brandon's tight expression.

Hanson glanced at him. "No."

The two men stared at each other for another second then Brandon pushed the button on the radio mic. "Mayday. This is November niner-niner-seven-two-three enroute from Coyote Creek to Falcon's Head. Will be attempting an emergency landing at Haven Lake."

The engine sputtered. Lucy watched the prop come to a near standstill. Instead of attempting to start it, Hanson steadied the aircraft and began looking ahead for Haven Lake. The silence filled her head. Where once the drone of the engine surrounded them, now only the noise of the wind rushing past interrupted the quiet, and that had to be the eeriest sound she had ever heard.

"Miss Cameron," Tom Hanson addressed her in a calm, level voice. "This is going to be a rough landing. No two ways about it. When we get closer to the lake, I want you to lean over. Put your face between your knees and grab your ankles. Don't turn your head sideways."

"All right."

Brandon set the mic aside for a moment and turned to grab her hand. She saw his Adams's apple bob a couple times before he said, "I'm sorry, baby. I—I love you, Lucy."

She squeezed his hand, nodded and choked out, "Me too. You can tell me after we're on the ground. Okay?"

He smiled. "Okay. You're one hell of a lady." He turned around and returned to broadcasting his mayday on the emergency frequency.

Lucy looked out the windows, the wild beauty she'd so appreciated on the way out now taking on a much more sinister aspect. Instead of majestic crags and the lush green of pine forests, she spotted boulders and solid trunks that could rip the small plane to shreds.

"Our glide ratio is short," Hanson growled.

Lucy had no idea what he meant.

"How close are we?" Brandon demanded.

"A few hundred yards. Start looking for any open space you can see. The snow will cushion some of the impact. And keep broadcasting."

While Brandon went back to his mayday, he also scanned the terrain in front of them. Lucy looked too. Another set of eyes couldn't hurt. Her mouth had gone dry, and a trickle of cold sweat slipped down her spine. In some ways, though, she was almost thankful for her ignorance. She glanced at Hanson and Brandon. They knew what was coming and their grim expressions told her more than she wanted to know.

"There." Brandon pointed. It wasn't much, a thin strip of bare ground that seemed impossibly short to Lucy, but then, perhaps their altitude made it seem so.

"I'll try it."

Brandon turned, his fingers stroking Lucy's cheek. She had seen his hazel eyes alight with laughter and sparkling with adventure. Now they held her gaze with tenderness. "It's time, Lucy. Brace for impact like Hanson explained."

"What about you?"

He tried to smile, but it was just a lifting of the corner of his mouth. "We'll fly her as far as we can. Hanson will do his damnedest to get her on the ground in one piece."

Lucy didn't want to let go. She swallowed, looked at Brandon one last time and put her head between her knees. While she grabbed her ankles, the thought occurred to her if nothing else in this life remained, she had at least known the love of a man she could admire.

Chapter 6

All hell broke loose. Brandon continued to broadcast their mayday. She heard him swear and Hanson yell, "Hang on!" She thought the plane's nose lifted slightly, then a piercing whine that confused her filled the cabin. Pointing up instead of down had to be a good thing. Right?

Seconds became minutes that became a lifetime of screeching metal, glass breaking and feeling as though everything and everyone was being tossed around like papers caught in a whirlwind. Lucy held onto her ankles for dear life, grunting when something struck her shoulder. At last there was one final, long metallic ripping noise and the small craft shuddered to a halt, hanging at an odd angle.

Silence. The only thing she could hear was her own breathing. And that frightened her more than the pain in her shoulder. She lifted her head, relieved to find she had room to move. Snow had flooded the cabin and the branch of a tree protruded through the window to her left.

"Brandon? Mr. Hanson?" She heard nothing. Not even a groan. The pounding of her heart, so hard it rocked her, finally spurred her to action. Her fingers fumbled with the harness, making it difficult to get the latches unbuckled. Free at last, she inched forward. Her shoulder felt stiff and painful, but she ignored it, her heart slamming ever harder in her chest at the continued silence from the two front seats. From the amount of snow jamming the cockpit around them, it was almost impossible to see anything.

"Brandon?" A note of hysteria crept into her voice, so she stopped and took a deep breath. She couldn't help if she fell to pieces. Okay, the first thing she needed to do was make sure they weren't dangling over the edge of a precipice or jammed in a tree. When she scooted to the right side, she could see what remained of the fuselage rested amidst a tangle of broken trees, but it did appear to be on the ground. She moved, relieved to find nothing shifted.

Lucy blew a puff of air out. She needed to get out, but trees blocked the left side of the plane. On Brandon's side, snow and no doubt his bulk blocked her access to the door. She searched, her gaze landing on the rear passenger window. It was broken, but not all the glass was gone. The way the window narrowed toward the back would make squeezing through hard, but it was her only option. Taking her wool scarf from around her neck, Lucy wrapped her hand and arm and began punching out the glass. Already weakened, the remaining shards broke beneath the pressure. Once the opening was clear, she brushed away the pieces. Much as she hated it, she was going to have to go through headfirst so she could get leverage to pull herself out.

Breath puffing out in little clouds, Lucy wiggled through the window. Once her hips were through, she put her arms down to catch herself and kicked free. Her shoulder protested when she tucked and rolled. Several branches scratched her face and hands, but at last she sat in the snow a few feet away, able to take stock of herself and her surroundings. Other than some scratches and a shoulder she suspected was severely bruised, she was okay.

Her gaze lifted to the plane. Brandon. She scrambled to the side and, balancing on the trunk of a tree, tried the door. It was jammed. She braced one foot against the fuselage and tried again, using the strength in her leg to add to her effort. With a lurch and a grinding of metal, the door cracked open about six inches.

"Holy Mary, please," she cried. "I need to help them!" She tried again, once more bracing her boot on the side. This time she leaned all of her weight into it, even knowing she was apt to fall backward when or if the door gave way. Another grind of metal on metal and this time it moved. Lucy's innate sense of balance was the sole factor that kept her on her feet.

Snow tumbled from inside, and now she saw the sleeve of Brandon's blue jacket. Tempering her desire to get him out as fast as possible with the knowledge she needed to be cautious, Lucy began removing the snow with swift, careful movements. She freed his face first, and gasped when she saw a bump and a jagged cut near his hairline. It was bleeding, but sluggishly. As a rule, didn't head wounds bleed a lot? Fingers shaking, she stripped off her glove and pressed two fingers next to his windpipe, sighing in relief at the pulse beating there. He was alive, his heartbeat regular, so maybe the lack of blood had to do with the snow.

"Brandon?"

He moaned. Scraping at the snow faster now, she uncovered more of him. When she reached his lower left leg, Lucy swallowed. His ankle was at an odd angle. She'd seen a broken ankle once when she was a teenager at her last foster home. One of the younger kids had jumped off a trampoline, landing on the hard ground in the backyard. The boy had screamed bloody murder. Looking at the ankle, and the cramped space, Lucy realized there was no way to stabilize it before she moved him. And moving him was going to be no easy task if he remained unconscious. He was tall and muscular.

She looked around for something to cushion his fall and gathered a few of the many pine boughs severed during the crash, piling them outside the door. With as much gentleness and care as she could muster, she pushed his slumped form back so she could get to his harness. This time she had to stop because her fingers were getting cold. Lucy blew on them, rubbed them together and then tried once more to unbuckle. Damn it. It was jammed. An image flashed into her mind of their first day out on the ski slopes. Her binding had jammed. In an instant, Brandon had produced a jackknife from his pocket. Would he still have it? She eased her hand into his jeans, her fingers just touching the knife. Digging a little deeper, she grasped hold and pulled it out.

She was hoping she could use it to give her leverage. If she had to cut through the tough nylon belt, there was no telling how long it might take. Luck was with her. At the point where she feared she would snap the blade, the latch released. She had just enough time to flick the knife closed and shove it in her pocket before Brandon's unconscious form started sliding toward her. His ankle smacked the plane and he moaned.

"I know," she whispered. "I'm so sorry, baby, so sorry to cause you any pain. And I wish I could bind your ankle for you right now, but I have to see if I can get Mr. Hanson out. I'll be as quick as I can." She wasn't sure if he could hear her, but talking to him calmed her too. The fact she'd heard nothing at all from Hanson turned her stomach, but she crawled into the cockpit anyway, pulling snow away from him.

She freed his face and gasped. His eyes were wide and staring into nothingness. Teeth chattering and hands shaking, she made herself look for a pulse, but she found none. Oh God. Frantic and frightened, she pulled at the snow, and her hands came away bloody.

"Hanson! Tom!" She shook him, but his head lolled, and then she uncovered the branch that had pierced his chest. There was nothing she could do for him. He was dead. Lucy's stomach lurched. She stumbled from the cockpit, barely missing Brandon in her haste and tripping over a couple of branches. Bending over, she threw up what was left in her stomach, heaving until nothing remained. Lucy had seen a lot of things during her life people shouldn't have to see, but never anyone dead. When she had control over her emotions and her stomach, she made herself return to the plane.

She found the mic Brandon had used and traced the wire to the control panel. A lot of things looked smashed, but she had to give it a try. She clicked the push-to-talk button, but there was no indication anything was working. She stared at it in frustration. Weren't these things supposed to have some sort of emergency beacon that automatically activated? Somewhere, she had read something about transponders and emergency signals, maybe in other crash stories that had made the news. She rubbed her hands up and down her arms for comfort and to ramp up her circulation.

The radio didn't seem to be working, so she would have to trust that some emergency locator signal was going out. She didn't know how flight plans worked, but even if no one official was expecting them, the kid at Air Service would be. He would call the guy at Coyote Creek when they didn't show… Someone would look for them. The question was how long until they did?

Lucy looked around. Hanson had said they would be short of Haven Lake. If she assumed the plane was facing in the direction they had been going, then she could use it to orient. From the glow of the sun, her assumption felt valid. She was no navigator, but she had spent time sailing, so she was used to figuring out direction. She forced her gaze back to Hanson.

"I'm so sorry, Mr. Hanson. I can't move you and Brandon both. There's nothing I can do for you, but I can still help him." She made herself climb into the cockpit and closed his eyelids. There was something spooky about his glazing gaze. A search behind the passenger seats uncovered an emergency kit containing a space blanket, bottled water and some granola bars. After jumping out, she pocketed the water and the granola bars and covered Brandon with the Mylar blanket. Maybe the cargo area had something she could use. She pulled open the door, rooting around for anything that might help her. When she pulled out two nylon tarps, several bungees and a long piece of rope, Lucy breathed in relief. She'd hit the jackpot.

With Brandon covered, she took the smaller tarp and climbed into the cockpit. She couldn't do much for Hanson, but she could at least cover him and do her best to secure the plane. All she could do was pray the rescuers would find them before any animal discovered his remains. She had no idea what kind of family he had, but she knew what her own feelings were…and Hanson was a virtual stranger to her.

It worried her that Brandon was still unconscious. What if he had internal injuries? How would she know? Going on instinct, she checked his pulse again. It felt strong and regular. If he was bleeding internally, shouldn't she be able to tell from his pulse? She huffed out a shaky breath. What the hell did she know? She was a stripper, a freaking city girl from back East out in the middle of nowhere with a dead guy and an injured, unconscious man.

Whoa. Hold on. She was losing it again. Step back, Lucy girl. She needed to decide what had to be done and in what order. Okay. Brandon's ankle needed splinting. They needed shelter. She needed to figure out another way to try to contact help. She looked around. She couldn't have much daylight left, so finding shelter meant she would have to move Brandon at the same time she searched. Hanson had mentioned fishing cabins. If they were near Haven Lake, then maybe one of those cabins was close enough to reach.

So how could she move Brandon? She looked at the tarp, the bungees and the rope. What if she wrapped him, almost like swaddling him? She could attach the rope to the grommets on the tarp and use it like a harness so she could drag him. She chewed her lip while she thought about his ankle. If she dragged him without doing something about it, she could damage it even more. Right. The splint had to come first.

By the time she had him wrapped and ready to go, Lucy was dripping with sweat.

"Okay, baby. This isn't going to be fun for either one of us, but it's the best I can come up with." She zipped her jacket and lifted the rope over her good shoulder so it crossed her body. Blowing out a breath, she leaned into the rope and began pulling Brandon, swaddled in the tarp, over the lighter snow blanketing the area beneath the trees. Ahead, she could see the woods thinned, and she prayed what she'd see when she came out was the lake. Even better, a cabin in close proximity because she was running only on adrenaline.

She reached the edge, crying with relief when lying in front of her was the smooth expanse of Haven Lake. Her relief soon disappeared. The closest cabin was along the northern edge of the lake. Even worse, out here in the heavier snow cover, the going was exhausting. This snow wasn't like the packed and groomed runs of the ski resort. It was deep natural snow. With every step, she punched through the thin top crust, but she had no choice. If she couldn't get Brandon to a cabin, he would die. And leaving him behind was not even in the equation.

Halfway there, she knelt in the snow, gasping for breath. The next thing she knew, she was crying. Blubbering, in fact.

"I'm losing it, Brandon," she sobbed. "I don't think I can do this."

Silence was her answer. This high, in the middle of winter, not even the chirp of a bird disturbed the crisp air. After a couple minutes, she swiped her hand across her eyes and nose. This wasn't getting it done. There was no choice to be made. She could either suck it up and get them to shelter or they'd both die because she wouldn't leave him. She'd already had to leave one man behind, but not this one. Never this one.

The light was fading fast by the time she reached the small cabin tucked in the edge of the trees surrounding the lake. Barely able to lift the rope over her head, she let it drop behind her and stumbled to the door. The latch turned with a small squeak of cold-stiffened metal. *Oh, thank God*. Something had gone her way. Just one small thing. It was enough to lift her up so she could face what still had to be done.

There was a wide cot in the corner, bare of any blankets, but that was okay. At least for now, she would concentrate on getting Brandon inside. She pulled him in, but instead of getting him all the way to the cot, she stopped in front of the fireplace. With exhaustion dragging at her, she wanted to cry with relief when she saw not only wood in the woodbox, but kindling, paper and matches. Building a fire was a task she could do. She'd practiced with a pit kiln two summers earlier until her neighbors had complained about the fire and she'd had to purchase her own kiln.

With the flames licking the dry wood, she shut the cabin door and turned to Brandon. Time to begin unswaddling. His color seemed okay. Once she got them both warmed, she would see about cleaning the cut on his head and taking another look at his ankle. She needed to try a last ditch attempt at reaching help first. Reaching into his left front pocket, she pulled out his cellphone. When she looked at it, her hopes crashed. The phone was cracked. She tried turning it on, but got nothing.

God in heaven… They were stuck until someone figured out they hadn't returned and initiated a search. Hanson was dead, Brandon was unconscious and they were without any kind of communication with the outside world. Could it get any worse?

From behind her, she heard movement. Brandon was waking. She spun and knelt next to him. With shaky fingers, she brushed his hair off his face, being careful to avoid the bloody bump.

"Wake up, baby. Come on. Talk to me and let me know you're okay."

"What happened?" His voice was nothing more than a hoarse croak.

"There was an accident," she told him, trying to keep her tone calm. "A crash."

"Thirsty," he whispered, his tongue touching his parched lips.

"Lie still. I'll get you some water." She pulled the bottle from her jacket, unscrewed the lid and lifted his head so she could tilt the opening against his lips. "Not too much, baby. I've got to get everything squared away here, then I'll get you some more."

He nodded, his hazel eyes tracking her movements around the cabin while he lay on the floor. Lucy took off her jacket and tucked it beneath his head, then began a systematic search of the cabin to determine what was there. A quarter of an hour later, she had lined up two cans of potted meat, a tin of saltines, some coffee and three pouches of dehydrated beef stew. What she hadn't found were any pots and pans or dishes.

She eyed the vanishing light. There was another cabin about two hundred yards away. She would have to search it before darkness fell. They were in the middle of nowhere, and it would be pitch black. She was reluctant to take her coat, but she needed it. Brandon had slipped into a doze. He stirred when she slipped the jacket from under his head, but then settled back to sleep.

"I'll be right back." Of course he couldn't hear her, but it made her feel better to say it anyway.

* * * *

Matt Petersohn tried calling Brandon again, and once again got dumped straight to voicemail. It wasn't like Bran to be out of touch. The guy was permanently plugged in. A glance outside, and Matt gritted his teeth. He'd gotten a call less than a half-hour earlier from Air Service at Falcon's Head Airport. Brandon and Lucy had flown out with the company's co-owner to Coyote Creek. They'd been scheduled back two hours ago. There'd been no radio contact, and despite checking, no emergency beacon. The plane and its occupants had disappeared. After Nick Hanson had called his dad to alert him, Jim had phoned Matt. Jim was letting the authorities know now that the plane was missing. While Matt was on tenterhooks about his friends, he knew it was even worse for Jim. Tom Hanson was his older brother. The two of them had been running the charter service for more than twenty years.

Matt's phone vibrated and he punched it on. "Yeah."

"We've initiated a search. According to Coyote Creek, they left on schedule. Problem is we're losing daylight, so unless someone can pick up an emergency beacon, there's not much we can do until tomorrow morning."

Matt sighed. "I'm sorry, Jim. I know this is tough on you. I'm not going to be able to wait too much longer before I notify Brandon Barrett's family. This isn't like some run-of-the-mill Joe. The guy's the COO of one of the biggest media companies in the United States. And I have to warn you, once this gets out, this place will be swamped."

"Then let's hope we find them in short order. Tom's a fine pilot, Matt. You know that. If they ran into trouble, he could land that little Cessna almost anywhere."

"God, I hope you're right."

After hanging up with Jim, Matt stared out the window of his office. He and Bran had been through a lot together over the years. When Matt had torn himself up skiing, Bran had been there for him. In fact, without his friend's support, Matt had wondered sometimes if he wouldn't have ended up a cripple. Brandon had been the one to bully, badger and bolster him through the surgeries and rehab. He'd been the one there to pick up the pieces when Matt had returned to the World Cup circuit and faced the knowledge his comeback wasn't quite enough. His dreams of reigning at the top of the competitive ski world were over, so Bran had given him the backing to get Falcon's Summit where it needed to be to become a world-class resort.

He owed Brandon's family. He couldn't keep this a secret any longer. With a reluctance born not only of what he would have to say, but also to whom he would have to say it, Matt picked up the phone. He had Bran's parents' phone number from way back, and he doubted it had changed. They didn't live in a house…they inhabited a kingdom. The phone was answered on the third ring by a supercilious-sounding British voice no doubt belonging to a butler. He was informed Mr. and Mrs. Barlow-Barrett were entertaining.

"I don't care if their guest list includes the president and the pope. This is an emergency regarding their son Brandon. I need Mr. Barlow-Barrett on the phone right now."

That appeared to get the man's attention. Matt drummed his fingers while he waited for the phone to be picked up.

"This is Alexander Barlow-Barrett. What is the meaning of this?"

Cold and imperious, just as Matt remembered him from the few—thank God—brushes he'd had with Bran's old man. "This is Matt Petersohn from Falcon's Summit in Colorado. There's no easy way to tell you this, sir. Your son is among three people missing aboard a charter flight out here."

Dead silence greeted him.

Chapter 7

For most of her adult life, Lucy had pushed herself to her physical and mental limits. And just how funny was that coming from a stripper? But it was true. She had demanded a lot of her mind through college, and of her body by keeping fit enough to have a long career as an exotic dancer. While other girls came and went like fans rushing through a turnstile at a rock concert, Lucy had been at Flamingo Road since she was old enough to dance.

Right now, she began to think she'd reached her limit. She trudged back to the cabin carrying a duffel bag filled with her booty from the other fishing cabin and wondered how much longer she could last before she collapsed. But collapsing was not an option. She had to take care of Brandon, had to stay alert in case anyone flew over tonight searching for them. She had found a flare, but didn't want to waste it, since the burn time wouldn't be long.

She opened the door to find him curled on his side toward the fire. What wouldn't she give at that moment to be able to stretch out next to him, to feel his arms wrap around her, his voice tell her everything would be all right? She shook the image from her mind. Practicality. That's what was needed now.

Lucy spooned coffee into the smaller of the two pots she'd found, put snow in with it and set it at the edge of the fire. She added more snow to the second pot and set it on the other side. Once that water was hot, she would stir in the beef stew. In the meantime, she could tend to Brandon's head. The other cabin had sported pots and pans, but it had also boasted a couple blankets and a first aid kit. Nothing elaborate, but enough to clean and disinfect his head injury.

He woke with a hiss when she cleaned the cut. "Damn! That hurts."

"I'm sorry, Brandon, but I need to get this cleaned some." While she worked, he watched her. She placed a butterfly bandage on the cut, thinking it needed stitching, and gave him a small smile. "There. That's the best I can do right now. I have coffee on and once the water is hot, it shouldn't take long to get the beef stew ready."

"Where are we?"

"At one of the fishing cabins at Haven Lake."

He looked confused. "I'm not familiar with Haven Lake."

A trickle of unease slid along her spine. "It's a lake in Colorado not too far from Falcon's Head."

His gaze shifted around the cabin. "You said we were in a crash. What kind?"

Lucy packed the first aid gear before answering. He didn't remember, but that wasn't any big deal. A lot of people had blurry memories of traumatic events. "A plane crash, coming back from Coyote Creek." She paused. "Do you know who you are?"

His gaze shifted to her. "Brandon Barlow-Barrett." She sagged in relief until his next words destroyed her world. "Who are you?"

Lucy had always wondered if she would be able to smile in the face of disaster. Now she knew. The answer was yes. She kept a small smile curving her lips, faced the man she loved, the man who had no idea who she was, and introduced herself. "I'm Lucy Cameron."

He hesitated. "Do we know each other?"

"We met a couple of days ago," she responded, keeping her tone casual, and turned to the fire to check the coffee and the stew, as if their meeting were no more important than what time of day it might be. No way was she burdening him with the intimacies of their relationship. Not on top of everything else. "What's the last thing you remember?"

He rubbed the uninjured side of his head near his temple. "Arguing with my father during a breakfast meeting at Barrett Newspapers headquarters over the future of *National News*."

Amazing. Her hand was steady as she poured some coffee. *National News*. His family's newspaper. Brandon hadn't been honest with her either. Saying his family was in communications was like saying Bill Gates worked on computers. She held the mug out to him. "Here. Be careful with this. It's hot."

She felt his eyes on her while she stirred the stew.

"How long have we been here?"

"A few hours. You and the pilot tried the radio when the engine started acting up, but you didn't have any luck." She saw him reach for his phone. He could remember what pocket he kept his phone in, but not the woman he'd made love to two nights in a row. Wow. That was a real ego adjustment. "Your phone's broken."

His gaze went to the window next to the door. "The plane's emergency transponder should have activated. Someone will be looking by first light, if they aren't already." He rubbed his head. "Where's the pilot?"

Lucy swallowed and shook her head. "Dead."

He looked around. "You got me here on your own?"

"Yes. It had to be done." Lucy scooted nearer the beef stew and dished some into a bowl. She didn't want to talk about this. She wanted them to eat and go to sleep, so she could lick her wounds in private. "Here. Eat."

"What about you?"

"There's one bowl. I'll eat when you're through." She stood and turned her back to him. "I'm going to bring in some more wood."

Anything to get outside, away from the man who'd forgotten her and everything they'd shared. She threw her coat on and walked out of the cabin. After stacking plenty of wood next to the fireplace and next to the door, she looked at the pile behind the cabin, and an idea came to her. Lucy toted armful upon armful of wood to the edge of the lake, well away from the cabin and in an area where the wind had blown away much of the snow cover. With meticulous care, she laid out the letters SOS along the lakeshore. She hoped it was big enough for someone to read from the air.

The cold whipped her cheeks as she looked over her work. It had to be enough. They had to be rescued soon because she just didn't know how much longer she could keep her pain and exhaustion under wraps. Even out here, she was afraid to let go. If she did, there was no telling if she could get herself under control again.

* * * *

Alexander Barlow-Barrett had always prided himself on being stoic. His wife, Patricia, was cut from the same cloth. Over the years, they'd worked well together because they both understood a good marriage was seldom founded on the heat of passion. It was built over time with care. They had paid attention to their relationship and their children, always felt they knew what was best for their progeny. In recent years, that had been called into question. First with Preston, who had been a constant trial, and then with Seth, whose rebellion he didn't quite understand. Still, Alex lived in hope Seth would be coaxed back into the fold. In the meantime, his younger brother had been doing an excellent job of running the company.

Brandon had surprised him. Prior to Seth's defection, Brandon had seemed far too flippant and carefree to be taken seriously when it came to running Barrett, but in the last few months, Alex had seen a whole new side to his middle son, a side he could respect even if he didn't always agree with the sometimes radical ideas Brandon set forth.

Now, for the first time since Preston had run away from her boarding school, fear gnawed at Alex. Following the phone call from Brandon's ski bum friend, he had broken the news to Tricia. With the calm that had always epitomized them, they had seen their guests out the door and instructed the servants to begin packing. Breaking from her usual after dinner sherry, Tricia had asked for a scotch on the rocks, just like Alex's.

He reached over across the armrest of the private jet seat and took her hand in his. "We will find him. He will be fine."

She shook her head. "I don't know why he had to come out here. We have such beautiful places to ski in the East. And what is wrong with the house in Stowe? This could have been prevented."

Alex's eyes narrowed as he glanced out the window. They would arrive in Denver before dawn. The authorities had discouraged them from trying to fly into Falcon's Head during the dark, but had promised they would get them in at first light. Of course, taking the Barrett jet was out of the question since the runway in Falcon's Head wasn't long enough. Alex chafed at the inconvenience. Once they found Brandon, he wanted to be able to get him to the best medical facilities without delay.

He reviewed what he'd learned. Because no emergency beacon had activated, authorities were already looking at maintenance records for the aircraft, and what they were uncovering was disturbing. While Tom and Jim Hanson had been in business for more than twenty years with an impeccable safety record, the maintenance logs for the missing C-182 showed the mechanic they'd hired a few months ago hadn't checked everything he was supposed to during the plane's last routine service. One of the things he'd failed to check was the batteries for the emergency transponder. It made Alex wonder what else had been overlooked or lied about.

They would get to the bottom of it, and someone would be held accountable, but first and foremost, they would find his son and he would bring Brandon home. Alex cleared his throat and kept his eyes averted from his wife. Seth had always been her favorite of their three boys, but Alex had found his eldest son wearing most of the time. Perhaps because they were both too stiff-necked and opinionated. Brandon was the most easygoing of the three, but still had a mind and a business sense that were flawless. And right now, Alex would admit it to himself, if no one else, Brandon had always been his favorite. He was a born negotiator who nevertheless stood up for what he believed in and charmed most people into agreeing with him.

If there was any way for anyone to survive an airplane crash, Brandon was the one to do it. Alex had to keep reassuring himself.

* * * *

Lucy let herself into the cabin. Brandon had set his cup and his mug to the side and was stretched out once more. When she saw he was sleeping, she let him be. There would be time enough later to get him to move from the floor to the cot nearby. In the meantime, she would get coffee and stew.

Her muscles were beginning to let her know in no uncertain terms that her body had gone through a trauma, and she had been pushing herself to the limit ever since then. Brandon had to outweigh her by at least seventy-five pounds, and she had managed to move him around a half-mile or more. The last thing she needed right now was to worry about what she ate. She needed calories to restore what she'd lost. Then she needed rest. The emotional disaster her life had become would have to wait until later, until after they were rescued.

In the back of her mind was the thought maybe Brandon would remember. She had read somewhere amnesia was most often a temporary thing. But she didn't want to try to live on hope that was true. Since he had suffered a head injury, he probably had a concussion in addition to the broken ankle. The best thing would be to keep him as quiet as possible.

Retreating to the small wooden table near the window, Lucy sipped her coffee while she waited for the stew to cool enough for her to eat. It wasn't the best meal she'd eaten, but thinking back to her teenage years, she'd also eaten meals a whole lot worse. This one warmed her and filled her. For now, that was enough.

Brandon woke again, and she helped him outside so he could take care of his personal needs. When they returned, she directed him to the cot, helped him get comfortable and gave him some over-the-counter pain pills, the sole thing she had to help ease the discomfort of his ankle. He didn't complain about his head, only the ankle, so she took the chance it was safe to give him some relief.

Once she had him settled, he looked at her. "What about you?"

"I'll bunk on the floor near the fire if I get sleepy. Don't worry about me."

She watched him most of the night, memorizing every feature of his face. It wouldn't take long to find them. After all, this was the heir apparent to one of the biggest newspaper companies in the country, maybe the world. Chances were, people were already searching. There wouldn't be room for Lucy Cameron aka Jasmine LeFleur, the main dancer at Flamingo Road, anywhere in the headlines that would surround Brandon Barlow-Barrett's brush with death. Nor should there be. At most, she would be a scandal, an embarrassment.

She stared into the flames crackling and snapping in the fireplace and could envision the headlines. *Newspaper Tycoon Holed Up With Stripper. Did In-flight Hanky-panky Lead to Mountain Crash?* Yeah. Not what the Barlow-Barretts would want published. Not what she wanted published either. Lucy had worked damn hard to keep her personal identity and her professional one separate. She lived in a quiet residential neighborhood. It was working class, but they were nice people. Publicity like this could tarnish Brandon's future, but it could annihilate hers.

* * * *

Matt spent the night pouring over maps of the area between Falcon's Head and Coyote Creek. According to Jim Hanson, there was a dead area in the vicinity of Haven Lake where it could be difficult if not impossible to get out a radio signal. But he knew he'd gotten out of there on his cellphone, yet when he tried Brandon's he still got dumped into voicemail over and over again. He and Jim both considered Haven Lake a logical starting point to begin looking at first light. It was one of the few areas between the two towns where it might be possible to land a small plane in an emergency.

If they weren't there, Matt knew the chances of finding anyone alive would be remote. He didn't even want to think about it. Brandon had been one of his best friends—was still one of his best friends, he corrected himself. They would find him. They would find Tom Hanson and Brandon's woman, Lucy. He'd seen the look on Bran's face. Brandon wouldn't let someone like her slip away without a fight. Matt was counting on determination from all three of them. Tom Hanson had survived Vietnam. He was an excellent pilot under pressure. Brandon, despite his rich-boy upbringing, was mentally and physically tough. Lucy, he didn't know well, but she had the same look about her. She was a fighter, not some weak-kneed woman who'd lie down and cry at the first sign of trouble.

He'd gotten a call from Brandon's father when the Barrett Newspapers jet touched down in Denver. Matt told him he and Jim were going up in a helicopter along with other search crews at first light. He wanted Brandon's father under no false idea he would be waiting on him to arrive before they began their search. That was not happening. Even if the three of them had survived an emergency landing, chances were they were all injured. Depending on the extent of those injuries, they were now in a race against time to save them.

* * * *

Lucy stirred as the sky began to lighten. She tried to remember how long they had been in the air when she'd noticed Haven Lake. It seemed to her it was closer to Falcon's Head than it was to Coyote Creek. The search would no doubt be based out of Falcon's Head. Out of habit, she checked her watch, then sighed. It too had become a casualty of the crash. She would have to guess the time. She wanted to give it about fifteen minutes past the point where she figured they would take off. Then she would light the flare and double check to ensure the SOS she'd created last night was still visible.

Brandon slept. For that she was grateful. She had checked on him a couple of times during the night, so she knew the sleep was natural, not something induced either by concussion or coma. She had no more pain medication to give him. If someone didn't find them today, she wasn't sure what she would do. His ankle needed attention, but she had no way to give it. With a soft groan, she slipped her boots on, followed by her jacket. After grabbing the flare and a box of matches, she stepped out into a world of white and gray. Little stirred in the morning light, just the sound of the wind whistling through the trees.

Lucy walked to where she'd laid out her crude SOS in logs. It was still visible. She looked over her shoulder at the cabin. The glow from the fire shone through the one small window, casting a patch of warm light on the snow. This would be over soon. She buried the end of the flare in the snow, feeling like she was closing the door on an entire life. In reality, it was four days, but they were four days that had changed her existence. She had believed for a while they had changed Brandon's too. But that was just a fantasy. He didn't remember them, didn't remember meeting her on the plane, teaching her to ski, dancing with her, making love to her. Those memories would stand out forever in her mind. She would never forget, never forget the moment he had turned around in the Cessna and told her he loved her. She would always remember, but it seemed he would not.

Lucy bent close to the flare and struck a match to the edge of the box. The first two went out before she could get the flare to light, but the third match connected. With a hiss and a sizzle, the flare lit, sending out its reddish chemical glare and highlighting even more the darker letters of her wooden SOS.

In the distance, she thought she heard the faint thump-thump-thump of helicopter rotors. Brandon would get help now. Wanting at least a moment or two alone with him, she jogged along the path and entered the cabin. He might not remember, but she would and she could at least savor these last couple minutes. He lay on his back with one arm across his chest and the other thrown above his head. His golden hair was tousled like it had been—was it just yesterday morning she had awakened with him next to her?—in his room. He looked like he would open his eyes any moment. She wished he would and tell her this had all been a dream or a joke.

The speed of the rotors increased and the sound of snow crystals peppering the cabin joined the rhythmic thumping of the motor. Her throat ached even more than her chest, but this wasn't a time for tears. She crossed the room to his side and rubbed his shoulder.

"Brandon? Wake up. Help's arrived. We're going to get you out of here now."

He blinked at her, and the blankness of his gaze was like a knife cutting her heart in two.

The next several hours passed in a daze. She vaguely remembered the arrival of a medevac chopper right on the heels of Matt and Jim Hanson's arrival. She remembered the look on Jim's face when he'd stepped into the cabin and seen Tom was not with them. As they left in the air ambulance for the hospital in Falcon's Head, she had answered the questions directed at her perfunctorily, her eyes glued to what was going on with Brandon. They hooked fluids to him, someone was unwrapping the ankle she'd splinted and taped. Lucy heard the word surgery bandied about. Not surprising. There would be only the best for Brandon Barlow-Barrett.

When they arrived at the hospital's landing pad, she saw a tall, silver-haired man in a long, black wool coat, a blond woman tucked into his side and wrapped from neck to ankles in fur. The man looked like Brandon, but he was harder, more arrogant. The couple's eyes skated over her, through her, as if she were not there. And to them, she wasn't. All but one of the paramedics rushed alongside Brandon's stretcher, the older couple hurrying in its wake. Lucy watched them go, a small twisting wrench in her gut leaving her feeling empty and alone.

"Come, Miss Cameron. Let's get you to the ER. They'll do an evaluation on you, but I suspect you'll be treated and released. You were lucky. The shoulder injury appears to be some blunt force trauma, but nothing serious. Your scratches seem to be healing fine on their own. It's a miracle."

"Thanks. Treated and released would be good." The only serious injury was to her emotions, but she would get better. Once she got home and back to her regular routine, she would get better.

With just a bruised shoulder, the medical staff had a few other cases that had to be seen in front of her. After a wait that seemed interminable, they got her into X-ray, satisfied themselves her shoulder was only bruised, then sent her out. With nowhere else to go, and too tired to think about it, Lucy sat and watched the news coverage on the television. Wow, if she hadn't experienced the crash firsthand, she'd never know she'd even been on board the same plane from listening to the reporter doing a live shot outside the hospital.

"Miss Cameron?"

She looked into a pair of flat, blue eyes.

"I'm Mike Lovelace with the National Transportation Safety Board. I need to ask you a few questions…"

She must have given him the answers he needed. When he finished, she asked, "Will you need me for anything else or can I go home?"

"To the resort or to your permanent address?"

"Home. I believe I've seen all I care to of mountains and snow for some time to come."

"We're through. I have your information if we should need to reach you. Someone may contact you for a formal deposition." He paused for a moment. "Do you have anyone here to give you a ride?"

"I can." The voice came from behind her. Lucy turned, somewhat curious, to find Matt Petersohn waiting, his fingers tucked into his jeans pockets. Lovelace nodded at them both, then walked down the hall. Matt squatted in front of her. "Have they seen you?"

Lucy tucked a strand of hair behind her ear. "Oh, yes. I just have some bruising, so there's no need for me to stay. I should be thankful for how lucky I was." She looked into Matt's steady gaze. "Why, in a week or so, I'll have absolutely nothing to remind me of this and can put it from my mind." Lucy stopped and clamped down on her lower lip with her teeth.

"Lucy…"

"Don't!" she hissed at him. "If you're going to give me a ride, then let's do this. You'll accept my apology, I hope, if I'm not the most scintillating conversationalist on the trip up the mountain. For some odd reason, it keeps sticking in my mind I had to leave a dead man sitting in his plane overnight with nothing more than a tarp wrapped around him. And after I hauled the other man out of the wreck to find us both shelter, he doesn't even remember who I am. But I'm sure I'll be able to put it all from my mind. It will fade like the bruises on my shoulder."

Their eyes met. In his, she saw an immense amount of understanding and she had to look away before she cracked. As if sensing her turmoil, he drew her to her feet and wrapped his arm around her waist. "Come on. Let's get you out of here. The news crews are so busy making sure they get the medevac chopper in the background of their live shots, I doubt they'll even notice us." Even saying so, he hurried her along the sidewalk and out to the parking lot, where a van from the resort waited. Matt made sure she was buckled in, then slid behind the wheel. "You know, his dad did ask about you. He wants to thank you."

Lucy stared out the window. "I think that would be a little awkward under the circumstances. I want to get my things packed, then I want to get on a flight home."

"Lucy," Matt grated, "amnesia like this is almost always temporary..."

She turned and put her hand on his arm. When he looked at her, she said, "I don't want him to remember. It would be better if he never remembers."

"You can't mean that."

"I do. You need to understand this. I am not anyone Brandon should even know. My real name *is* Lucy Cameron, but I have a work name— Jasmine LeFleur. I'm an exotic dancer at a high-end club in DC. How well do you think that will stack up in Brandon's life? If it became public, rival media outlets would have a heyday with it. And I saw his parents. My God! She practically flies a DAR banner behind her, and he's got Yacht Club written all over him. I doubt they'd appreciate the finer points of pole dancing." Lucy jerked her head away and mumbled, "Just let me get out of here, and when I'm gone, do everyone a favor—lose any records of my stay here, especially my home and work addresses."

"I think you're making a mistake."

"If you are the good friend to him he believes you to be, you will do this."

Chapter 8

"I don't know if this will help me remember or not, Matt, but I need to do it." It had been six weeks since the crash and while Brandon still carried the cane the doctor insisted he have, it was now more a decoration than a necessity.

"We'll take the helicopter. That way if you want to set down, we can, but I'm warning you right now, if you get away from right around the lake, the terrain is too rough for that ankle of yours."

"I'm not planning on hiking." Brandon set his cane inside the helicopter and then stepped onto the skid before folding himself into the seat next to Matt. "I appreciate you doing this."

Matt grinned at him. "It gives me a chance to see how much skiing we might have left, and how much melting's already occurred. I get some guests who like hiking to Haven Lake."

After slipping on his headset, Matt pointed to Brandon's set and then picked up his clipboard and began going through his preflight checklist. As the rotors started and picked up speed, Brandon stared out the side window at the mountain where they would be heading. He hoped this trip would start giving him a feeling of being back in control of his life. Right now, that was something lacking. Having a chunk of his life disappear was fucking with his head. What pissed him off even more was no one else seemed to want to discuss it, including Matt. Whenever Brandon had brought up those missing days and the mysterious woman who'd also been a part of the plane crash, Matt went tight-lipped and silent.

All he'd learned was her name. Lucy Cameron. Not a common name, but not so rare it was easy to find her. On top of everything else, he'd been so out of it following the crash he didn't even remember her from its aftermath. Tall and blond with haunted gray eyes. He would dream of the expression in those eyes when he was able to sleep at night, but whenever he tried to reach out to her in his dreams, she vanished, no more than a puff of smoke from a magician's trick. And somehow, Brandon was sure he needed to remember her, was positive she held the key to what he was missing.

His father had tried to get him into the office, but Brandon had skirted the none-too-subtle hints until Alexander had lost his temper. "This is about that woman, isn't it?"

"Why didn't you find her? Why is there no mention of her?" Brandon had raked his hand through his hair as he'd confronted his father. "She saved my life. Couldn't you have at least *thanked* her?"

For once, his father had seemed almost embarrassed. He fiddled with the antique brass sextant on the desk in his study. "We tried. She was already gone."

Brandon had sighed in exasperation. "What do you mean, 'gone'?"

"She'd left the resort, and your friend…"

"Matt. His name's Matt."

"He refused to divulge any information."

"Well, I'm going out there."

"You cannot be serious!" Alex's face had flushed an unbecoming red. "Brandon, it's time to put this behind you and move on. You're alive. That's all that matters!"

"Not to me. I've lost more than four days from my life. I want to know what happened. I want to know what I was doing on the plane. I want to know why Lucy Cameron was a passenger." He hadn't added that every night an aching sense of loneliness almost brought him to his knees. On some level, his life had stopped the day of the crash, some part of him dying as surely as the plane's pilot. "I want to see the crash site again."

His father had slapped the smooth, polished surface of his desk. "Then go, but I want a promise from you. I want you to promise you'll get this nonsense out of your system, and when you return you'll be ready to go back to work. Barrett Newspapers needs you, Brandon." His father had paused, the telltale tic in his temple revealing the clenching and unclenching of his jaw. "I need you."

They had stared at each other, eyes narrowed, for several seconds.

"I promise."

So now, with the helicopter tilting forward before lifting clear of the pad at the base of Falcon's Summit's parking lot, Brandon hoped something would trigger his memory. Matt's tinny voice crackled through the headset.

"When we come around this ridge, you'll be able to see Haven Lake. We'll be coming at the site backward. I figured we'd do an overview, fly beyond it, then turn around and approach along a similar path to what Hanson would have flown while you were going down. Can you handle that, bro?"

"Yeah." Brandon spotted the two cabins sitting at the edge of the woods not too far from the lake's shore. "Which one were we in?"

"The one farther away. According to her reports and the tracks investigators found, she turned you into a kind of human travois and hauled you out."

They were over woods now.

"Where was the wreckage?"

"At the north end, a couple hundred yards in."

Brandon took in the scene with the eye of an experienced pilot. "Hanson was attempting the impossible, wasn't he?"

Matt's sunglass covered gaze met his. "Yeah. He almost succeeded too. One person walked away. Two people lived. That was a freaking miracle." Matt took the chopper up and out in a wide arc. "They brought Hanson's mechanic up on charges. He's in jail awaiting trial."

"I guess there's some justice."

"They may ask you to testify, especially with your own pilot experience."

Brandon's laugh held a bitterness he couldn't conceal. "A witness who can't remember shit about what happened won't do the prosecutor any good."

"We're coming around now. I'll go in lower and slower so you can get a good look."

"Are those sheared off trees from the crash or from investigators?"

"Bit of both, I think. When we arrived the following morning, I don't remember it being quite this open."

Brandon stared at the raw, scarred trunks of pines. He kept waiting for some memory to surface, like a submerged ball bouncing to the top of a tub of water. But it didn't happen. He had read the NTSB reports, the details of which must have been supplied to them by Lucy. From those, he knew he had been on the radio broadcasting a mayday over and over. The plane's engine had already seized and they were gliding in. There would have been only the sound of the wind and their voices. Then Hanson probably attempted to lift the Cessna's nose. The transcripts had described what could only have been the little plane's stall horn sounding right before impact.

Why the fuck couldn't he remember? He'd read the cause of death for Tom Hanson. The guy had been gored by a pine limb that came through the plane's window. A few feet one way or the other, and it could have been him rather than Hanson. And the woman? What had Lucy thought and felt and heard in those last few seconds? What had she thought in the immediate aftermath? He could imagine how quiet it must have been. She had described having to crawl out the rear window of the aircraft. According to the investigator's notes, she had worked on freeing him first. Why? Why hadn't she gone after the pilot? Had she already known he was dead? Or was there some other reason?

The unending circle of questions with no answers haunted him.

"Is any of this helping?" Matt's voice interrupted Brandon's tortured round of thoughts.

"Not yet."

"I can set down near the cabin. You want to get out and look around?"

"Yeah." Brandon followed the line of trees to the lakeshore with his gaze. "How far is it from the crash site to the cabin?"

"Nearly a mile."

She had splinted his ankle, wrapped him up and then dragged him and herself to shelter.

Matt set the chopper down and cut the engines. "Take a look around. I'm going to inventory the two cabins so I can make plans to restock them."

Brandon stripped off his headset and put a restraining hand on Matt's arm. "You and I have been friends for a long time, Matt. We've been through a lot together. I appreciate what you're doing for me today."

Matt dropped his gaze to Brandon's hand and swallowed. He slipped off his sunglasses and met Brandon's gaze. "You saved my life years ago. I don't know if you realized how close I was to ending it. When I thought I wouldn't walk again? That was a dark time. I owe you for that…" When Brandon started to interrupt him, Matt shook his head. "No, let me finish. I do owe you, but I also owe Lucy because if it hadn't been for her, you would have died here. I made a promise to her. She asked me to destroy the records of her stay at Falcon's Summit. I did what she asked in repayment. I won't tell you where she works or what her address is. I promised her."

"But you are going to tell me something, aren't you?" Brandon's gut clenched. Somehow he knew already his world was about to be rocked.

"The two of you?" Matt's voice choked. "You were inseparable for those three days before the crash. You taught her to ski. You'd gone to Coyote Creek together. She wasn't just some random female along for an afternoon jaunt. You were together in every sense of the word."

Laura Browning

Brandon's throat tightened. He'd suspected it. Late at night, he'd even experienced some of those snippets of passion. When he'd unpacked his belongings, he'd pulled out his Nationals sweatshirt and inhaled the scent of her. He had never let anyone wear that sweatshirt. God, that was such a guy thing, like letting other people drive his car or relinquishing control of the television remote. She had worn his sweatshirt…and he had let her because they were together.

"Why didn't she stay?" The question was wrenched out of him with a world of pain trailing in its wake.

"I don't know the answer."

"Then how the fuck do I find her so she can tell me?"

Matt let his head fall back against the seat and expelled his breath on a loud sigh. "She lives somewhere around DC, man. That's all I can or will tell you." Matt climbed out of the chopper. "The museum owner in Coyote Creek sent me a handmade pot a few weeks ago. According to her, you bought it for Lucy and were supposed to get back to her with a shipping address. I have it at the lodge."

Brandon nodded. With the use of his cane, this time for real, he walked from the chopper to the cabin, studying the surrounding terrain. The snow was melting now. It had thinned in some spots to the point where rocks and tufts of tough grass were showing. Six weeks ago, it would have been coated in deep snow. She had brought him through that. Such perseverance had to mean something. He wished he knew what. Most of all, he wished he could remember. There had to be some reason she'd walked away.

* * * *

"Sugar, you need to add a little more blusher," Tiffany told Lucy when she stopped behind her and peered at her reflection in the lighted makeup mirror backstage. "We got a big bachelor party coming in tonight. They gonna spend plenty of time staring at your tits and your ass, but if you don't brighten up your face some, they might be tossing dollars on the stage instead of tens and twenties."

Lucy picked up a blusher brush and dusted her high cheekbones once more. She'd had to take another couple weeks off once she'd returned so her bruises could fade. Roberto hadn't been happy to have his best dancer sidelined, but once she'd come back to work, he'd been all smiles. She'd taken to working an extra night a week in order to make up for some of her lost revenue, and she was sure it had helped make up some revenue for Roberto too. Lucy wasn't conceited, but she knew her acts brought in crowds and helped attract groups like the bachelor party making an evening of it at Flamingo Road. This next routine was one she had put together as a joke before going on vacation. While Jasmine LeFleur was her stage name—and that's who she'd be in her last dance of the night—this routine she called "Snow Bunny Baby," complete with some strategically placed pom-pons and a long ski scarf she used to tease her audience. After this, she would have a break and then finish for the evening with Jasmine's erotic strip tease. When a bachelor party came in, she made sure to stage most of it right in front of the poor groom.

Tiffany massaged Lucy's shoulders. "You okay, sugar?"

"Yeah." She patted Tiffany's hand.

"I worry about you. You just never seemed to bounce back since that vacation of yours."

Lucy added bright pink lipstick, glad to see her hand was rock steady. This was work. She could fall apart on her own time, and very often did. "I'm okay, Tiff. Really. Maybe I am working a little too hard."

"Two minutes, Jasmine!" the stage manager called, knocking as he passed.

Lucy smiled at her friend. Tiffany had started as a dancer and taught Lucy everything she knew. Most of her time now was spent overseeing the waitresses and checking on the dancers. She looked like she wanted to say something else, but shook her head instead. "Break a leg, sugar. You know where I am if you need me."

Their eyes met in the mirror. "Thanks."

She stood behind the curtain a minute later, waiting for her introduction, then bounced out onto the stage to a rousing round of applause and whistles. The smile she turned on for the crowed was designed for effect. She was no longer Lucy Cameron, aspiring artist. She was Jasmine LeFleur. With a jaunty smile and a cock of her bare hip, she waited for the heavy thumping beat of her music to begin, then launched into a routine physically challenging enough to get her mind off Brandon. As she slithered along the pole, holding it with her thighs, she arched her body almost horizontal to the ground. The eyes of the men in her audience traced the curves of her body so revealingly displayed. When she pumped her hips from a low crouch near the flushed faces of the wedding party and the rest of their buddies, the first of the money was tossed at her feet.

It was a game, a very profitable game, but one Lucy no longer had the heart to play. The fun-loving part of her had disappeared in a few minutes along the edge of a mountain in Colorado, and she didn't know how to resurrect it.

When she put on the silky lingerie for Jasmine LeFleur's final act of the evening, Lucy let herself drift into the persona she always thought suited this final dance. It was a departure from the strident, hip pumping beats of her earlier routines. This last dance of the evening was one long, slow seduction. If there was a man in the audience who didn't have a hard-on when she was finished, then he was either dead or women weren't his thing. The props she used were one chair and one subdued spotlight. The music was jazzy, silky and sexy. She never allowed herself to get close enough to any of the patrons in this routine for them to tuck money in her costume. It would have ruined the effect, cheapened what was meant to live in each man's mind as his own personal seduction.

Tonight she played to the groom to be, seducing him with her eyes and her body. When she trailed off the stage with her long hair teasing the taut globes of her golden ass, tens, twenties and even a few hundred dollar bills littered the stage. Men sat with their jaws agape and Lucy put her hands over her face and cried.

Tiffany shooed Roberto and the stage manager away, wrapped an arm around Lucy's shoulders and guided her into the dressing room. Most of the other girls were in the showers, so they had the area in front of the mirrors to themselves.

"Sugar, you can't go on like this. I know you were in a plane crash out there, but something else happened you ain't talking about."

Lucy wiped her eyes. "And I won't now. I need a couple of days off. Then I'll be fine."

"You need more than a couple days off. You still making those pots and things?"

"Yes."

"You get cleaned and changed, sugar. You and me are gonna talk to Roberto."

When Lucy stood in the shower, all she could feel was a sense of relief someone else was taking charge for a change. The water from the wide showerhead sluiced over her body, leaching some of the fatigue from her muscles. She hadn't been sleeping well since her return from Colorado, haunted by dreams in which Tom Hanson wasn't the one who'd died in the crash. In those dreams, it was Brandon's blank green-gold gaze staring at her. And wasn't that the truth of the matter?

He might as well have been dead to her. Part of her wondered if what she was going through wasn't in fact worse. At least if he had died in the crash, he would be gone and she would know, just like she'd understood the permanence of her grandmother's death. This way, there was always the possibility torturing her that someday he might remember. What then?

Her movements were pure habit while she toweled dry, removed any makeup still remaining, and then dressed in the jeans and sweatshirt she always arrived and departed in. With her face makeup-free and her hair in a long braid, she resembled neither Jasmine LeFleur nor the Lucy Cameron Brandon had first met. She sighed and stared in the mirror. This was who she was. This was what and who she would be when she went into her studio in the morning and began working on the pots she'd been building.

In the meantime, she needed to sit down with Roberto. He and Tiffany were waiting for her when she came out of the dressing room. Lucy had always thought there was a sad, empty feeling to the club once the customers were gone and the lights had come up. Flamingo Road was a glitzy establishment, but like the women who entertained there, Lucy supposed it was often best seen in low light, not the glare of fluorescents.

"Have a seat, Lucy," Roberto ordered, his voice its usual deep rumble. "When my star dancer comes backstage and breaks into tears, I need to know why. Am I working you too hard?"

Lucy shook her head.

"Then what is it? Have you reached the end of being able to dance?"

"I don't think so, but I keep wondering. It's always been fun for me in the past. I don't feel it right now."

Roberto took her hand in his. He had been almost like a father to her, though he wasn't old enough, but she suspected he'd endured a tough childhood on the streets. Once or twice he'd mentioned taking off from foster homes. She never questioned how he'd come to own a place like Flamingo Road. Sometimes, Lucy had found, it was better not to delve too deeply into a person's past.

"Look at me," he ordered now. "What is it you want to do, Lucy?"

She swallowed, her hand trembling in his rough palm. "I want to be a potter like my grandmother. She didn't make a great living, but it was enough."

"That is a very solitary occupation," he observed. "You would be content with such a life?"

Would she? It was a question she didn't need to think about for more than a split second. "Yes. I would like to take it beyond what my grandmother did. I would like to exhibit my work, not just create pots and mugs to sell in some trendy tourist traps."

"Are you good?"

She was taken aback by his question, but after she had a moment to think, answered, "Yes. Yes, I am."

"Do you have a plan of how to make this career you want happen?"

Lucy shook her head. Roberto smiled. She had seen a similar smile before. She had seen the same look months ago when he had found a place for Tessa Edwards in his business office once the girl's pregnancy began to show. Lucy hadn't thought about her friend in a while. She would be getting ready to have her baby soon, but Tessa was no longer working at Flamingo Road. She had given her notice and explained she would be moving to the shore with the man who was now her husband. Lucy talked to her every once in a while.

Roberto had pulled out a pen and paper. He scribbled a couple names and phone numbers on it and then pushed it toward her. "Two people who can help you. One is for your head," he told her and smiled. "The other is to help you follow your heart."

Lucy's gaze darted from the paper to his face. "Are you firing me?"

Roberto leaned back and laughed. "No, love. Until you tell me you are through, I would like Jasmine LeFleur on my stage whenever she wants to be, but when she is there? I want all of her in the game, so you call the first number. She can help you with what's bothering you…"

"A shrink?"

Roberto shrugged. "She is a good listener. We all need someone to talk to every now and then. Even me."

"You?"

His mouth quirked. "Even me. Angelina, she has a good head and a good heart. Now, the second name? He is a friend of a friend—a gallery owner in Georgetown."

Lucy stared at the names and numbers on the paper. When her lip began to tremble, she clamped down on it.

"Now, you have three days off scheduled. I want you to add two more. When you come back, you can tell me if you will still dance for me or if you are ready to move on. Okay?"

Lucy picked up the paper, stuffed it in the pocket of her jeans and stood. "Why couldn't I love someone like you?"

Roberto's dark eyes widened. "You are a woman any man would be proud to have at his side, but me? I am not a man women would be proud to have with them. You take care of your business, and I will see you next Saturday, okay?"

Lucy leaned down and kissed his cheek. With a wave at Tiffany, she grabbed her duffel bag and headed out to her car. Her fingers touched the paper in her pocket. Roberto was just full of surprises. Who knew?

Chapter 9

Brandon sat in Matt's private quarters at Falcon's Summit, a bourbon at his fingertips and his gaze on the fireplace. They had returned about an hour ago. Matt had promised to bring him the pottery piece, but an emergency in the kitchen had taken him away. Brandon could wait. It seemed all he was good for. He'd had to wait to make this trip while he went through first surgery and then recovery on his ankle. He hadn't waited, rather he'd put off going back to work at Barrett. On one level, while he might be back to normal, the hole in his memory—now a much more vital one than even he had realized—had affected his confidence. If he couldn't remember four days of his life, how could he run a multi-billion dollar company? What if his mind went blank again? What if there were already blank spots he wasn't even aware of yet?

His cellphone vibrated against his hip. Brandon grabbed it and answered, "This is Brandon."

"It's Seth."

The tone in his older brother's voice put him on the alert. "What's up?"

"Dad's in the hospital. Mild heart attack, but the cardiologist is making noises about doing a bypass. Where are you at, bro?"

Brandon knew Colorado wasn't the answer Seth was seeking. He wanted to know where Brandon's head was. It was tempting to put this off on Seth, but they had done that to him for too many years. Brandon had wanted control of the company, now it seemed he would have it. Sitting straighter, he asked a question in return. "Where do I need to be?"

"Here. Mind and body. I can return on a temporary basis. Tessa and I had planned to move to the brownstone in Georgetown anyway with her due date getting so close, but I've been out of the loop. I'm your backup. You're the main go-to guy."

Brandon raked his fingers through his hair. Shit, he needed a haircut. He needed to get his ass in gear. Most of all, he needed to quit looking at the past and move on. "Tomorrow morning's as soon as I can get out of here. How's Dad?"

There was a short, sharp bark of laughter. "Not anywhere close to kicking the bucket and still the biggest son-of-a-bitch I've ever had to deal with."

"What about Mom?"

"As stoic as ever, rushing about making arrangements in case any of our other siblings decide to visit the lion in his den." Seth paused. "If Tessa's due date weren't so close, Bran, I'd let you do what you need to get done, but this time I got to use my membership on the Board of Directors to pull rank. The corporation needs someone at the helm."

"I can do it."

After hanging up, he phoned the company pilot to let him know they'd be leaving first thing in the morning. He had just finished his call when Matt returned.

One look at Brandon's face and Matt asked, "What's up?"

"My dad's in the hospital facing bypass surgery. Seth called. I'm needed at Barrett headquarters."

Matt nodded. "When do you leave?"

"Right at dawn."

"Let me get you the pottery piece."

Brandon had already steeled himself to feel no reaction. If seeing the lodge again, the crash site and the cabin had done nothing to stir his memory, what could a freaking clay pot do? Matt set it in his hand. Brandon's eyes widened. He had expected something bigger, like a flower pot or at least a soup bowl. This thing wasn't big enough to hold much more than a flower bud. He brushed the pad of his thumb over a surface smooth and polished like a gem. When he turned the pot resting on his palm, he saw it had been worked to resemble a seed in the first stages of germination.

Another image came to mind, this time of a slender woman's hand with fingers that were elegant and strong. He heard suppressed excitement in her voice as she talked of the heritage of Native American pottery.

"Brandon? Are you okay, dude?"

"What?" He glanced at Matt feeling like he was just starting to resurface from beneath the depths of some thick, viscous liquid.

"Did you remember something?"

Brandon rubbed his forehead. "I—I don't know. Can I take this with me?"

Matt's gaze was troubled. "It's yours, dude. You paid a thousand dollars for it."

* * * *

Lucy stared at Roberto's handwriting the following morning. Angelina O'Daniel. Now there was a true American melting pot. She tapped her finger on the paper while she sipped her coffee and stared out the window of her tiny breakfast nook into her postage-stamp-sized backyard. Spring flowers brightened the border of the patio. At the back of the yard, her kiln sat idle. She set her coffee cup down and picked up the phone.

Roberto was right. Everyone needed someone to talk to at some point. She had reached hers. After dreaming once again of the crash last night, Lucy knew she couldn't continue. The nightmares were getting worse, not better, with the passage of time. That didn't seem right. Luck was with her when she called. Angelina had time late in the day to meet her. Lucy hung up, feeling she'd made an appointment not with a doctor, but with a friend.

Buoyed by her success with Angelina, Lucy called the second number. At the upper crust sound to the voice on the phone at the other end, her nerve failed. Instead, all she asked was what the gallery's hours were.

Chicken. That had always been part of her problem. She was scared to put her talent on the line. Scared to lay it out there where someone might tear her work—and thus her fragile ego—to shreds. Just thinking about it made her somewhat queasy.

Well, she knew the cure. She loaded her dirty dishes in the small dishwasher, then walked down the stairs leading to the glassed-in porch she'd converted into her studio. There was plenty of natural light and lots of shelving where she could allow pottery to dry before she glazed. Although she'd been working with techniques of hand-building pots, this morning she wanted the comfort of the wheel. The rhythm of the clay moving beneath her fingers would soothe her because it reminded her of her grandmother.

She used her foot to start the wheel, selected a ball of clay and centered it with her hands, dipping one in water to remoisten hands and clay while she worked. How many times had she sat nearby in her grandmother's studio, watching? There had never been anything fancy about what she'd made, but the practical, serviceable bowls, cups and dishes had been turned with an attention to detail and craftsmanship. She had always stuck with light, earth-toned glazes because she said they reminded her of the ocean and the shore where they lived. They had also gained the interest of the tourists.

Lucy's work differed there. Her glazes were a bold meshing of vibrant colors, the hues and tints of a sunrise or sunset, the vibrant energy of a night in the city. Maybe that was the part of herself she was still trying to accept. She had not carried on her grandmother's tradition. Lucy had taken it and changed it. She'd made it her own. Her foot stopped pumping the pedal. The wheel halted. After cleaning the surface of the wheel around the pot, Lucy used a wire to separate it, then lifted the bat to the side to let it rest.

She washed her hands and examined some of the last items she'd glazed and fired. She recalled some of the techniques she'd seen in Falcon's Head and Coyote Creek. As painful as it might be because those memories were tied to Brandon, she needed to think about them. Her glazing techniques weren't enough. She needed more to make her pottery stand out, not an amusing conversation piece, but fine art people wanted to display. There would always be room for turning utilitarian pieces, but if she was going to make a name for herself, then she had to separate her work from the thousands of potters already out there. And she needed to market it.

An hour later, Lucy was stepping off a bus in Georgetown, her gaze seeking out the discreet numbers over the doors until she found the one she wanted. There was just enough of a display window to let passersby know this was a business, not a private home. She studied the area. Historic homes, trendy restaurants—a place where locals and tourists might be tempted to look and buy.

A discreet tinkling bell announced her arrival. It seemed not even a moment passed before a willowy brunette in a classically tailored suit greeted her. "Welcome to Mason's. How may I help you?"

Lucy swallowed. This was the same cool voice she'd heard on the phone earlier, and she was as intimidating now as she had been then. Maybe more so. In her classic clothes and understated jewelry, she managed to make Lucy feel too everything—too tall, too busty, too casual. She had changed into jeans and high-heeled short boots, but she now wondered if the tunic-styled sweater was a little too figure-hugging. *Fuck this.* This must have been Roberto's idea of a joke.

"Belinda?" a masculine voice interrupted from the rear of the gallery. "Senator Hughes's wife would like to make arrangements to have the vases delivered." A dark-haired, dark-eyed man of about Lucy's height with the addition of her heels strode into the room, raking an agitated hand through his shoulder-length hair. He came to an abrupt halt. "Hello."

Lucy smothered a laugh. Belinda looked irritated, then angry when she noticed the man's gaze raking Lucy's figure. Belinda had no doubt already determined Lucy was not a potential commission. With a dismissive nod at her, she excused herself and disappeared through the same door the man had come through.

He approached her, his dark eyes warm with appreciation. "I'm Mason Hatch. You are?"

She held out her hand. "Lucy Cameron. I'm a friend of Roberto…" She wasn't sure how much to reveal.

Mason laughed, taking her hand and holding it. "Ah! So you are that Lucy. Roberto called me last night." He glanced around her as if searching for something. "Did you bring anything to show me?"

"No. I just came by to introduce myself."

"And check us out, right?"

Lucy laughed. "Well, yeah. I suppose so."

"Then let me show you around. I'll explain how we operate, and if you like what you see and hear, you can bring some pieces by for me to look at…or I could drop by your studio."

Whoa. Mason Hatch was good-looking, but he was moving way too fast for her. Besides, nobody but nobody who could connect her to Flamingo Road knew where she lived. "I'll bring some pieces by."

He backed up a step and held up his hands. "Sorry. I'll back off. I appreciate beauty in all its forms, so I'm sorry if I came on a little strong."

Lucy smoothed her hands along the thighs of her jeans. "Yeah. Well, you did. Look, I don't know what Roberto told you, but I'm not sure…"

"Come. Look around. We cater to a variety of clientele, not only social-climbing Washington wannabes. I carry everything from the practical to high-end art. See if you think your work will fit in. If not, I can recommend some other places."

She stopped. "You would do that?"

He shrugged. "I wouldn't like it, but I would do it—a favor to Roberto."

It seemed to her Roberto had a lot of people who did him favors. Mason escorted her to a large open area where a variety of practical ceramic and stoneware products were on display. "This is our bread and butter, practical items that are purchased by both tourists and those making the area home—at least until voters get a second crack at them."

"That's a little cynical."

Mason chuckled. "Maybe. It does have its advantages. It means we have a steady stream of potential new clients." He gestured to a display of dishes. "We have a huge demand right now for custom-made dishes. If you can supply the merchandise, we can pay your grocery bill."

The dishes were fine. Each set was beautiful and unique. "I know how to do that," Lucy began.

"But it's not what you want to concentrate on," he finished for her. "I understand, and there's nothing wrong with feeling that way. You just need to understand it sometimes means a longer waiting period before you're self-sufficient."

"I can support myself." If she had to continue to dance for a while, it would be easier to do knowing there was light at the end of the tunnel.

"All right. Well, let me show you what we have in higher-end fine art."

This room was smaller, with fewer items on display, all arranged and lit to show them to best advantage. Some pieces with practical application: vases, bowls and plates. Others were for beauty alone: tiles glazed in elaborate geometric designs, abstract works that drew on vastly differing techniques. Lucy's attention focused on a couple pots on a low shelf near the window.

"What beautiful pinch pots. This takes such an incredible amount of patience." She looked around her. "This is amazing."

Mason stepped to her side. "What is it you do that will garner the same reaction from someone else?"

With a wellspring of cynicism she'd never acknowledged, Lucy replied, "I take off my clothes."

Mason surprised her then by laughing. It was a rich, deep sound, rife with amusement. "I'm not talking about how you earn your living. I meant your art. What makes you unique when it comes to ceramics?"

She ran her finger along the edge of one pinch pot. "My glazing—at least when it comes to what I turn—but I build by hand too. I've been experimenting with larger pieces blending coil and slab work."

"Bring me samples of both."

* * * *

If Lucy thought Mason was an eye-opening experience, Angelina O'Daniel was another. She stood eyeball to eyeball with Lucy, her long, black hair curling over her shoulders and down her back. She dressed like an upscale sixties hippie-holdover and the art collection on display in her living room seemed to confirm the image.

Mason and Angelina. They were so different yet both friends of Roberto.

"So Roberto tells me you were involved in a plane crash a couple of months ago."

Lucy raised her brows. "I'm beginning to wonder why Roberto even gave me names and phone numbers. He seems to have already touched base with you and the art dealer he had me contact. He also seems to know a lot more than I've ever shared about what happened to me."

"Does it upset you?"

Lucy wandered the room, feeling a little restless. "I don't know. I guess there's a part of me that's amazed he cares so much."

"Is there some reason why people who know you shouldn't care about you?"

Lucy glanced at Angelina over her shoulder. "They just never have."

"Including the man in the plane crash?"

"Ouch. You don't waste time, do you?"

"I don't let people distract me."

Lucy laughed and sat on the couch positioned in front of a large, bay window. "Is that what I was doing?"

"Yes. I asked you about the plane crash. You don't want to talk about it, so you tried to refocus attention onto Roberto." Angelina smiled. "We can talk about either one. Or you can start further back. I figure this is a chance for me to get to know you."

Lucy crossed her legs at the knee. "Why don't I tell you about my vacation? We can start there because it had a lot of firsts for me."

"All right."

"The ski trip was the first vacation I've ever planned and taken."

Angelina arched her brows. "No vacations when you were a child?"

"No. My parents died when I was quite small. My grandmother raised me, and there wasn't money for extras like vacations. Besides, we lived near the coast. Most people figure living near the beach is already a vacation. Gran had a stroke when I was twelve. It eventually killed her. I was moved to foster care. No vacations there."

"But you make good money stripping. A lot of young women would be spending it hand over fist."

"I went to college and got a masters degree in art history. Then I paid off my loans."

"That's a big undertaking. So was this vacation a reward?"

"Yes. A celebration of having finished those payments."

"What were some of the other firsts?"

"My first flight in an airplane. I thought that was great, even the cramped commuter flight from Denver to Falcon's Head." Lucy paused and took a deep breath. "That's where I met him."

"Tell me about him."

Lucy swallowed. Her chest ached. She hadn't talked to anyone about Brandon. It hurt too much. "His name is Brandon. He has the most amazing eyes. They're a mixture of green and gold. I guess you'd call them hazel. He hit on me as soon as he met me, but in the nicest possible way."

"What do you mean?"

"He offered to teach me to ski."

"Did you take him up on it?"

Lucy tucked her hair behind one ear. "I did. The skiing was another first. He was a wonderful teacher, patient and very knowledgeable. He even had his friend, the owner of the resort, check out my skiing skills before he took me to some higher level slopes. It was funny, because on the surface he seemed to be such a risk-taker kind of guy, but he was careful when it came to me."

"The two of you clicked?"

"We were inseparable."

"So why were you flying the day of the crash?"

"Brandon set it up for me. He'd discovered my love of pottery and my knowledge of art. A dealer recommended a museum in another town. He had planned rent a plane and fly himself…" Lucy trailed off. It occurred to her, had Tom Hanson not needed to fly to Coyote Creek himself, it might have been just her and Brandon in the plane. He would have been the one sitting in the pilot's seat. He would have been the one with the branch jammed through his chest and his eyes staring vacantly.

"Lucy?" It seemed as if she had only blinked but now found Angelina at her side, holding her hands. "Do you want to put your head between your knees? You look a little pale, sweetie."

"No. It occurred to me Brandon could have been the one piloting the plane. He could have been dead." She stopped and gulped a couple of times before she whispered, "And what made the realization worse was the relief I felt that it was Tom Hanson who died and not Brandon." Lucy covered her face with her hands and started crying. "How can I be glad someone died?"

Angelina handed her a couple tissues. "There's a big difference between feeling relief someone's alive and being glad someone else is dead. Yes, you feel relief the man you loved survived, but that doesn't translate into being glad this other man didn't. You have some real issues about the crash still, don't you?"

"Yes." Roberto had been right. She did need to get all of this out in the open, and Angelina was safe. Anything Lucy shared would be confidential.

"Have you talked to anyone about what happened?"

Lucy shook her head. "Just the investigators right after it happened. I still don't even know what happened to cause it."

"Don't you want to know?"

"It's complicated."

"I have time. You can uncomplicate it now, or I can come to your place in the morning. I'd like to see some of your pottery, see where you work."

"I don't normally invite people to my home." Lucy looked out the front window to the green lawn and overflowing garden areas. They were deceptive. At first glance, it seemed haphazard, but the more she'd glanced at them, the more she realized the plantings were designed to keep flowers blooming through the season. She returned her attention to Angelina, who watched her with a Madonna-like patience. "But everything I tell you and show you is confidential. Right?" At the other woman's nod, Lucy continued. "Can we do both? Now I've started, I need to get some of this out."

"That's fine. Would you like some tea?"

"Yes, I would."

"Come with me. I see you studying my yard. If you like the front, you'll love the back. We can sit in the sunroom there. Plenty of plants and sunshine, plus a wonderful view of the patio."

Angelina let her wander along the length of the sunroom, and Lucy began to relax. For the first time since she'd flown back from Colorado, she wasn't whipping in the wind like a loose spinnaker. Angelina had grabbed her line, and the security soothed her.

"Sometimes it helps to talk about the traumatic event that's got you tied in knots. When you share the horror, it doesn't lessen its significance, just helps share the burden. When the weight is carried on your shoulders alone, it can wear you down with sheer fatigue."

Lucy sipped from her tea and set it down. "That's a lot how it seems, and it worried me. I kept feeling like it should be getting better, but instead the memories and the nightmares seem to prey on me more and more."

"Why don't you begin with going to the airport that day?"

Lucy thought. "Brandon had planned to fly. He said he was a licensed pilot, and when he mentioned the amount of flight time he had, the kid at the air service place seemed impressed." She shrugged. "I know so little about it. Anyway, the kid was about to tell us there weren't any planes available when Tom Hanson came in and asked where we wanted to go. When Brandon told him, he said he could take us there if we'd planned just a day trip because he had to pick up some parts. It seemed like the perfect solution."

"Were there any problems on the way there?"

"No. Not at all. I sat up front, and it was the most amazing view with everything spread out right in front of me. I'm sure Tom and Brandon both got a chuckle out of it, but they were patient with my excitement. When we got to Coyote Creek, Tom drove us into town. We grabbed some lunch and went to the museum."

"How was that?"

"As incredible as we'd been led to believe. I had a wonderful time, and I think Brandon did too. Sometimes I caught him looking at me…"

"How?"

Lucy cleared her throat. "Like I was precious. There was something different in the air between us. I didn't understand until later." She stopped and closed her eyes for a minute. "I'm getting ahead of myself. Anyway, we got to the airport and Tom had the parts he needed crated and stored in the cargo area. This time he made me sit in the back of the plane. He said he needed to distribute the weight so it was even."

Angelina nodded as if she understood. "And everything seemed fine?"

"Absolutely. We took off and I joked that since I was in the rear, I would take a nap. I guess I did for a few minutes, at least."

"What woke you?"

Lucy took a deep breath and let it out. She could feel once more the fear that had made saliva pool in her mouth. "The engine didn't sound right. I think Tom said the plane was losing oil pressure. He and Brandon began discussing what they could do, something about glide ratios and how it still wasn't enough to get the plane either to Coyote Creek or to Falcon's Head." She paused. "It didn't hit home until Tom started going over crash procedures."

"What was Brandon doing?"

"He was on the radio broadcasting a mayday. He did it the whole time, except right when Tom finished explaining what I needed to do when we landed, Brandon turned to me."

"What did he say?"

She looked into Angelina's kind, dark eyes with their patient understanding. Lucy's chin wobbled. "He apologized and told me he loved me," she whispered. "Then he went right back broadcasting that damn mayday."

Angelina came over and rubbed her shoulders. "Do you want to quit for today?"

"No. You need to at least hear the rest of this." Lucy tried to smile, but she knew it appeared pretty shaky. "Not long after, all hell broke loose. It was like being a rowboat in a hurricane. Then there was this awful, awful silence. The only thing I heard was my own breathing, and that scared me the most. I couldn't even see Tom and Brandon. Snow and debris filled the plane. I managed to crawl out the rear window. I braced my leg on the plane and yanked open the door on Brandon's side."

She stared out at the verdant green of the yard. "I think that's why I feel so guilty."

"What you did was only natural, to help the man you loved first."

"But what if I had gotten to Tom faster? Could he have lived?"

Angelina shook her head. "You did what any human being does. We go first to those we love, and you did save him. Without you there that day, Lucy, Brandon would have died too."

"I knew I had to find shelter for Brandon. He looked so hurt and helpless."

"Right at the point when you could have used his strength the most. Is that part of your guilt too?"

"Yes." Lucy looked at Angelina, holding her gaze. "It was so hard to move him and myself. I found one of the cabins near the lake where Hanson was trying to get us, got a fire going, found supplies and bandaged Brandon as best I could. Then when he woke, he had no idea who I was. On top of the hurt, God help me, for an instant I wanted to scream at him. How could this man who had spent the last few days making love to me, spending every moment with me and even telling me he loved me not have any idea who I was?"

Lucy clapped her hands over her mouth and sobbed in pain. After a moment, she took a deep breath and dropped her hands into her lap. "He made love to me. He told me he loved me and all of a sudden he didn't know who I was?"

Angelina let her get the pain out and then handed her a tissue once Lucy had herself more under control.

"Is that why you left? Because you were angry at him?"

Lucy stared at her, dumbfounded for a moment. She wiped her eyes and sniffed. Was that part of it? "Maybe, but there were other things too. Things I didn't know about him. Maybe I should have. He'd never tried to hide his name. I suppose I should have realized Brandon Barrett, whose family was in communications, was the same thing as Barrett Newspapers, the publishers of *National News*."

"I think what we've talked about is enough for today, Lucy. It sounds to me like there are some other issues at work here, but you've had enough for now. I just want you to remember everything you did on that mountain was out of love and instinct—and your reactions were those of any normal person."

"Thanks, Angelina. You've helped more than you know."

When they walked out to Lucy's car, Angelina took her hand in both of hers. "I will see you in the morning. Is nine too early?"

"No. I'll be back from swimming by then."

"Nine it is."

Chapter 10

"You know I will support you if you want to go ahead with developing the marketing of *National News* through e-reader and phone subscriptions." Seth paused while Brandon continued to stroke his thumb over the small pot in his hand. "You know, I'm the one who's supposed to be distracted here. My wife is ready to go into labor any day now."

Brandon shook his head, set the pot down and focused on his elder brother. "Sorry."

"Souvenir from your trip?" Seth asked.

Brandon shook his head. "A gift that never reached the recipient."

Seth arched one thick, golden brow. "The woman in the plane with you? What was her name?"

"Lucy Cameron."

"She did a disappearing act." There was a critical tone in Seth's deep voice that put Brandon's nerves on edge, but he tried to remind himself no one but Matt knew Lucy had been more than just a casual acquaintance. "It seemed like it might have been polite to at least see how you were doing."

"Shut up, Seth." There was a long silence. Brandon sighed, stood and limped to the windows of his office. He'd kept the office on the opposite corner of the same floor where Seth's still was, though his elder brother seldom spent any time in it anymore. He showed for board meetings. However, until their father's heart trouble, most of his attention focused on the small paper he was overhauling in the beach community where he now spent most of his time. He and Tessa were busy furnishing a nursery when he wasn't in DC working on his novel.

"Rude's not your usual style, Brandon. What's up?"

He jammed his hands in the pockets of his slacks and turned away from the view of the Potomac. "Some things I learned on my trip out there."

"You're remembering the crash?"

"No. Her. Lucy." Brandon raked one hand through his hair. "Matt says she and I were together from the time I arrived until the crash."

"Together, as in lovers?" Seth's voice deepened with concern.

"It would seem so. I mean, I'm sure I didn't have sex right in front of Matt, but according to him I taught her to ski, took her out to dinner and dancing. I was the one who suggested the trip to Coyote Creek." He nodded toward the little pot on her desk. "I liked her well enough I forked over a grand for that little pot for her. I was supposed to contact the museum owner with where to ship it. She brought it to Matt."

"Flowers and a couple of baubles are more your usual style. You bought this woman a little clay pot?"

Brandon's lips quirked. "Must be love, huh?"

Seth threw back his head and laughed. "Only you could conclude that. What are you going to do about it?"

"Fuck if I know. She made Matt promise to destroy the records of her stay. The only thing he would tell me was she lived somewhere around here. You're the reporter. How do I find her?"

"Tax records, credit reports, driver's license. Tessa could have you a complete dossier in under five minutes, but I'm not about to ask her to help. She's been a little on edge the last couple of days."

Brandon raised both brows. "Hello. She's getting ready to have your baby. I'd be nervous and grumpy too. You're mighty big, and she is a little thing, after all."

Seth sighed. "Yeah, don't remind me. She's also mean as a rattlesnake right now. I almost walked out of the house without my BlackBerry this morning and I thought she might go for my throat. But seriously, Brandon, if you want to find this Lucy, hire a private detective. That will keep it private."

Brandon paced the office, still favoring his ankle some. "That's just it. I'm not sure I do want to find her. God, Seth. What did I do to her that she would leave without a word? That she would beg Matt to destroy the records of her visit and not even freaking tell me anything about her? I mean it was obvious he was betraying a confidence, and he was only doing it because of the length and depth of our friendship."

Seth joined him near the windows and put his hands on Brandon's shoulders. "Bran, think about it. If you were close like Matt says you were, imagine how she felt following the crash. She had to be scared out of her mind."

Brandon nodded. "I saw the site. Jesus, Seth, she dragged me through snow that had to be more than knee deep for close to a mile."

"And what do you remember of her?"

"Almost nothing. And I was so out of it after the crash, I still don't have a clear image of her other than she was tall with long blond hair." He paused and shook his head. "I don't remember, but she does."

"And?"

Brandon swallowed before he continued. "How would you feel if Tessa looked at you and didn't know who you were?"

Seth's golden eyes narrowed. "I don't know, but you have someone who can tell you that."

"Anna." Brandon wasn't sure why he hadn't thought of their sister earlier, but then, he wasn't thinking with complete clarity. "Not quite the same thing because Anna also had reasons at the time, at least, for not wanting Chris to remember."

"You should give her a call." Seth paused as they both heard the buzz of his BlackBerry. "Shit. It's Tessa." He snatched the phone out of his pocket. During a brief conversation in which Brandon saw his face first flush and then get pale, he jammed the BlackBerry in his pants pocket with a hand that shook. "She's in labor. I have to go."

"I'll drive you."

"You don't…" Seth started.

"Yeah. I do. You're a nervous wreck. We'll swing by, pick her up and I'll get you both to the hospital. Then I'll arrange for her brother to get home from school."

"Yeah. Okay."

Brandon grabbed his suit jacket. He would have to put off finding Lucy, and if he was honest with himself, he was half afraid to launch a search. He didn't remember her, and there was a big part of him that was pissed off. If what they'd shared had mattered so fucking much, couldn't she have stuck by him?

Now it was Seth who had his attention. He'd never seen his older brother quite so bent out of shape other than the morning of their sister Stacey's wedding, right after he'd found out Tessa was pregnant and had no intention of letting him anywhere near her. Good thing she'd changed her mind because their baby was about to be born.

"Come on, Seth. Make sure you remember all that coaching stuff you've been learning."

"Right." While they rode in the elevator, Seth went through the list Tessa had drilled into him. When it came to organization, she had Seth firmly in hand. Up until the last couple months, it had been a source of secret amusement to Brandon. He was now beginning to understand the emotional heights and depths being in love could cause. Whoa. Where had that come from? And how the hell could he be in love with someone he couldn't remember?

He leaned his head against the wall of the elevator. He might not remember, but he knew from Matt's description of him and Lucy, from Seth's reaction to the pot he had intended as a gift—there was no question, he'd cared for her. And he would find her, but first there was getting Seth and Tessa to the hospital, taking care of business until his dad could take charge, and...damn, he was beginning to understand how confined Seth had felt.

* * * *

Lucy felt much better following her swim the next morning. She'd slept better than she had since the crash. Angelina had been right. Just talking about it, admitting to her feelings and her fears and hearing she was normal had made it easier to bear. As she puttered around the kitchen, making coffee and setting out fresh fruit slices with yogurt dip while she waited for Angelina, Lucy thought about what she needed to talk about today. Somehow, she wasn't sure Angelina would have an easy time putting this into perspective.

The doorbell rang, and Lucy headed to the front hall. Angelina stood on the stoop, her hair still loose and curling around her shoulders, but instead of the long, flowing skirt and tunic, today she was dressed in tight jeans and cowboy boots.

When Lucy, still in her sweats, arched her brows, Angelina laughed. "Hah, you're wondering about the dramatic change in fashion? Easy enough. Roberto and I are meeting at his farm in a couple of hours so I can test drive a horse he's picked out for me."

Lucy laughed. "I don't know much about horses, but somehow I doubt it's called test driving like you do a car."

Angelina waved a careless hand. "Roberto promises me this one will be—what did he call it?—push button, like driving a car, so I figure it is a test drive."

"You and Roberto are close?" Lucy couldn't contain the fascination filling her about these new facets she was discovering in her boss's mysterious personality.

Angelina's lips curved. "Sometimes. He is not an easy man to be around." She stepped inside. "Is that coffee I smell?"

Lucy showed her the studio first and was flattered by Angelina's enthusiasm, especially for her glazed bowls. Once they'd settled in the living room with the coffee and fruit tray, though, the other woman got down to business, picking up the thread of their conversation from yesterday as if there hadn't been more than half a day's pause in it.

"So what I heard from you yesterday was you didn't know who Brandon was?"

Lucy sipped her coffee. "I guess that sounds a little stupid. I mean, he did introduce himself as Brandon Barrett, but all he said was he worked for his father in their communications business. After the crash, when I discovered the communications business was Barrett Newspapers, I felt…" She sighed. "I don't know, like he'd been vague on purpose, hoping I wouldn't know who he was, hoping I was stupid enough…"

"You shouldn't let your anger attribute words or thoughts to him he might never have had."

"But why wouldn't he just say it was Barrett Newspapers?"

Angelina's eyes darkened as if at some thought of her own. "Perhaps he gets tired of people looking at his family and his business first before they ever see Brandon Barrett, the man."

"How could anyone notice his name instead of him?" She shook her head. "And that tells you how fast I was falling."

"Then why does such a minor discrepancy make such a difference to you?"

"Because someone like him would never hang around me. How could he? The business tycoon and the stripper? Please."

Angelina sat back, her eyes narrowing. "Who did that to you?"

"Did what?"

"Made you feel like what you do somehow defines you as a person."

"And doesn't it? What person with his background is going to show up at the family compound with Jasmine LeFleur in tow, unless it's to entertain at a bachelor party?"

"Was there someone in your past with prominent social connections like Brandon's?"

"Yes!" Lucy hissed. "I was fine to have on his arm, fine to fuck, but never to bring home to Mommy and Daddy. I didn't have the pearls or the sorority girl accent. I didn't spend my summers at the beach house. I was the kid working behind the scenes, babysitting and earning money any way I could. I saw the way Brandon's parents looked, and how they stared right through me…"

"So you walked away rather than risk being hurt?"

Lucy's hands balled into fists. "I was already hurt! Inside and out. No, I didn't have his injuries, but from the moment we arrived at the hospital, I ceased to exist. I had to get away. Not just because of that but because

I feared the scrutiny. If everything I had done became public knowledge, after the cheers for being a hero died out, speculation would have started soon enough that something going on in-flight had led to the crash. We've all heard those stories about pilots who crash because someone wants an initiation into the mile-high club when what they should have been doing was flying the plane. What better person to be involved in that than a stripper?"

She jumped up and took her coffee mug into the kitchen. Angelina followed at a slower pace.

"So you will put this behind you and forget about him?"

Pain suffused her from head to toe. "Yes. Like he has me. It's better this way."

"For whom? Don't you think you could be a key to helping him remember? And what about you? Would you have gone on with the nightmares and the overworking yourself until you got sick and couldn't work?" She touched Lucy's shoulder. "If you want to make the decision to put Brandon Barlow-Barrett in your past, then do it for the right reasons. Do it because you're ready to move on with a new stage in your life, not because you're running from what's happened in your past."

Lucy raised her chin. "I am moving on. I'm taking several pieces of my work to Mason Hatch this afternoon."

Angelina leaned in and kissed her cheek. "Good. That's a start. Drop by my place tomorrow afternoon. I want to hear about how things go with Mason's evaluation of your work."

Lucy nodded. "Thanks, Angelina."

Once the other woman left, Lucy dressed with care for her meeting with Mason. She kept trying to tell herself it was neither to impress him nor was it in defiance of her feelings for Brandon. She wanted to look her best. Angelina was right. This was an opportunity for her to begin again. She could cut back on her hours at Flamingo Road, just dance the weekends, so she could spend all week long working with her clay. Once her work started selling… Lucy stopped. She was where she needed to be. She had a plan. And wasn't that what Roberto had asked?

Two hours later, she was standing with her arms crossed across her chest and her stomach muscles fluttering while Mason took his time analyzing the pieces she'd brought in. He had said very little while he'd picked up each piece, turned it in every direction then set it again on the table in his office. Lucy's stomach churned.

"You hate it, don't you?" she blurted.

He paused and looked over at her as if he had forgotten her presence. "No." He lifted a brightly glazed cup and saucer. "Can you recreate this glazing pattern with any consistency?"

"Yes."

"Do you have an entire place-setting?"

"Yes."

He raised one brow and smiled. "More than one?"

"Not at the moment, but I have enough pieces ready for glazing to create four place-settings."

He smiled and waved her to a chair. "Have a seat, Lucy. Let's talk about how we can work together." He glanced at his watch. "Even better, let me take you to lunch so we can discuss it."

She wasn't sure she would be able to eat a bite, but she nodded. The next thing she knew, Mason was holding the door of a four-door Porsche. Lucy smiled.

"What's the smile for?" Mason asked.

"A sports car you can carry people in?"

"I don't like feeling cramped. It's a good car."

Lucy looked away to hide her grin. A good car. Right. Chances were good it had cost what she made in a year. Mason slid in behind the wheel and took her to a rather noisy deli a couple blocks off the water. It must have been a favorite of his because the waitresses greeted him by name, and the manager stopped by to speak to them while they waited for their sandwiches. When Lucy started to say something business-related, Mason stopped her.

"Eat first. We'll talk business over coffee. They make a mean cheesecake here, too."

Lucy ate, but could only get down about half her sandwich because she was so nervous. "Mason," she said to get his attention. "Can you please just let me down easy and let's get this over with."

"Let you down?" He wiped his hands on his napkin and set it aside. "We're here to talk about getting enough of your slab and coil abstracts in so I can set up a showing. While your glaze work on your practical pieces is superb, I can market it as high-end houseware, but your abstracts? You've hit on a technique and style that works. Now the smallest piece..." He went on to name a price tag for it that made her eyes widen.

"People will pay that?"

Mason grinned. "They will when I'm done marketing you."

"I can't believe it."

He chuckled. "You will when I set the first check in your hand. Now, if you're willing to have my company handle this, there is some paperwork we need to complete. If it's agreeable with you, I'd like to do it over dinner tomorrow evening. Consider it a celebration."

It was hard to refuse his invitation when it was phrased that way. Lucy was more than aware of the way he regarded her with warm appreciation, and she had the feeling he would be willing to take it further if she gave him the go ahead. But that wasn't going to happen.

Lucy tilted her head to one side. "As friends, Mason, I'll accept. But only in that light."

His eyes narrowed. "You're involved with someone else?"

Lucy tucked a strand of hair behind her ear. "It's complicated, but yes."

Mason pursed his lips. "Friends it is. Friends and business associates. Suit you?"

"Yes."

"Good. Give me your address and I'll pick you up at seven tomorrow. None of this meeting me there."

Lucy laughed. There was something appealing in Mason's brashness.

Chapter 11

"We'll get you there in time, Tessa." Seth sat with his wife in the backseat of his SUV while Brandon drove as fast as he dared to the hospital. "You remember your breathing."

"Seth," Tessa said with infinite patience. "I don't think I need it yet. We're a few hours away, but the doctor did want me to go ahead and check in. You know he's been a little concerned about the size of the baby."

Brandon glanced in the rearview mirror. Tessa looked and sounded calm, her tone now designed to reassure Seth. It was an eye-opening experience to see the elder brother who had chewed his way with little regard through secretary after secretary now pale and a bit sweaty-looking at the thought of his wife giving birth. This was the same brother who had, on several occasions, dodged Muslim extremists in order to get stories out of Afghanistan.

But the idea of his petite wife facing childbirth brought him to his knees. Brandon glanced in the rearview mirror yet again and saw Seth rest his head atop Tessa's. For a second, his golden eyes filled, then he blinked, turned his face and kissed her dark red hair. Brandon shifted his gaze to the road and swallowed around the tightness in his throat. He hoped Seth realized how lucky he was, but he had a feeling his brother was more than aware. Seth and Tessa hadn't had an easy time of it. Some of the fault lay at the feet of their father, now part of the reason they were even in town.

Brandon pulled into the emergency entrance of the hospital. "Stay with Tessa, Seth. I'll find someone to help."

The next hour passed in a flash. Brandon carried Tessa's bag to the room, then promised to call their mother and siblings. When the doctor came in, he excused himself to begin those calls. Dad was now resting at home, but was by no means ready to be out and about following his bypass surgery, so Mother was staying close to his side.

Brandon informed her the birth of Seth and Tessa's baby was imminent, but his mother's response was typical. "My place is with your father right now. However, after the baby is born, you must let me know. I shall have Morgan bring me into town."

He hung up the phone, wondering if his mother had ever done anything independently of her husband. His personality dominated the whole family. For Stacey, Phillip and Morgan, it had never seemed to be a problem. Seth and Preston—Anna, Brandon reminded himself—had actively fought the constraints. Brandon had managed to slip through, around and under them whenever possible. His skiing had kept him away a lot, but Seth had also been a shield. While his elder brother had knuckled under to the pressure to take on the mantle of Barrett Newspapers, Brandon had been able to play at it, no one ever taking him as a serious voice in the business.

He wandered to the hospital's coffee shop and got something to eat. When he was through, he took his coffee to the maternity floor. He knocked on the door to Tessa's room and heard Seth's deep voice tell him to come in. She was seated in a rocking chair while Seth rubbed her feet.

Brandon quirked a brow. "Is this part of what you learn in the childbirth classes?"

Seth glared at him, once again on more of an even keel. "If you mean keeping her relaxed, then yes."

Brandon chuckled. "I wanted to let you know I would hang out in the waiting room if you need me for anything."

Tessa smiled. "You could hang out here if you want. It will be a while."

Brandon's stomach fluttered with nerves. "Uh, no. While I appreciate the thought, I think I'll let the whole process remain a mystery for a while."

Once he was in the waiting room, he pulled out his Droid and logged into the company email. He could at least get some work accomplished while he was there. Once he'd sorted through the business mail, he switched to his personal account, discovering Matt had sent him mail to let him know the mechanic investigators had questioned in the Cessna crash had been convicted of manslaughter. Brandon made a mental note to look up the court files and see if he could get hold of the transcripts. He also wanted to contact a private detective to help him find Lucy Cameron. They had unfinished business he wasn't about to let go.

Right around the time he began to think about dinner, Seth appeared at the door of the waiting room, a broad smile on his tired face. Brandon shoved his Droid in his pocket and stood.

"It's a girl," Seth stated, then laughed. "A healthy, squalling, beautiful baby girl."

Brandon wrapped him in a hug, felt Seth shaking. "How's Tessa?"

Seth squeezed Brandon's shoulder. "Tired, but okay. You want to come see?"

"I do." Brandon surprised himself. He'd never had any interest in kids, and made a studied effort to stay away from them. In the wake of the crash, he'd begun to feel a need to draw closer to his family.

He followed Seth into the room with its subdued lighting. Tessa's vibrant hair tumbled around her shoulders. There were shadows of exhaustion beneath her eyes, but a smile on her lips that made even Brandon pause. Beautiful. Just then, a tiny fist reached into the air.

"Good Lord," he murmured. "She's so tiny."

Seth had already moved to their side, sitting now in the chair pulled close to the bed so he could lean in to watch his daughter's face. Tessa patted the other side of the bed. "Come on, Uncle Brandon. Take a look at your niece."

He started to tiptoe toward the bed, and then thought how stupid that was. Shaking off the feeling, he stepped over to the bed. The baby was sleeping, which disappointed him a bit, but he supposed she needed rest, like Tessa, after working so hard to get into this world. Everything about the baby was delicate. He didn't envy his older brother. Brandon feared he wouldn't have the nerve to handle anything quite so fragile-looking.

"She's beautiful. Have you decided on a name?"

Seth glanced at him. "We're still debating. I want to make sure she doesn't get hung with one of the Barlow-Barrett monikers like poor Preston did."

Brandon nodded. "I'm with you there, bro. It doesn't seem fair to saddle such a delicate being with a ten-ton name." He gathered Tessa's hand in his. "I'll grab a cab and head home." He tossed the keys to Seth. "I know you'll stay, but if you decide to go home and grab a shower, you'll have your SUV."

By the time Brandon got to his house, fatigue and a vague feeling of depression dragged at him. He was happy for Tessa and Seth. Just like he was happy for Anna and Chris. He poured himself a glass of bourbon and took it over to the couch, realizing he was limping again. It seemed that would be his reminder of a trip gone terribly wrong.

* * * *

Lucy was feeling better than she had in recent memory. She'd gone running that morning, then returned home to work at the wheel. She turned out several more pieces, which she set aside so they could dry enough before being removed to a drying rack, and began glazing the pieces Mason had asked her to finish. When the phone rang in the middle of it, Lucy almost didn't answer it, but wiped her hands on a rag and dashed into the kitchen at the last minute.

"Lucy, it's Tiffany. How you doin', sugar?"

"Great, Tiff, and I mean that. I can't thank Roberto enough. In fact, tell him I'll be there Friday night to dance, but I'm getting there early to talk to him."

"You aren't gonna quit, are you?"

Lucy laughed. "Not for right now, but the time is coming. Did you call just to see how I was doing?"

"No. Remember Tessa?"

"Of course."

"She and her husband had a baby yesterday."

"Oh! That's fantastic. A boy or a girl?"

"A little girl. They're not going home until tomorrow. You should drop by and see them. I know she'd like you to. Her married name is Barlow. Tessa Barlow."

For a moment, the similarity to Barlow-Barrett had made her stomach clench, but when the second name didn't get tacked on, Lucy relaxed. "What hospital?"

Lucy took all the information, deciding she would leave early for Angelina's house and stop in to see Tessa and her baby on the way. She hated to spend the additional money, but cabs would be the best way to go, though she'd have to call one to come pick her up from Angelina's house. Lucy dressed in casual attire. It was a warm day, so she opted for capris and sandals. With her hair in a braid and only a touch of makeup, she was sure no one would ever associate her with her alter ego. Heaven knew, the last thing she'd ever want was to embarrass Tessa in front of her husband.

As soon as she walked into the front lobby, Lucy's breath caught. Between her brief brush with the hospital in Falcon's Head and the occasions she'd visited her grandmother, Lucy had made it her business to stay far away from doctors and hospitals. When she stepped up to the information desk, an older woman looked at her and smiled.

"May I help you?"

"I came to visit a friend. She's on the maternity ward."

"What's her name and I'll look up her room number."

A couple of minutes later, Lucy was in the elevator headed up. She clutched the gift bag she held, hoping her gift wouldn't embarrass her friend. Wrapped inside was a small pot she'd made a couple of years earlier. Its hand carvings and vibrant glaze would look good in a child's nursery. The floor nurse smiled and directed her to Tessa's room.

The door was ajar a fraction. From behind it, she heard the quiet murmur of voices and soft laughter. She tucked a strand of hair behind her ear and hesitated, then tapped on the door.

"Come in," Tessa called. Lucy pushed away a flash of nerves. It had been a few months since she'd worked with Tessa at Flamingo Road. In fact, it was through Lucy Tessa had gotten a job there as a waitress. Roberto had kept her on even after her pregnancy had become obvious, moving her into his business office. Once she hooked up with her baby's father, though, she'd handed in her resignation.

Pushing the door open enough to step through it, Lucy paused, her gaze drawn to Tessa. She was dwarfed by the big hospital bed, and the even bigger man sitting with his back to her. For an instant, Lucy's heart had skipped a beat at the sight of his golden head and broad shoulders. Brandon? Just then the man turned and Lucy almost dropped the bag holding her gift. No. Not Brandon, but the similarity in their looks was unmistakable.

"Lucy!" Tessa's voice overflowed with surprise. "Oh! What are you doing here? Did Tiffany come too?"

Ignoring the suddenly narrowed tawny eyes of the man sitting with her friend, Lucy shook her head. "No. She has a kid home sick. I told her I would stop by." The man still regarded her in an intent way that made her want to squirm. She stepped to the bed. "I can't stay long. I have another appointment, but I wanted to bring you a gift."

Tessa took the bag and lifted out the small pot. "Oh, Lucy! This is beautiful. Is it something you made? Look, Seth. Isn't this lovely?"

"Indeed." He held out his hand. "Seth Barlow-Barrett." He introduced himself as if trying to gauge her reaction.

With no other option, she took his hand. "Lucy Cameron."

He smiled. "Pleased to meet you, Lucy. I'm going to step out to get some coffee. That will give you and Tessa some time to talk."

Lucy's heart was beating so hard she felt it flutter in her throat. She fought the panic. She couldn't run out. Tessa was her friend. But, oh merciful heaven, there could be no doubt her husband was related to

Brandon. They bore an amazing resemblance to each other. She watched him walk out the door with the sneaking suspicion he knew who she was. Panic threatened again. She was putting all this behind her.

"Lucy?" Tessa questioned. "Is something wrong?"

She released her breath and forced a smile. The last thing she wanted to do was to worry her friend. "No. Gosh. It's so good to see you again. You look amazing for someone who just gave birth less than twenty-four hours ago."

Tessa laughed. "And you look amazing, period. As always." She glanced at the pot. "This is beautiful. Does this mean you're still pursuing pottery?"

"Yes. I'm going to be doing more pottery and less dancing. Roberto is the one who gave me a nudge to go after what I want."

Tessa arched a brow. "His best dancer?"

Lucy shrugged, not wanting to go into it too much. "Yeah. It's a good move for me." She glanced at the bassinet in the corner of the room. "May I?"

"Sure. Take a look at her. Emily Rose."

Lucy studied the tiny, sleeping infant with her delicate features and perfect doll-sized fingers. "That's such a feminine name. It suits her. She's like a fragile little blossom."

"Thank you. And thanks for coming by too. You helped me at a time when my world had crashed, Lucy."

She turned in surprise. "We're friends." She looked around the room at the stuffed animals and flowers. "Life has worked out well for you. Are you happy?"

"Ecstatic." Tessa's pale blue eyes watched her. "What about you? What's wrong?"

She wanted to tell her but couldn't upset her. Not right now. "Changes. You know how it is. Deciding to pursue the pottery. It will be different. Change always makes me nervous." She rubbed her hands along her upper arms. "Look, I can't stay long. I just wanted to drop by and wish you well." In fact, she needed to get away and soon. With each passing minute, she became more and more paranoid, as if a whole group of Barlow-Barretts would show up and trap her.

"I'd love for you to stay longer…"

"No. I—I have to go. I'll call you. I'm working with a gallery on a showing."

"That's great! You will invite me, right?"

Lucy smiled. "I wouldn't dream of not inviting you." She leaned over and kissed Tessa on the cheek. "I'll be in touch, I promise."

She turned and fled the room. Starting toward the elevators, she saw the doors open and Seth came out. What shocked her was Brandon following right on his heels. He had a cane and he looked thinner than she remembered. For an instant she was frozen, just long enough for both men to see her. Brandon's gaze met hers with nothing more than the blank stare of a stranger for a fraction of an instant, and then she saw awareness dawn.

She wasn't ready for this, and all the reasons why she shouldn't be a part of his life flooded through her in a horrible rush. Lucy spun away, found the staircase and fled. As she pounded down the stairs, she heard the door open behind her. Heard him call her name, but she didn't stop, not until she sat, panting, in the backseat of a cab.

* * * *

"Lucy! Wait." The slap of her soles on the stairs picked up pace. "Damn it! Wait, Lucy." He stared in impotent frustration at the yawning staircase before him. He still didn't trust his ankle enough to follow her, not at the speed with which she'd taken off. With another muttered curse, he slapped his hand against the wall in frustration.

He hadn't been able to believe it when Seth had called him. He'd already been on his way over. After he hung up, the only thing he could think was how the hell Tessa knew the very woman he'd been trying to find. When the elevator doors had opened, he'd seen Seth go rigid. Then his brother stepped out of the way, and he'd seen her. For an instant, he'd wondered who she was. Then it had flooded in like the time had never been missing.

And she'd run from him.

Stepping back from the stairway, Brandon let the door shut and turned. He met Seth's gaze and found his brother regarding him with sympathy. He knew Tessa and Seth had gone through some rough times, knew his brother was one of the few people who did understand how he felt right now.

"Come talk to Tessa," Seth told him. "I don't know how the hell they know each other, but maybe she can tell you how you can find her."

Brandon ground his teeth. Every instinct told him to pursue her, but how damn stupid was that? She was long gone and he had no idea where or how to find her. "Okay," he responded at last to Seth's suggestion.

"You missed my friend Lucy," Tessa said before her smile faded. "What's wrong? Has something happened to your father?"

Seth sat in the chair next to her bed, but Brandon couldn't be still. He paced the room until he limped over to the window and parted the blinds so he could see outside. She was out there somewhere. All this time, she'd been within reach. He nearly growled in frustration.

"Nothing's wrong with my father. He's still as big a son-of-a-bitch as ever," Seth reassured his wife. "Tess—how long have you known Lucy?"

Brandon turned his head away from the window to watch his sister-in-law. She looked at Seth in confusion. "Since last summer. I met her at the Y. She helped me get that job after your father fired me."

"She helped you get the job at the strip club?" Something inside Brandon twisted with pain. Then familiarity niggled him. He remembered going there the night of their sister's fiance's bachelor party. "Does she work there?"

Tessa looked from Seth to Brandon. Something in his expression must have alerted her. "She's the one, isn't she? She's the woman from the plane crash. But that's impossible. Lucy never takes vacations. It was a running joke at Flamingo Road."

"It was her first vacation," Brandon stated. He cleared his throat. "It was the first time she'd flown." He already knew, in his heart, he already knew, but he still had to ask. "What does she do at Flamingo Road?"

Tessa looked uncomfortable. Her gaze shifted from him to Seth to the small, decorative pot sitting in her lap. Brandon's chest tightened. The pot combined vibrant glazes with cleverly carved designs. Had Lucy made it? He raised his eyes and met Tessa's pale gaze. "She's the headline dancer. Jasmine LeFleur. Brandon, is she the woman who was on the plane? I thought you couldn't remember. How can you be sure?"

"I wasn't until I saw her just now. It's come back." God, he needed to think, wanted to be someplace on his own where he could take in the shock of remembering along with the shock of finding out who Lucy was. He swallowed, trying to fight down the bile rising in his throat. It wasn't because of what she did. That wasn't it at all. What made him sick was she had known who he was, known he was so close, but she had chosen not to find him.

"Bran?" Seth's voice was soft. "You okay, bro?"

He blinked, raked a hand through his hair. "No. I'm not." He tried to smile. "But I guess I'll get there."

"I'm sure there must be some explanation—" Tessa began, but Brandon cut her off.

"Don't. Don't make excuses for her." He jammed his free hand in the pocket of his slacks. The other clenched the head of his cane. "Thanks for the information, Tessa. I don't think I'm great company right now, so if you two will excuse me."

Seth stood. "Bran. Don't do anything rash. Take some time to think."

It wasn't what he wanted to hear at the moment, but he knew it was good advice. "Thanks, Seth."

Brandon didn't remember driving to Barrett's glossy steel and glass headquarters, nor did he remember the ride to his office. Now he stood near the windows looking out over the Potomac and he wasn't even sure what he felt. Too many emotions churned inside him. His ability to empathize had enabled him to get along with all his very diverse siblings, had enabled him to live almost conflict-free with his irascible father and brother, but now when it touched him on such a personal level, Brandon wasn't sure he could empathize.

There were moments of the day of the plane crash he would never have any memories of because he had been unconscious, or so barely aware he knew it would forever be a fog to him. But he did remember the days leading to the trip he and Lucy had taken to Coyote Creek. He also remembered turning to her in the minutes before the crash and telling her he loved her. She'd told him she felt the same way.

Then she'd walked away from him. Knowing he was so close, knowing how to find him, she had walked away and stayed away. And Brandon couldn't figure that out.

"Mr. Barrett?" His secretary opened the door. "Don't forget, you have a meeting with the department heads at two."

He nodded. "Let's hold it in the conference room upstairs."

"Yes, sir."

There was work. There was always work.

Chapter 12

"Lady, are you all right?"

Lucy's gaze skated to the cabbie watching her in the rearview mirror, then away again. She shook her head. She had managed to mumble the address to him. Not home. She was going to Angelina's. Brandon had recognized her. His amnesia was gone. He'd remembered her, but in his recognition she had not seen any gladness, only shock.

He hadn't expected to see her again, that was obvious. How long had it been since his memory had returned? Lucy rubbed her fingers across her aching forehead. Had he been shocked to see her because he had just remembered? Or was he shocked to see her because he'd written her off as a holiday fling?

The cab pulled up in front of Angelina's well-tended bungalow. Lucy wiped beneath her eyes, hoping she'd cleared the worst of the smeared makeup. After digging the fare out of her wallet, she paid the cabbie, and he asked. "Lady, are you sure you're all right? Do you need me to wait?"

Taking a deep breath, she tried a smile she was sure must have failed. "No. I'll be okay, but thank you for your concern."

He touched the brim of his ball cap to her.

Lucy rushed up the walk. Ignoring the bell, she rapped on the door. As soon as Angelina opened it, Lucy burst into tears. With gentle hands, Angelina tugged her through the door. Lucy heard it shut behind her before Angelina turned her and wrapped her arms around her.

"Get it out. Whatever it is, get it out and we'll work through it when you can."

She followed Angelina, who led her to the couch in her living room. The other woman stroked her hair and her arm with one hand while she used her other to hold Lucy's in a grasp designed to give comfort, her thumb stroking the back.

Although she had told Angelina she was ready to move on and put Brandon behind her, seeing him, seeing he recognized her, had reopened it.

"I saw him," she choked out between sniffs and hiccups. "At the hospital. Another mistake on my part." Lucy jumped up. "What's with these stupid hyphenated names anyway? Can't they use the whole thing or at least use the same part? How the hell was I supposed to guess my friend Tessa's husband, Seth Barlow, was Brandon Barrett's brother? Or that they all belong to the same richer-than-the-Vatican Barlow-Barrett family who own half the known media universe?"

"You're ranting," Angelina inserted in a calm tone. "I guess I would rather see you angry than so wounded, but what I would like is for you to know which one is the true emotion."

"I feel them both," Lucy murmured, grabbing a tissue and wiping her eyes and nose. "Both of them are real. I feel like Brandon set out to deceive me. That makes me angry. And the look on his face today? He wasn't glad to see me. Do you know how it hurts?" Lucy was losing it. "I dug him out of a fucking crashed plane, dragged him... Oh God, listen to me? I sound so bitter. I don't want to feel this way. I don't want to feel anything. I want it to go away!"

"So put it behind you and move on." Angelina's voice was irritating in its calm, logical tone.

Lucy spun, hands on hips. "Right. And how do I do that?"

"Either confront him or find someone else."

"It's a little late to plan a confrontation for today." Lucy shook her head. "I can't believe I'm even having this discussion."

"The fact we're now discussing it is a good thing."

Lucy's mouth tilted. "That's so shrink-sounding."

Angelina shrugged. "So if the first thing's not an option, how about the second?"

"I do have a dinner date with Mason Hatch, but it's business. We'll be signing the paperwork for my consignments, and he wanted to do it over a celebratory dinner."

"Sugar, if a good-looking man like Mason is taking you to dinner, business or not, it's a date. I'd dress the part and leave the rest to him. He'll make you feel better about yourself even if he doesn't make you tingly."

Lucy gaped. "You know him?"

Angelina laughed. "Not in any biblical sense, but Mason's built a reputation and a lucrative business on being able to furnish the homes of

Washington newbies fast and on whatever budget they give him. Along the way, he's started handling some high-class art. If Mason's wants your work, you can pretty much write yourself a check."

"Okay, I'm feeling a lot better now, but I've already told him it's just friends."

Another burst of laughter. "Trust me, Lucy, if you give Mason any sign you want it to change, he'll be happy to oblige, but don't expect forever."

Lucy frowned. "So he screws around? Even if I was interested in him that way, I'm not sure I want the high-end equivalent of a man ho."

"He's not. In fact, he might be one of the hardest men in the area to catch. In the last year and a half, even more so—though nobody knows why—but he is a good man, Lucy. He'll treat you right, and he'll run interference for you if that's what you decide you need."

She thought about Angelina's observation while she got ready to go out with him. When the doorbell rang, she checked to make sure it was Mason and opened it with a wide smile for him. He brought his hand from behind his back and presented her with a bouquet of spring flowers.

Lucy's eyes widened. "Thank you, Mason."

"To new beginnings. May I come in while you put them in water?"

"Sure." She stepped out of the doorway and led the way into the kitchen. After grabbing a vase her grandmother had made years ago, she filled it with water and set the flowers in, manipulating them into a casual arrangement.

"Lovely," Mason murmured.

"It is a beautiful vase. My grandmother made it."

"I meant you." He grinned and winked at her. "But the vase is nice too. Talent must run in the family." Lucy sighed and put her hands on the counter. Mason touched her arm. "What is it?"

"Look. Could you dial it down a notch? I'm nervous. I've had a really, really tumultuous day, and I would like to be able to relax and have a good time tonight."

He turned her to face him. They stood eye to eye, unlike when she was with Brandon, who had towered over her even when she wore heels. "Accept my apology. Strictly business?"

"I think that would be best."

"You want to talk about it?"

Lucy took his hand from her shoulder and held it for a minute, calmed by the warm, hard texture of it. "At some point, maybe."

"I'm a good listener, and if it makes you feel more comfortable, I've got my own hang ups I'm dealing with. Friends is fine with me."

She smiled, once more relaxed. "Do we have time for you to see my studio while you're here?"

Mason's grin was back. "Of course."

* * * *

Once the department head meeting had concluded, Brandon's confidence soared about the direction in which he was taking Barrett Newspapers. It might piss off the old man, but then Alexander was home recovering, and Brandon was sure if his father returned to a done deal, it would make life a lot more bearable for everyone. So, on a business level, well…life was good.

It was his personal life that sucked. Big time.

Brandon checked his watch. Just past five. He was scheduled to meet his younger brother for drinks at seven. A few drinks might be the very thing. If he dropped the car by his house, he could change clothes, grab a cab and be there in plenty of time. If he were his dad, it would be a simple matter of ordering the chauffeur to take him, but like Seth, Brandon had eschewed some of his father's more overt displays of wealth.

And pretending to be what he wasn't… Wasn't that what had gotten him into trouble with Lucy? He'd downplayed who he was, and it was pretty fucking obvious she'd done a fantastic job covering up who she was. That was funny. A stripper doing a cover-up. Yeah.

He arrived at the restaurant after seven. It was a little upscale for drinks, but Phillip's law practice wasn't far and it was the place he'd named. Brandon hadn't been in the mood to suggest anything different.

"Good evening, Mr. Barrett," the manager greeted him at the door. "Your brother's expecting you. He's seated at the bar. I could find a table for the two of you…"

"Not at the moment, thanks." Brandon tried to smile with the refusal, but wasn't sure he'd been quite successful.

Phillip slid from the bar stool, his jacket gone, but his starched white dress shirt and red power tie were still in place.

"Court today?" Brandon inquired. "You're not this dressed up as a general rule. If I'd known I might have kept my king of capitalism look going. Instead, I'm down to khakis and deck shoes—and still the manager wants to give us a table in the dining room."

Phillip's grin was lopsided. Like all the rest of the Barlow-Barretts except Anna, his younger brother was blond and tall. When the bartender approached, Brandon ordered bourbon up.

"Stoli Elit," Phillip murmured.

Brandon arched a brow. "Vodka? What would Father say?"

Phillip's mouth twisted. "He's already said plenty ever since I told him I was going to law school and not into the family business."

The drinks appeared at their elbows. Brandon lifted his and sipped. "You and Anna, the family rebels."

"Because we want careers outside of the media?" Phillip shook his head. "Don't you ever feel confined, Bran?"

Every day. Right now even more so since I suspect the woman I loved latched onto me in hope of a free ride, then bailed when the going got tough. "Now and then," he admitted aloud. "Seth absorbed a lot of the flak over the years."

"But now it's on you."

"Yeah. Look, where's this going, Phillip? In the grander scheme of things, today has sucked. I'm not sure I'm up for a psychoanalysis of my career decisions."

"That's just it, bro," Phillip said. "What decision did you or Seth have? Seth at least has broken from the mold, though I suppose he's back now with Father laid up."

"Temporarily only. He's made that plain."

Phillip swirled the Stoli in his glass. "And you. Can you say, in all honesty, you would have chosen Barrett? You were one hell of a skier."

Brandon shook his head, frowned. "I would never have been the best. It was fun. That was it. But Barrett?" He paused. "You're right. I didn't choose it, but I'm good at it, Phillip. Seth hated the wheeling and dealing, hated everything other than the journalism side of it."

"You like it?"

Brandon swirled his drink. "I do. I don't always see eye to eye with Father, and we've had a couple of real battles, but overall I don't feel trapped."

"So why have you turned into such a morose prick?"

Brandon set his glass down. "Pardon me?"

Phillip finished his Stoli and signaled the bartender for another. "You heard me. I haven't seen Bran, the brother I've always hero-worshiped, since you went on that damn ski trip and ended up in a plane crash. Is it that? Was the near-death experience what turned you into an asshole?"

Anger flared. He tossed back his bourbon. "What the fuck do you know about it, *little brother*? Either about what happened to me or about running one of the biggest media companies in the US?"

"Not a damn thing, but if you don't let some of what's roiling around inside of you out, you're going to blow a gasket."

Another bourbon appeared in front of him. "And I suppose you think you're my father confessor now?"

Phillip grabbed a couple cocktail peanuts from the bowl in front of them, popped them in his mouth and began chewing. "No priest here. That was Mom's suggestion for me since I was the youngest male Barlow-Barrett, but I nixed the idea pretty fast. No, Bran, I just want to help."

A faint flush stained Phillip's cheekbones. Brandon swallowed, his throat tight. "Have I really been so bad?"

"Like a wounded grizzly? A pissed-off wolverine? Nah…it hasn't been so bad."

Brandon started to smile and lifted his gaze to the mirror behind the bar while he raised his glass to sip the smooth, amber liquid. He froze. Walking into the dimly lit bar was Lucy, dressed in a form-fitting green dress that showed off all her curves, and heels that made the eyes of every male in the bar gravitate to her legs and ass. Behind her was Mason Hatch.

"Fuck me."

"Huh?"

Seeing his brother start to turn his head, Brandon growled, "Don't look. Damn it. It's her with him."

"Okay Brandon, not one of your more erudite moments." Phillip didn't quite manage to smother a snicker and Brandon glared at him through narrowed eyes.

"Lucy Cameron. The woman I met in Colorado. The woman in the plane crash with me. The woman I…" He managed to stop right before he uttered the word *love*. God, she looked beautiful. She had looked lovely at the hospital. Now she was stunning.

And she was with Mason Hatch.

"She's with Mason Hatch," Phillip observed.

Brandon gritted his teeth, barely suppressing a *duh*.

"Do you think she's *with him* with him?"

Now he ground his teeth together. The thought had snuck into his brain too. His temper flared. She'd said she loved him. Had she cast him off with such ease? Brandon downed the rest of his bourbon, intent on confronting them. When he started to push to his feet, Phillip clapped a hand onto his shoulder and shoved him onto the stool again.

"Think, Brandon!" Phillip hissed. "The COO of Barrett Newspapers can't start a fucking bar brawl, and you know that's what it would become. You know Mason."

"That's the problem. I do know him. He picks women up and throws them away like paper plates at a company picnic. Lucy…" Brandon's voice dwindled to a whisper. "He'll hurt her."

Phillip's glass slapped the polished wood of the bar with a thunk. "You love her. Jesus, Brandon. You're in *love* with her?"

He tossed back the refill the bartender had slid his way. "I thought I was. What I loved doesn't exist."

* * * *

Right when they entered the bar, the skin on the back of Lucy's neck tingled. She hesitated, and Mason was right there behind her with a casual hand at the small of her back.

"Is anything wrong?" he asked.

She scanned the room, but didn't see anything. "No. Just nervous, I guess."

He smiled at her. "Let's get a table and have a drink while we get business out of the way."

Lucy couldn't shake the feeling she was under scrutiny. In the years she'd danced at Flamingo Road, she had never encountered anyone who could identify her as Jasmine LeFleur outside of the club. Part of her anonymity, she was sure, was due to the fact she slathered on the stage makeup at work, and outside of it always kept her makeup tasteful and minimal. The other factor was she seldom socialized or went anywhere she might encounter people who'd seen her act. Even exercising at the Y, she was careful to keep to herself and tried to hit the weight room when she was least likely to encounter men. However, an upscale restaurant like this meant all bets were off. Flamingo Road had always drawn a high-class clientele.

"What would you like to drink?" a white-coated waiter asked.

"A glass of merlot," Lucy murmured. Mason ordered a dry martini. After the waiter returned with drinks, Mason pulled the paperwork out of his jacket pocket with a grin.

"I hate briefcases, so I try to keep contracts short and sweet. Page one outlines our responsibilities to you as an artist. Page two defines what you agree to provide us along with the terms and timing of payment. Take your time looking it over."

Lucy tried to concentrate, she did, but it was so difficult. The problem wasn't the language of the contract, which was straightforward like she had found Mason to be. No, the problem was the feeling of being watched that she couldn't shake. Mason had to think she was the world's slowest reader by the time she finished it and murmured, "Everything seems to be in order."

When he handed her a pen, Lucy glanced toward the bar. Her breath caught in shock as she met Brandon's reserved gaze in the mirror over the bar. She noted he was seated with another blond man who bore a remarkable resemblance to him. The pen fell from her hand.

"Lucy?" Mason touched her hand in concern. "What's the matter?"

His head started to turn, so she put her hand on his arm to stop him. "It's someone I know. Don't look."

Mason halted and returned his gaze to hers. "From your work?"

"No." Lucy stared at her hands. "Someone I'm…I was…involved with."

He covered her hand with his. "We can go somewhere else if you'd like."

She shook her head. "No. I suppose it was naive to think I would never run into him." Squaring her shoulders, she took a sip of her wine, then picked the pen up again, proud her hand was steady. She had just finished signing her name above Mason's when she heard his hissed expletive.

"The someone you're talking about wouldn't happen to be Brandon Barrett would it?" Her expression must have told him the answer. "Jesus, Lucy. Where did you meet him?"

She caught his gaze with hers and held it. "In Colorado."

"*You're* the woman who survived the crash with him?" His glance slid to the two men at the bar. "You saved his ass and he doesn't speak to you?" There was a world of outrage in Mason's quiet voice.

"It's complicated." His eyes narrowed and she swallowed. "Mason, he didn't remember anything…including me."

He touched her cheek with his fingertips. "Let me take you someplace else." He was already signaling to the waiter for a check.

"No. Look. Can we go into the dining room to eat? I refuse to make it appear I'm running away." She sighed. "I already did that earlier."

The waiter appeared at Mason's side.

"If our table is available, we're ready to dine."

"Of course, sir. Let me make sure and I'll be right back."

Mason's dark gaze narrowed on her. "Tell me what you want me to do. If you need a shield, I can provide one." His smile was disarming. "Instant boyfriend, at your service. In fact, I'm onboard for anything that will piss that family off."

Lucy darted a look at the two men at the bar. Brandon's gaze was no longer reserved, it was hostile. She thought of the innocent touches on the arm, Mason's fingers on her cheek. "I don't think you need to do anything, Mason. He already looks like he could rip my head off. Yours too, for that matter."

Mason chuckled. "You know, I went to school with him."

"Some Ivy League bastion of learning, I'm sure."

"Well, yes. But I was there on scholarships and loans. Daddy forked out his tuition."

Lucy smiled. "If you were a woman, that comment would be bitchy."

Mason arched a brow. "If I were a woman, I wouldn't be as interested in how you hold your dress up, in a purely academic way of course."

A discreet cough and the waiter said, "Your table is ready, Mr. Hatch."

Lucy braced herself for Brandon's scrutiny after she stood. When Mason stepped to her side and placed his hand on the small of her back, she raised her chin. What right did Brandon have to glare at her? She wasn't the one who'd looked right through him earlier at the hospital. For a second, she held Brandon's gaze, then turned to Mason and smiled.

* * * *

"Bitch," Phillip muttered. "You're well rid of her, bro."

Brandon swirled what remained of his bourbon without saying anything. He couldn't help remembering what she'd been like in Colorado, couldn't believe it was all a put-on. For a split second, he would even have sworn he saw pain in her beautiful gray eyes. But then he'd watched Mason's hand resting just above the curve of her ass, and anger surged. He swallowed the rest of his drink.

"Let's go grab something to eat somewhere a little less formal. Staying will only piss me off. Lucy and I are through. It's history."

Chapter 13

Lucy called Roberto's cellphone the following morning after she felt sure he was awake. That was still early because she also knew he was anything but a late sleeper.

"Lucy! How wonderful to hear from you. Are you feeling better?"

She laughed. "You are a dog, Roberto."

"*Querida*! How can you say such a thing?"

"You give me names of people to see…for my head and my heart… then talk to them yourself before I can even get there."

"But it has worked for you?"

"Although I suspect you already know the answer… Yes, it's helped. Angelina is as she is named. And I signed a contract with Mason last night."

"Ah, so your days dancing for me are numbered."

"I would like to cut back to Friday and Saturday nights. I'll start this Friday. I want to return to work now I've made the decision."

"I will not say no. The customers have missed you. We have missed you."

"Then expect me Friday."

When she hung up, she couldn't believe how much lighter she felt for just having made decisions in different areas of her life. Maybe that had been part of the problem all along. She had wandered around without direction. Sure, she'd gotten a masters degree, but rather than try to either do something with it or her art, she had drifted along. Okay, there was a certain lure to pulling in a six-figure a year income, and exotic dancers did have a rather limited career life, kind of like professional athletes except it was gravity, not injury that most often sidelined a stripper.

Now she had more to look forward to. Mason had spent time over dinner talking to her about marketing her pottery. She had discovered that while his conversation was about business, Mason Hatch was a very tactile person. He touched her hand, her cheek. When they left the restaurant, he'd kept his hand at her back. He tried to talk her into going dancing, but she'd declined. Brandon was the last person she'd danced with, and she thought it would stir too many memories. So Mason had brought her home…and tried to kiss her at the door. He'd taken her refusal in stride, grinning at her.

"You can't blame a guy for trying. You might have said yes."

"You're incorrigible."

He'd taken her hand in his, rubbing it with his thumb. "I am your friend. If you need more, I can be that too. Whatever you need, Lucy." His smile had been sincere, even sweet.

"You know, Mason," she'd observed, "I get the feeling your interest would be less in me than in getting back at someone else."

He'd smiled, but she'd seen the shadows in his dark eyes.

Lucy shook her head, remembering the evening. Mason was easy to be around. He was handsome, but he wasn't Brandon, and even though she had made the decision to move on with her life, it didn't mean she was ready to move to another relationship. Lucy wasn't sure she would ever be ready. She swallowed as a vision of Brandon's unconscious, bloodied face flashed before her eyes. She wouldn't risk herself like that again. It had been too painful.

She put the remaining time until she returned to Flamingo Road to good use, working like a fiend in her studio. Deciding she would get the dishes done first, she completed plates and bowls, mugs and saucers, moving them to drying racks after they dried enough to be removed from the bats. Before they dried, she did whatever trimming needed to be done. In between work in her studio, Lucy kept to her schedule of running, swimming and lifting.

By Friday afternoon, she was happy with the work she'd accomplished and ready to return to Flamingo Road. She had missed her coworkers, Roberto and Tiffany too. Those two were more than coworkers, they were friends. She knew when she did leave Flamingo Road, she would miss them.

Pulling into the parking lot that evening felt almost like coming home. The building was still empty. Even though she went on stage later in the night, Lucy liked to arrive in plenty of time to relax and spend time stretching out and limbering up. Only when she had, did she sit down to apply stage makeup. From backstage, she could hear the club begin to fill, and the throb of the music intensify. She would perform three times during the evening.

Tiffany stopped in while Lucy was at the small practice room in the rear. She had her foot on the barre and was stretching her hamstrings.

"Welcome back, sugar. We sure did miss you around here. Roberto's been a bear."

Lucy dropped her foot to the ground and gave Tiffany a hug. "I am glad to be here, Tiffany. I am cutting my hours, just Friday and Saturday nights, but Roberto says he's cool with that."

Tiffany leaned against a wall while Lucy continued to stretch. "So things must have gone well with the gallery owner?"

Lucy grinned. "Very well. Mason wants dishes from me, but he also wants to display some of the work I consider fine art. He's even talking about putting together a showing to publicize me."

"Oh, sugar, that's fantastic! Will you still visit now and then when you're rich and famous? You know Roberto always lets the ladies in free."

"Of course I will." Lucy laughed. "But I'm nowhere near rich and famous yet."

Roberto stepped into the room, his swarthy face in a mock frown. "You're famous enough around here you'll leave a big hole when you're gone."

Lucy put her hands on her hips. "Well I'm not gone yet, and not likely to be anytime soon, so you can quit looking like a down-in-the-mouth hound dog, Roberto."

He winked at her. "I'm glad you're back, *nina*. You look beautiful."

"Thanks."

* * * *

Brandon tossed his car keys on his dresser, unloaded his pockets and then hung his suit and tie. He wasn't a neat freak by any means, but he was careful with his belongings. His upbringing might have been rich, but his parents had still kept the kids on a pretty tight line, not throwing money without necessity at anything other than their home and business. With Seth so close in age, Brandon hadn't even been a stranger to hand-me-downs. After stripping off his dress shirt and tossing it in the stack to go to the laundry, he pulled on sweats and grabbed a duffel bag. He still couldn't run because of his ankle, but he would get in a swim.

Friday night at the gym. Some social life. His smile was not pleasant. Brandon doubted most people would believe how unexciting the life of a major corporate COO was. He had managed to wiggle out of an invitation to a party and didn't have to go to his parents' compound until Sunday brunch, so right now, the brunt of the weekend stretched in front of him—a vast, empty expanse. To be honest, before the trip to Colorado, he would not have been at loose ends. There would have been a party, a date or some business function, but since his return, he had scaled back his social life.

Maybe Phillip was right. He was turning into a morose asshole. He swam up and down the length of the pool, his arms cutting through the water with an economy of motion. For a long time, he'd known something was missing, but he was unable to revert to where he had been before the ski trip. He hadn't understood why until a couple days ago when he'd stepped off the hospital elevator and seen Lucy. The recognition had slammed into him, followed by the memories.

Even now, he could see her laughing up at him and taking his hand after she'd fallen on her fanny for the umpteenth time the day he'd taught her to ski. Had that been an act? Had she known all along who he was and hoped to get her hooks into him? He didn't want to think that, but a cynical part of him, the part that had been latched onto time and time again throughout his life just because he was a Barlow-Barrett, could think nothing else. For God's sake, she was a stripper. He knew she had aspirations to become an artist. How much easier would life be if she had someone willing to bankroll her lifestyle? Maybe the whole thing about it being her first vacation was a lie then too. But no, Tessa had said Lucy never took vacations.

He didn't know. What he did know was he couldn't get her off his mind. He'd tried. Neither exercise nor booze had worked.

Brandon climbed out of the pool, his ankle sore but not painful, and limped into the locker room. A little time in the whirlpool and he should be good as new. On his way to his house, Brandon found himself taking a detour. He hadn't intended to but realized, turning into the parking lot, he'd driven to Flamingo Road. It was already crowded. For a few minutes, Brandon sat in the car. Why was he doing this? Why was he punishing himself this way?

He needed to see. He needed to be able to picture Jasmine LeFleur instead of Lucy Cameron. Maybe when he saw the stripper he would be able to work her out of his system. It would be like aversion therapy. Once he saw her dancing, he could walk away.

The bouncer, a guy who looked like even his ears had muscles, stopped him at the door. "Coat and tie are required, sir."

Jesus. He was still in his sweats. Brandon nodded. It had been a stupid idea anyway, but it wouldn't go away. He drove home, started to flop on his couch to watch a sports documentary and found he couldn't get the idea of seeing Lucy-Jasmine out of his head. With a sigh of self-disgust, he went upstairs and changed clothes. Ignoring the khakis and blue blazer which would have been enough to get him in the door, Brandon pulled on a conservative navy pinstripe. After tightening the knot on a custom-made silk tie, he checked his money clip to make sure he had plenty of cash and headed out again.

This time the bouncer waved him forward into their VIP section, a discreetly lit area very near the stage. A waitress, clad in a bikini-style top and a skirt not much bigger than a dish towel, came over to take his drink order. While he waited for her to return with the burgundy, he watched the girl on stage. The dancing was mediocre at best, but he supposed the size of her no doubt surgically enhanced breasts more than made up for the lack of skill. That seemed to be the case because a couple noisy patrons managed to reach forward enough to shove some bills in her g-string. His jaw clenched. He forced himself to study the dancer once again. Her body wasn't as fit as he remembered Lucy. This was a woman who would run to fat in no time at all. Another dancer he didn't recognize took the stage, and Brandon began to wonder if Lucy was even working, but he remembered seeing her name on the marquee when he came in.

He ordered a second glass of wine. As the waitress set it down, he stopped her.

"A friend of mine mentioned a dancer—Jasmine—does she still work here?"

The waitress smiled. "She's next. Jasmine's the reason we're so busy tonight. She's been off a few days, but she's back now. The place is packed and Roberto is a happy man."

He nodded and smiled. He picked up his wineglass and grimaced to see his hand shook the smallest bit. As if he weren't the only one in the crowd awaiting her appearance, he began to hear the name Jasmine being whispered among a nearby group of men.

"She's been here forever," he heard one man say. "But damn, she's got a body that just won't quit. The way she moves... She must be a maniac in the sack."

When the men snickered and picked up their beer bottles, tension knotted Brandon's stomach in an even tighter coil. The faint throbbing of a headache beat behind his forehead.

"And now, gentlemen," the stage manager announced, "by popular demand...Jasmine LeFleur!"

A hard-driving hip hop tune blared. Brandon leaned into the shadows. At least for now he would prefer she didn't see him. She spun out onto the stage with a move that would have made a professional dancer proud.

While he watched her combine grace and athleticism with the fast pace of the music, he understood why she was so demanding of her diet and exercise. There was nothing soft or half-assed about this performance. In your face hip pumping, ass wiggling and chest shimmying had the crowd hooting and hollering. Money fluttered on stage as soon as she ripped the lower half of her dress away to reveal a skirt barely covering her tush. Long legs flashed and twirled. By the time she finished, she was out of breath—and so was every man watching her, including him. As she bowed and waved, he saw her glance around. He leaned away from the light even more.

He gulped the wine. The waitress reappeared. "Another, sir?"

He nodded. He wanted his mind to be numb. His cellphone buzzed. "Yeah."

"Hey, Bran… Where the hell are you?" Seth barked into his phone.

"Flamingo Road. Torturing myself."

"Shit." There was a pause on the other end, then Seth said, "I'll be right there."

"I'm trying not to be noticed," Brandon snapped. "Two giant, blond Barlow-Barretts will be a lot harder to keep incognito."

"Nevertheless, I'll be there if for no other reason than to drive you home."

The connection cut before he could tell his brother how much of his ass he could kiss. Another dancer was on the stage, but she was nowhere near the caliber of Lucy. The next time she came out, she was dressed for skiing. His heart nearly stopped. This was the Lucy he remembered, but the makeup and expression were all wrong. His Lucy was fresh-faced and laughing. The Jasmine version of her was… Holy Mary. He almost swallowed his tongue when she wrapped herself around the pole. His eyes widened and his cock swelled. After another swallow, he glanced around the room and his lips thinned. He didn't want these men seeing her. His fists clenched. He had started to rise when a hand clamped on his shoulder.

"Sit down, Brandon," Seth hissed close to his ear. "No matter what you're thinking or feeling right now, you cannot create a scene. Remember who you are."

"*Fuck* who I am," he snarled.

"Sit." Seth signaled to the waitress. "Bring another glass of wine for him and one for me."

"I thought this would help," Brandon muttered, "but it's torture."

"It's her job. Not her. Remember, I found Tessa in here too."

"Waiting tables. She at least had the important things covered." Lucy turned her back to the audience, sliding down the pole until she was squatting with her legs splayed and the taut muscles of her butt and thighs on display. Brandon groaned. "God help me."

Customers tossed money onto the stage. Seth tossed a bigger bill on the table and tapped Brandon's shoulder. "Come on, Bran. We're leaving. You did need to come here, but you don't need to stay."

Brandon nodded. He couldn't do anything else. His throat was tight and his groin was aching, but what hurt the worst was his heart. As they left the club, he bumped a smaller, slighter guy just coming in.

"Watch it, dude," the guy said, giving him a hostile look.

"Sorry," Brandon muttered, not liking the way the guy still stared at him, eyes narrowed with speculation.

"Whatever."

* * * *

Lucy bowed and stood. Two towering blond men in the process of leaving caught her eye. For a moment, her heart skittered, but it had to be her imagination. Brandon wouldn't be here. No way. She slipped backstage with a wave and into the dressing room. One of the other dancers grinned at her.

"The customers sure love you."

"Thanks. A few days off, though, and I'm feeling this tonight, especially that last dance. Thank goodness the final one is a lot slower."

The other woman chuckled. "For you, maybe. Not for the customers. When you go out there for the last act, the heat level in here climbs like a thermometer in boiling water."

Lucy smiled. She took off her costume, threw on a robe and slipped into the warm-up room to stretch. She was always tight following the first two dances because of the pace and the type of movements choreographed into it. The final one, however, required her to be super flexible, so stretching was a must. By the time she slipped into the dressing area, she had just enough time to touch up her makeup and change into her final costume.

When she went on stage for her closing routine, Lucy closed her mind to the men in the audience. Instead, she pretended there was one man there. Brandon. And she danced for him. The applause and the whistles were thunderous. The stage was green with cash. Lucy picked up her robe and walked backstage.

Right after she slipped the robe on, Roberto came around the corner. He pulled her into a friendly embrace. "You amaze, as always. Welcome back, Lucy."

She nodded and rested her cheek along his for an instant.

Lucy slept in the following morning, but not too late. She wanted to wake in plenty of time so she could work in her studio. Once she checked her newest projects, she went to the racks and found the pieces ready for glazing. As the morning sunlight slanted through the wide windows, Lucy worked with complete concentration. She had opened a window so the sound of the birds and someone mowing their grass in the distance accompanied the dip of her brush in the glaze. She knew some people enjoyed working with music in the background, but she had always preferred either quiet or the sounds of the outdoors when it was warm enough to leave windows open.

She was a bit stiff this morning and knew it was from dancing last night. She had discovered over the years that deviating from her routine would leave her sore. She would have to include some dance practice into her exercise schedule if she was going to confine performances to Friday and Saturday nights. Perhaps Roberto would allow her to come in a couple days in the late afternoon to practice in the warm-up room.

With that idea in mind, she arrived a little early the next evening and ran the idea past her boss. He leaned back in the chair in his office and smiled. "If it will keep you dancing Fridays and Saturdays, then by all means."

"Thanks, Roberto. You are the absolute best."

He grinned. "Remember me when you're the famous Lucy Cameron."

She spent more time warming up, loosening tight muscles until she felt relaxed and supple. Once again, the club was packed. There were two bachelor parties with front row seats, so like the other dancers, she tried to focus the direction of her dancing on the grinning young men who were more than willing to order plenty of beer and toss plenty of bills on stage. Unlike some of her fellow dancers, Lucy kept just out of reach. She allowed no one to touch her. Never had, never would. It had been the one thing that had creeped her out about the job when she first came to talk to Roberto, but he had assured her it was not required. In fact, following the letter of the law, it wasn't even allowed, but because it was such a tradition in most strip clubs, cops tended to overlook it if it wasn't shoved in their faces, so to speak.

During her second dance, when she was wrapped around the pole with her ass pointed at one of the soon-to-be-hitched, she noticed a pair of long, elegantly clad legs in the VIP section, a cane resting next to the unknown patron's chair. Try though she might, she couldn't see the man's face. All she could see was he was alone, his almost untouched wine, and while she danced, his foot tapped—not in rhythm with the music, but with a cadence of irritation or impatience.

She forced her attention away from the mysterious VIP and slithered around the pole, shimmying up and wrapping her legs around it. As she leaned back and stretched out, she saw one of the man's hands reach for his wineglass. Gold flashed on his pinkie and the elegant cufflinks, like the ones Brandon had worn the night they went dancing in Falcon's Head. Lucy slipped, which would have sent her head-first into the floor, but she caught herself, swung around the pole, and improvised to cover the mistake.

Coincidence. It had to be. She finished, gave a quick wave and bounced off the stage. After wrapping her robe around herself, she attracted Tiffany's attention. When her friend came off the floor, Lucy pulled her out of view. "I need you to do me a favor."

"What, sugar? We're crowded tonight and Laquisha didn't show for her shift so I'm covering."

"Please, Tiff," Lucy pleaded. "I need you to cruise through the VIP section and tell me what the man there in the corner looks like."

"All right. It might take me a while."

Lucy nodded. "Thanks. I owe you."

While she waited, she threw on sweats and a t-shirt and retreated to the warm-up room. She stretched, spending extra time on the floor forcing her body beyond its normal range of motion. She had just finished and was wiping sweat from her face when Tiffany returned.

"Big. Blond. And scowling. His waitress says he's barely touched his wine, but insists everything's fine."

"Thanks."

"Someone you know?"

"I hope not."

"I can have Roberto check him out, maybe ask him to leave before you go on stage again. I noticed you bobbled in your last routine."

Lucy shook her head. "No. Everything's cool."

But as she slipped into a g-string that was more bare than there and pasties that hardly deserved the name, Lucy's hands shook. She covered up with the silk robe in which she started this final routine then sat to reapply her makeup. She had to stop for a minute and do some deep breathing before she finished.

It wasn't him. It couldn't be. Brandon Barlow-Barrett would never be seen in a place like this. *But your other blueblood boyfriend was*, her conscience pointed out in its own annoying way. Seth had discovered Tessa working here. They were brothers.

No. She had to clear her head. She couldn't go on stage this way. And Roberto, friend though he was, would be livid if she didn't perform this last routine. It wrapped up the night. Lucy stood and stared at herself a moment. Please God, let the pottery be everything Mason thought it would be. She could quit, return to being plain Lucy Cameron and forget Jasmine LeFleur ever existed.

For this dance, the lights were down low except for the single chair on stage on which a spotlight was trained. When the first jazzy strains of music floated through the room, she stepped out on stage. This time, no laughing, smiling Jasmine LeFleur performed gravity-defying gymnastics with the pole. She was much more serious. The dance was choreographed to mimic the act of making love. While she went through her routine, her eyes strayed from the heated, drooling expressions of the grooms and their parties to that dark corner. The cufflinks and ring glinted, and the wineglass dangled from his fingertips. He had his legs crossed at the knee, and this time everything about him was still, silent, as if he were waiting for something.

The dance began to wind down, tips fluttered onto the stage, but Lucy didn't see them. She stretched upward just as the mysterious VIP leaned into the light. Her gaze locked with Brandon's, and he coolly dumped five one hundred dollar bills at her feet. She swallowed. No one tipped like that unless they were hoping a dancer would provide them with some other services after hours. Her gaze darted to his and she saw the contempt in his eyes. For a split second, tears welled. She blinked, spun away from him and grabbed her robe from the chair.

Trailing it behind her, she sauntered from the stage, making sure she wiggled her ass more than usual. Only when she was in the shower did she allow her emotions free rein. No one could see her cry there. While the water sluiced over her and she scrubbed at her skin, Lucy let the tears fall.

Chapter 14

He was in a foul mood. He had been since he'd left Flamingo Road Saturday night. Now sitting in his office, he had his chair turned toward the windows and a cup of coffee in his hands.

He heard the quiet opening of the door. "I've brought the morning papers," his secretary stated.

"Set them on my desk."

"Uh, Mr. Barrett, I think you should look at *DC Nightlife*."

Now he did turn, rotating his chair to arch one brow at his assistant. *DC Nightlife* was the regional equivalent to the national scandal sheets at the grocery store checkouts. Brandon grimaced and grabbed the paper off the top. He nearly dropped his coffee. Staring at him was a shot of him dropping money on the stage at Flamingo Road with the headline *Media Mogul Tips Big at Local Strip Joint.*

"Fuck. Me." How the hell had someone gotten a picture? He was hardly a recognized face. The club should have been off-limits too. His office phone rang. Brandon snatched it, knowing it would be Seth on the line.

"Have you seen it?" Seth barked.

"Yes."

"We're going to need to strategize some damage control."

"Fuck."

"Why the hell did you go back, Bran?"

He ran a hand through his hair, tousling it until he was sure it must be standing on end. "I don't know. I keep saying it's to get her out of my system…"

"And dumping five hundred dollars? Jesus! It looks like you're trying to set up sex with her. She had to have thought the same thing."

His fingers clenched in his hair, pulling until it hurt. He had thought for an instant when their gazes met he'd seen tears in those deep pools of gray. He swallowed, his throat tight and painful, but at that point he had been too pissed off and jacked up to care. His cock had been ready to explode—and he was sure every other guy in the place was the same way. That had just pissed him off so much more. He'd wanted to hurt her, wanted to strike out and make her feel the pain he felt. He'd succeeded. He'd seen the proof in those expressive eyes of hers before she'd tightened her jaw and given him her little fuck-you ass wiggle as she'd slinked away.

"No. She knew what it was," Brandon responded. "It was a *fuck you, bitch*, she couldn't fail to understand."

"Well, expect a call from the acting chairman. In fact, I wouldn't be surprised if you get a call from Father as well."

* * * *

Lucy had gotten up right at sunrise to go for a run Monday morning. She'd gone out the kitchen door and stretched on the patio, inhaling the sweet scent of the flowers blooming in her garden. Using the alley behind her house, she'd cut over to a quieter side street than the road her home fronted on. The alley was a shortcut to the small park nearby with its mile-long walking track. This early in the day, it was deserted so she could run with no interference. When she reached the park, she paused at the first of several little exercise stations and stretched. She'd do five circuits, then call it quits and jog home.

By the time she finished, she knew the morning paper would be on her front sidewalk, so she took a different route home, only slowing to a walk after she rounded the corner to her street. Her walk became a halt when she saw several cars parked near her home. In addition to a couple of unmarked sedans, there was an SUV from a major daily, another from the community paper and one from *DC Nightlife*. While she gaped, a marked car from one of the area television stations cruised to a stop. In front of her house was a small gaggle of people, some armed with video cameras on their shoulders, others with still cameras dangling from their necks, impressive zoom lenses mounted on the camera bodies.

To her utter horror, as she stood and stared, one of the photographers turned, lifted his camera and began snapping pictures. When the others noticed, more turned and she heard someone announce, "There she is! It's Lucy Cameron…the stripper!"

Not waiting for them to catch her, Lucy turned on her heels and ran back the way she'd come. She raced through the park to the other side and out to a busier street where she could hail a cab. Dressed in running shorts and a sports bra, it wasn't long before someone picked her up. With no money and no cellphone, though, her options were limited. Lucy gave the cabbie Angelina's address and prayed no one had followed her. She slumped against the vinyl seats, letting her head fall back, and closed her eyes.

"You're lucky I came along, miss," the cabbie told her. "I don't normally start this early in the day."

She opened her eyes. "Well, I'm glad you were there. Look, you may have noticed, I didn't come prepared to catch a cab. If you'll be patient, the owner of the house where you're taking me will cover my fare."

"If you'll pardon my saying so, miss," the grizzled driver remarked, "you look a lot like the woman on the front of this paper I picked up along with my coffee this morning." Reaching over on the bench seat, he picked up a paper and passed it to her.

Lucy took it to be polite and unfolded it. *DC Nightlife*. While she looked at the picture, her hands began to shake. *Media Mogul Tips Big at Local Strip Joint*, the headline screamed. Next to it was a page number for what she assumed was the story that went along with it. She fumbled through the pages and saw another photo inside. She scanned the story and, sure enough, there was the explanation for the vultures gathered around her house. "Jasmine LeFleur, aka Lucy Cameron, is Flamingo Road's featured dancer."

After folding the paper, she pushed it back to the cabbie. "You know, I've changed my mind about where I want to go. Do you know where Barrett Newspapers' offices are?"

"Sure do." His eyes darted to her reflection in his mirror. "You sure about this? I can wait for you once we get there."

Lucy smiled. "That would be a good idea because I'm sure I'll still want to go to the first address I gave you." She leaned on the seat and looked out the window. "And by the way," she added, "it is a picture of me. What I want to know is who took it and how they got my real name. I returned from my morning run to find half the media outlets in the district parked in front of my house." She sighed and brushed a weary hand across her forehead.

"Wow. I'm sorry."

When the cab pulled up in front of a monstrous steel and glass structure, saliva pooled in her mouth for a moment. Somehow, the building made who and what Brandon was a horrifying reality. Gathering her courage around her like the coat she wished she had, Lucy climbed out of the cab.

"Good luck. I'll wait."

She waved at him and jogged into the building. A brawny security guard, with his eyes bugging out, met her a few feet inside the door. "Excuse me, miss, but this is not a gym. I think you must be in the wrong place."

"Oh no, I'm not. I need to see Brandon Barlow-Barrett."

"I'm afraid that won't be possible." He didn't need to add he wasn't about to allow some wild-eyed, wild-haired half-dressed woman inside this bastion of journalism and big business, Lucy could see it in his expression. Well, hell, she didn't keep so physically fit for nothing. With a smirk at the overweight guard, she dashed around him straight toward the door she assumed led to the fire stairs.

"Hey! Stop!"

She ignored him, barely registering the fact he was chasing her while he spoke into a walkie-talkie. So there must be more of them. She would have to be creative. After dashing up three flights, she burst through the door onto a floor of deserted offices. A quick glance at her watch showed her it was still fifteen minutes to eight. Chances were most of the floors were this way. Good. She paused a second to grab her breath while she reasoned what floor Brandon's office would be on.

She stepped onto the elevator and punched the button for the floor second from the top. From what little Brandon had said about his father, she had the feeling the top floor would be his alone. She was surprised to find no one waiting for her as the doors swished open to reveal a thick-pile carpeted floor and a corridor as quiet as a church. Almost. From the far end she heard the ringing of multiple phones.

* * * *

"Mr. Barrett, Mr. Frank is holding on line one and your father is on line two."

Brandon blinked. "Just a minute." He stared in horror at two words in the article. *Lucy Cameron.* She would never have planted this and given them her real name. Someone had set them both up.

His intercom buzzed again. "Uh, Mr. Barrett, Mr. Frank and your father are still holding and there is a… Hey, you can't…"

His door burst open. Lucy stomped in, dressed in skimpy running shorts that showed off long, toned legs and a sports bra that left a strip of golden midriff bare. Her pale hair was confined in a long braid…and her expression was furious. "Did you have to give them my name? What did I ever do to you to make you hate me so much?"

Brandon pressed the intercom. "Tell Frank and my father I will call them later. Don't let anyone else in here, even if you have to body block the door." He released the button and braced his hands on the desk to stand. When he limped around the corner, he saw her eyes darken before she looked away.

"What? Not perfect enough for you anymore?" he snarled.

She stared at him wide-eyed. "That was never the issue," she whispered. "And I'm not here to talk about the past." She took two steps toward him until she was almost within arm's reach. "How could you give the paper my name?"

"I never…"

She wiped a hand across her face. "I finished my morning run and couldn't even get back to my house! Reporters and photographers were everywhere. The minute they saw me, they started coming after me. Lucy Cameron…the stripper. They knew my name. How *could* you?"

"I didn't…" He watched her start to prowl around his office. She was like a restless lioness and just as sleek. He looked at her attire. "How did you get here?"

"I grabbed a cab. He's waiting…" She ended on a frustrated huff. "You know, this was a bad idea." Her hand sliced the air. "Forget I even came by. I don't know what I was thinking."

She turned to go. No. Brandon moved between her and the door. "Don't go."

Her hands went to her hips. "What? Is it time to pay off on the five hundred dollar tip? Is that the deal?"

Behind the anger he saw the shadows she tried hard to hide. He punched the intercom behind him. "Linda, there's a cab out front. Have someone pay the fare and send him on his way."

"No!" Lucy protested. "You can't do that. I don't have any way to get… God, I can't even go home."

"Where were you going to go from here?" He sure as hell hoped she didn't say to Mason Hatch. He could take almost anything but that.

"To my shr—friend's house."

Brandon had noticed the switch. She had been about to say shrink. "Why are you seeing a shrink?"

"I'm not. Angelina is a friend." Lucy's jaw had hardened into stubbornness. When he continued to regard her, he saw her shiver and realized she must be chilled.

"My sister Stacey keeps an office on the floor below. You're both about the same size. I could have Linda bring some clothing."

Lucy shook her head. "No."

Brandon sighed, feeling like they were getting nowhere. The past was rising between them, something they would have to deal with if they were ever going to move forward.

"Why did you leave?" he asked.

Her expression shut down. "I told you. The reporters…"

"I'm not talking about this morning. Why did you leave Colorado without seeing me, without any word at all?"

She wrapped her arms around herself, rubbing her hands up and down her upper arms. So many emotions skittered across her face it was like watching clouds crossing a spring sky on a blustery day. She started to shake her head. He could almost see her backing away and closing herself off.

"Damn it, Lucy! Talk to me! I went back, you know, to the crash site. I made Matt take me there." Now she was shaking her head. Her hand went up to tuck hair behind her ear. "But I still couldn't remember it, couldn't piece any of it together, not until the day I stepped off the elevator at the hospital and saw you. Did you get a kick out of it? Was that the idea?"

"No!" Her arms were wrapped around her middle again, and she rocked back and forth on her feet. Brandon got the feeling she was about to shatter, and he didn't know what to do. "You didn't know who I was. You didn't remember! We got to the hospital and your parents were there." She stopped, swallowed. "No one looked at me. And there you were, a person I didn't know either. Maybe I should have known your name, but I didn't. I couldn't handle the attention you were getting. I didn't want people to start digging into who I was."

"So you ran?" he snarled.

She pointed to the *DC Nightlife*, still sitting on his desk. "Yes! From this. That's what I ran from. For years, I've managed to keep my real life separate from my job at Flamingo Road because no one cared." She stared at him. "But all you had to do was walk in, and the equation changed. Why couldn't you just leave it alone?"

She was cutting her emotions off, stepping back from any involvement, and if she succeeded, it was over. He was desperate. He stepped over to her and yanked her into his arms. "Why? Because of this, damn you!"

He brought his mouth to hers, intending to kiss her hard, but at the last minute, his mouth softened. He tasted her, smelled her, felt her velvet skin beneath his hands and groaned. The kiss teased, then demanded, as he pulled her into the heavy, aroused ache in his groin. He kept kissing her until he tasted the salt of her tears. Throat tight, he pulled her face onto his shoulder.

"Don't cry, Lucy. Please," he whispered.

The door opened behind them and Brandon spun. Seth stood there with Linda hovering behind him.

"What the hell are you doing, Brandon?" his brother demanded.

"Mr. Barrett," his secretary spluttered, "I tried…"

"The board will be here in five minutes. Is this what you call damage control?"

Lucy went rigid in his arms. "Turn me loose," she hissed.

"Lucy!"

"No!" She glared at all of them. "Just get the hell away from me."

"Wait. I'll take you…"

"Nowhere," she whispered in a flat, dead voice. "I don't want your help. I don't need it. You've already done more than enough. Believe me."

She pushed away from him, avoiding his hands while she stalked from his office. He started after her.

"Brandon!" Seth growled. "Let her go for now. Tessa can help us find her, and you know she's tied in with Mason Hatch. Right now you've got to meet with the board."

Brandon's heart thudded. She stepped into the elevator, and the doors closed, blocking her from view. He swallowed, blinked a couple times, then smoothed his hair.

"Linda, make sure there's a cab waiting for her. Have the bill for her fare sent to me." He would at least make sure she could get wherever she was headed safely.

* * * *

She didn't question the different cab out front, but slid in gracefully and gave Angelina's address. When they reached the house with its verdant, blooming yard, she told the man to wait until Angelina could come out and pay him.

"No problem. Your fare's taken care of, and I was instructed to wait unless you no longer needed me."

"You can go." Even if Angelina wasn't there, Lucy was staying. She would wait until her friend returned. One thing was for sure, she was in no hurry to get to her house. Oh God, she needed to call Roberto and let him know what was going on. He would be so upset someone had taken pictures inside the club. She dashed up the sidewalk and pounded on the door. As soon as Angelina saw her, she pulled her inside the house.

"Lucy? What's up?"

"Oh, Angelina, you will never believe it." She launched into her tale, and the other woman pulled her into the kitchen, seating her at the table. While Lucy continued to talk, Angelina poured coffee and set a plate full of fresh, yeasty rolls on the table for them.

"Drink some coffee and eat something. If I know you, you ran before breakfast and haven't had anything to eat, have you?"

"No." But then, she hadn't wanted anything either and still wasn't sure she could eat. Still, she would be polite. So she drank and ate, and surprised herself by being able to do so. "Thanks, Angelina."

"No problem. Hang on, I'll be right back."

The other woman appeared a few minutes later with a serviceable pair of gray sweats with *Hoyas* emblazoned in blue across the front of the hooded sweatshirt.

"Your alma mater?" At Angelina's grin, Lucy smiled. "Mine too."

"Now, let's discuss what we need to do. You've already seen Brandon, though it doesn't appear that was productive."

"At least I know I'm considered 'damage' that needs to be controlled."

Angelina arched one brow at her. "I'm not sure that's accurate, but we can visit that line of thought some other time. Have you talked to anyone else?"

"No. But I need to call Roberto. He should know someone took pictures in the club last night."

"I think he should also know someone in his employment gave out your real name."

Lucy's gaze snapped up from where she was buttering a roll. "Huh?"

"Be realistic. There's no rational reason for Barrett to do that to you."

Lucy swallowed. "You didn't see the look on his face Saturday night when he slapped his money on stage."

Angelina leaned back in her chair. "Think about it. Think how angry you were to discover the communications company he made sound so minor was Barrett newspapers? Doesn't he have a right to be angry you never mentioned you were a stripper?"

Lucy looked away, tucked a stray hair behind her ear and snatched her coffee cup. "I—I guess so."

"Well, I think we can attribute his reaction to that, but no one in his position is going to seek what's in *DC Nightlife* on purpose. So that leaves only the people you work with."

"Or Mason."

Angelina shook her head. "No. Not his style, and not the way he would choose to get you noticed, but I think you can add him to the list of people you need to call. Anyone else?"

"No. I don't have any family, and I never kept in touch with any of my foster families."

"The next thing we need to do is figure out how to get you into your house…and out again."

"Don't you think they'll give up? I mean, it can't be that big of a deal."

Angelina leaned forward and covered Lucy's hand with hers. "They've already dug enough to find out where you live. Someone will make the connection to the plane crash in pretty short order. You can bet on it."

Lucy pushed her plate away. Now her appetite had vanished.

* * * *

Brandon saw no friendly faces in front of him. At best there were only less hostile ones. And those consisted of Seth, Phillip and his sister Stacey. The rest of the board members were stone-faced. Bill Frank sat at the head of the table as acting chairman. Brandon sat at the foot of the table with Seth at his right hand.

"Brandon," Frank began, "I think we know why we're gathered here, but in case there's any question—" He looked around the table. "Has everyone seen *DC Nightlife?*"

There were nods around the table.

"This is a serious slap in the face for Barrett Newspapers. This company has always maintained a very low profile, conservative image, and in the competitive market in which all media companies find themselves right now, this type of situation has the potential to do irreparable harm."

"What I would like to know," one of the other directors said, "is what the hell someone was doing with a camera in there?"

"I have a call in to the owner," Seth murmured. "His reputation is impeccable, and I know for a fact he would never sanction or countenance such an invasion of privacy, either of a client or a dancer."

"It's not the dancer I'm concerned about," Frank stated.

At last, Brandon had heard all he wanted to. "Well, that's exactly who I'm concerned about, damn it. Her name is Lucy Cameron, and she's not some bimbo stripper." When Frank started to interrupt, Brandon held up his hand. "She's an artist—a potter—with a master's degree from Georgetown, but more than that… She's the woman who saved my life following the plane crash in Colorado. If for no other reason, I owe her for that. I can assure you, she's been far more damaged by this than me."

Bill Frank's expression was cool. "Unfortunately, in my position as acting head of this board, it's not her reputation or yours I have to be concerned about. It's the company's. Right now, we need to decide the best way to effect some sort of damage control."

Brandon's temper boiled. Added onto his uncertainty about how Lucy was doing, it was not a good combination. He was about to snap again when Seth kicked him under the table.

"I have an idea," his elder brother said. "Rather than try to sweep this under a rug, I believe our best bet is to meet it head on so we can put our own spin on it."

"What are you suggesting?" Brandon gritted out.

"Bran." Seth leaned forward, his hands clasped on the table. "Those reporters aren't going to quit until they know everything they can find out about you and Lucy."

Brandon leaned back, his arms folded across his chest. "Is that supposed to be news to me, bro? Because they're already camped outside her damn door. Why do you think she showed up here in her running shorts? She couldn't even get to her house, for Christ's sake."

"Then it's even more critical we hit this head-on right away. Here are the options I see. We can publish the story in our own papers, but the complete story, including Lucy's role in the plane crash, or we can call *DC Nightlife* and promise the reporter an exclusive. The problem with the second option is *Nightlife* is a weekly. We can cover about thirty percent of the U.S. with our dailies…even more with our websites. If we own the story, then it loses its punch and will blow over."

Brandon couldn't argue with Seth's logic. He saw most of the board nodding their heads in approval. From a business standpoint, it was a sound move. From a personal one, he knew it could very well turn Lucy against him forever. They would sacrifice her privacy. He tasted again the tears on her cheeks, saw once more the hurt on her face.

He shook his head. "You can't do this…"

"Brandon, the separation of her life as Lucy Cameron and her life as Jasmine LeFleur is already gone," Seth pointed out. "There's not much of a choice here. The rest of it—her involvement in the plane crash—is a matter of public record no one's bothered to check into so far, but that's over now. The question you have to ask yourself is do you want those details coming out with our spin on it or the speculation of people who don't know all the facts?"

Brandon's jaw clenched. He looked around the table then to Bill Frank. "Could I have a few minutes with my family please? I'm sure you understand, there are more issues involved here than the company."

Frank nodded and looked around at the other men and women on the board. "I think we can allow that. Why don't we give you a quarter of an hour, then we'll meet here?"

Brandon stood. "Let's meet in my office." He directed his gaze at his brothers and sister. Uncaring whether they followed, he left the room and headed for the elevator. Seth, Phillip and Stacey filed in behind him. No one said anything until they were in Brandon's office and the door had shut.

Then Stacey let loose. "What the hell were you thinking, Brandon. A strip joint? Tossing down five hundred dollars? For God's sake!"

"Bro!" Phillip added. "I thought you were done with her after seeing her out with Mason Hatch."

Stacey's face blanched for an instant, then she latched on like a terrier. "Done with her? You mean you have a relationship with a stripper?"

"Lucy," Brandon snarled. "Her name is Lucy." He turned from his sister and brother toward Seth. "If we do what you suggest… Will they leave her alone? Will the press let her get back to her life?"

Seth put his hands in his pockets and scowled out the window.

"Seth?" Brandon prompted.

"Eventually. And sooner than if we do nothing and make them ferret out the information on their own." In Seth's eyes, at least, he saw sympathy. Tessa and his brother had gone through their own rough spots, Seth even being led to believe at one point Tessa had stolen money from the company. While they were happily married now, Brandon knew they'd almost not made it. What brought them together had been Zach, Tessa's younger brother, by running away. Knowing how much Zach admired Seth, Tessa had turned to him for help.

Lucy would never turn to him for help. With her independent streak, Brandon would lose her no matter what he did. He looked around. Phillip regarded him with pity and Stacey still looked outraged. Oh yes, she was very much their parents' daughter. Brandon knew he would still have to endure their reactions, but he had other concerns he needed to deal with first.

"I need to try to reach Lucy," Brandon said at last, running his fingers through his hair. "I don't want her blindsided again, especially not if the story's going to run in Barrett papers." He looked at his brother. "Seth— will you write it?"

His older brother nodded.

Brandon cleared his throat. "All right, then. Let's finish this board meeting."

Chapter 15

Angelina called Roberto on his cell. When she handed over the phone, Lucy could almost feel his temper sizzling through the air waves.

"I cannot even begin to tell you how sorry I am, Lucy. I will find out who is responsible. The question now is what you wish to do."

Lucy swallowed several times, glad Roberto couldn't see the tears welling in her eyes. "I can't dance anymore, Roberto," she choked out. "We both know this is where it was headed. I guess I'll just need to take the dive into making pottery fulltime sooner than I thought."

Silence on the other end told her how much Roberto disliked what he was hearing. His next comment caught her off guard and made the tears overflow. "I could help you…with your finances…like a patron." He laughed. "Hey, and how funny is that? The boy from the streets would be a patron of the arts."

She laughed through her tears. "Oh, Roberto, I love you."

"You listen to me, *nina*. I'm serious. I will help however I can to get you past this. You need a place to stay for a while? You let me know."

Angelina handed her the box of tissues. "One of the things I hope you will realize while we work through this is you have friends, Lucy, people who care about you and are willing to step up to the plate to help you."

"I know," she whispered. "This is just additional confirmation. Let me call Mason."

This phone call was more difficult. Lucy felt like she had somehow violated the contract she'd signed with him the previous week. His snotty assistant answered the phone, her tone going frosty the moment Lucy identified herself. Still, a second later, Mason came on the line. The first question out of his mouth made her reconsider her opinion about him being superficial.

"I saw the article, Lucy. Are you all right?"

Why couldn't she feel mushy and tied up about this man? Why did she feel only friendship? "I'm okay, Mason, but there's one problem."

"What's that?"

"My house was a media circus this morning. I'm afraid to go there right now, so it kind of puts a crimp in being able to complete pieces and get them to you."

"I can fix that."

Lucy laughed. "How? Are you a miracle worker with a secret studio hidden somewhere?"

"Close enough. I have a house along the Chesapeake Bay in Maryland. I seldom use it and it's got plenty of room for you to set up a studio for however long you need."

"I won't have a job to pay you rent."

"You do have a job. And believe me, Lucy, once I get your stuff in stock, you'll have income from it."

"I don't know, Mason. How are you going to get my stuff out?"

He laughed. "Trust me, and don't ask questions. I'll have someone pack your clothes too."

It seemed too easy. From the disaster confronting her this morning, her friends were helping her pick up the pieces. She was more than damage that needed to be controlled. She was a person, their friend.

"What about my car?"

"Leave it for now. I'll get you a rental in my name. I have the feeling this will get worse before it gets better. The media have sniffed out a good story here and they're going to come after you. If you're driving your car, they'll find you."

Lucy tugged at her braid. "Mason?"

"What?"

"I'm so sorry. I feel like I've let you down."

"Not at all. This situation is not your fault. You hear me. Not. Your. Fault."

"But will I be able to use my name with my work?"

"Sure. We'll wait till the hoopla dies, and we'll be able to put a spin on it, if we even need to. The press and the public have a short memory. That can be good or bad. We'll make it work for us."

She took a deep breath. "You're a good friend, Mason."

His laugh sounded rueful. "I doubt anyone with the name Barlow-Barrett shares your opinion."

* * * *

Two hours later, Seth was shaking his head at Brandon. "Getting anything out of Roberto at Flamingo Road is like talking to the Sphinx." At Brandon's raised brow, his brother continued, "All he will say is he believes her name was leaked by someone in-house. Once he finds out who…they're history. As for the photos, he's going with the theory they came from someone's cellphone. Up until now, he's avoided asking people to turn phones off because he has such a large business clientele, but now he's going to have to weigh that alongside potential privacy issues."

"And that helps me not one bit as it pertains to Lucy."

"You got that. He's shut tighter than a clam about her. Won't say where she is or how to get in touch with her. Look, I have her address. You want to ride by there?"

Brandon rolled his sleeves and loosened his tie. "Yeah. I would." He pressed his lips together before he blurted, "You know, every once in a while I wish we didn't stand out so much in a crowd."

Seth laughed. "It does make it a little hard to sneak around when you're blond giants who bear more than a passing resemblance to your father. But come on anyway. We'll use my SUV. It's a little less conspicuous than your Porsche."

While they rode down in their father's private elevator, Seth glanced at Brandon. "You didn't say… How did your phone call to Mason Hatch go?"

"He told me I was a fucking asshole. Then he told me hell would freeze over before he breathed a word to me about Lucy."

"Wow. Way to schmooze."

"Stuff it, Seth."

As they set off in Seth's black Escalade with its tinted windows, Brandon scowled at the passing landscape. "How did you find her address?" he asked.

Seth glanced at him. "I did an internet search for L. Cameron within a twenty-five mile radius of the district, then narrowed it based on sex, age and areas I know to be closer to Flamingo Road. I came up with two. I called one. It turned out to be a guy—Larry Cameron. On the other I got an answering machine that was already full."

"How could you tell?"

"It cut me off when I tried to leave a message."

Brandon fumed for a minute. "I feel like such an ass. Why didn't I do that? Why did I go by Flamingo Road?"

"Look, Brandon. When you're in love, you do stupid shit. You just hope and pray the woman loves you enough to forget what a total dumbass you've turned into."

Despite himself, he laughed. "That doesn't sound like my brilliant older brother. It sounds more like something that would come out of Phillip's mouth."

"Phillip doesn't know enough about women yet to have my brilliant insight."

"Yeah, but it sounded like such a guy thing. Not your usual style."

"But see, I've had to learn to relate to a preteen. Zach only understands stuff put in guy speak."

Getting through the midday traffic took them about a half hour. The first things they saw when they turned down Lucy's street were several news vehicles camped out in front of a brick bungalow. The journalists had knotted together in front of the house. When the Escalade cruised past, Brandon watched the way the reporters' eyes focused on them and then dismissed them.

"She would hate this," he murmured. "I know it must seem odd, what with her dancing at Flamingo Road, but she's not someone who seeks attention, Seth. She would really, really hate this."

"Her car's still in the driveway," Seth remarked, "but I doubt she's there. I'd be willing to bet Roberto's not an option either. Let's cruise past Flamingo Road. I'm guessing there'll be a similar media stakeout going on there too, but let's make sure."

"No one knows about her relationship with Mason Hatch…"

"Oh? Is there something more than their business association?"

Brandon's heart flipped. "Business association?"

"Yeah. I did manage to get that out of Roberto. The guy was livid your stupidity might ruin her deal with Mason's gallery to take on her work."

Brandon shut his eyes and leaned against the seat. Could this get worse? Could he have been any more of a fool about Lucy? "God, it didn't look like a business dinner."

"Huh?" Seth's gaze swiveled his way.

"I saw her the other night when I was out with Phillip. She came into the bar with Mason. It sure as hell looked like more than a business dinner, at least on his part."

Seth flipped his turn signal and guided the SUV into the parking lot at Flamingo Road. The only car there was a shiny black Mercedes. "I don't know about that, but I do know Roberto gave her the intro to Mason to help her with her artistic career." Seth looked around. "No media in the area, at least that I can see. You want to try to talk to him?"

Brandon shook his head. "No. Let's cruise past Mason's gallery. No one will suspect why we're there. We could be looking for something for the newest little Barlow-Barrett."

Seth grinned. "Emily Rose. Yeah. You know, she might be tiny, but she roars like a lion. Maybe they'll have some broken glass she can gnaw on to take the edge off her temper."

"Making life tough?"

"Let's just say sleep's in short supply right now."

A slender brunette greeted the two men when they walked through the door. Smooth as she was, she couldn't quite disguise the recognition when she looked at Brandon. "May I help you gentlemen?"

Brandon looked around what he could see of the gallery. Was any of Lucy's work already on display? He wanted to find out, but he'd learned his lesson. "I was hoping to speak with Hatch. Is he available?"

The brunette's expression remained bland. "Oh, I'm afraid you missed him. Mr. Hatch will be out of the office for a couple of days working with one of our artists. I'm his assistant—perhaps I could help you?"

Brandon dug his hands in his pockets. Just because Hatch was out and working with one of their artists didn't mean it was Lucy. "No. Thanks anyway."

They headed toward Barrett's offices, and Seth broke the silence. "You made more than a good faith effort to reach her, Brandon. I'm sorry we didn't. But if we're going to get this in our papers for tomorrow, I need to write. I'm fast, but I'm not careless. I want to make sure this has gone through several sets of eyes before we print."

"Go ahead, Seth. If all it does is get the people away from her house so she can get inside, then it will have served some good purpose."

* * * *

Mason Hatch didn't waste time, Lucy thought after she pulled up in front of a modern home, not far from Annapolis and nestled in a grove of trees with a spectacular view of the bay right behind it. She parked the rental car in the driveway and palmed the house keys Mason had given her. Angelina had sent her off with some loaner clothes and handed her a pay-as-you-go cellphone.

"You call me when you get there," she had ordered.

Lucy had stared at the phone. "You didn't need to do this."

Mason stood nearby, his dark eyes somber. "Yes, we did. There's no phone at this house and I don't want you there by yourself with no communication." His mouth quirked. "How can I ride herd, making sure you get work done, if I can't hound you by phone?"

Lucy rolled her eyes. "No potting wheel, remember?"

Mason had just smiled.

As she stood outside his house, she decided her idea of little and Mason's were definitely not the same. The place looked like it could sleep an army. He had mentioned a sunroom in the rear she could use for a studio if she wanted. Deciding to get a look at it first, Lucy wandered around to the shore side of the house and gasped. Almost the entire wall was glass, but she could see the room he meant. More casual than the rest of the house, it appeared to be set up as a porch right now, kind of like how she had done her studio at her house. Tears stung her eyes for a minute. Damn. She blinked. Angelina was right. She was learning a whole lot about having friends who cared for her.

The shadows were lengthening around the house when she let herself in and toured the interior. Mason had warned her he used it to get away to fish and sail, so it was kind of a man cave, not set up to entertain. Lucy laughed out loud a few minutes later when she walked into a living room dominated by a large screen TV at one end and a pool table at the other. After she walked to the rear of the room where the pool table was, Lucy stopped to enjoy the view again. That was when she noticed the little dinghy bobbing at the end of the dock. Somehow, the boat wasn't quite what she'd envisioned when Mason mentioned sailing, however, she was more than comfortable with the dinghy. Maybe he'd let Lucy take her out. She hadn't sailed in years, but Lucy was sure it would be like riding a bike.

Shaking herself, she fetched her groceries in from her car, stowed everything, then made a salad for dinner. Her appetite wasn't keen, but she forced herself to eat. Because the day had been so hectic, she had managed to keep thoughts of Brandon at bay, but when the night and the quiet settled over her, that was no longer the case.

For a moment, they had connected. His kiss had been gentle, exploring, ardent…like the kisses they'd shared in Colorado. The press of his arousal along her hip had mirrored her response. And when her emotions had overwhelmed her and he'd tasted her tears, his voice had soothed. Then it had all blown up in their faces with the arrival of Seth and Brandon's secretary.

Lucy rolled out of bed and curled in a chair near the window, staring at the smooth, dark water of the bay. She knew from past experience she would get scant sleep, and now she sat with no studio in which to work, nothing, in fact, to help take her mind from her memories.

She knew she looked like hell the next morning. Her reflection in the bathroom mirror had told her in no uncertain terms, and even an early morning run had done little to energize her. She was finishing a morning cup of coffee at the table in the breakfast nook of the kitchen when she heard what sounded like a truck engine rumble up the drive. A knock sounded a moment later, so she set the cup down and stood just in time to hear the door open and Mason's voice.

"Lucy? You awake?"

She walked into the entryway and stuck a hand on her hip. "Awake and already back from a run."

Mason's expression turned concerned, and she was sure he must be seeing the same dark circles beneath her eyes that she'd seen reflected earlier. "You've seen the papers, haven't you?" he growled.

"No. I look like shit because I couldn't sleep last night, but now I guess I'll be able to blame it on something else." She tucked a strand of hair behind her ear. "Why don't you show me these papers." Mason looked so abashed, she squeezed his arm. "It's okay. I would have seen them at some point.

"Pour me some of the coffee I smell while I get them."

When he returned, Lucy was waiting for him at the table, sipping another cup of coffee while his steamed across the table from her. The number of papers he carried made her cringe. This was so much worse than she might have imagined. Mason sat and slid them toward her. She turned the top one over. *National News*, Barrett Newspapers' flagship publication. The story wasn't front page, thank God for that, but it was on the inside cover. *Barrett COO Finds Plane Crash Heroine in Local Club*, the headline read, and beneath it was the byline Seth Barlow-Barrett.

Lucy realized the paper had begun to shake in her grasp when Mason removed it from her hands. "You don't have to read it. The articles are pretty much the same thing. They're in most of Barrett's major dailies around the country. After seeing it in *National News* and the Boston paper, I checked their websites."

Lucy shook her head, her gaze intent on the bay beyond the windows until it began to blur and she realized she was crying. "He told me he didn't do it, that he wasn't the one to release my name," she whispered, "but those papers tell a different story." With a sweep of her hand, she knocked them on the floor and jumped to her feet. "He lied. Jesus, Mason, his own brother wrote these stories!"

Mason pulled her into his arms. Weary beyond measure, Lucy leaned her forehead on his shoulder. While sobs shook her, he stroked her hair. "God knows, Lucy, the last thing I want to do is defend any Barlow-Barrett but this isn't about you. These articles by Seth, they're an attempt to take away the ammunition from all of their competitors and put the whole story to bed. I know you don't want to read them right now, but they put you in a very flattering light."

She snorted and pulled from his arms to wipe her face. "No doubt they put Brandon in a good light too."

"Yes. That's part of the game."

Lucy picked up her coffee mug. "You'd think I would have learned my lesson years ago. I dated a guy, Edward Montgomery, who showed up at the club. He courted me, was a gentleman, but then when push came to shove, I wasn't good enough for his blueblood family. This is the same shit, different day, different year, but I still fell for it just the same. It hurts, Mason."

He eyed her with an understanding she'd never encountered before. "You're not the only one to be looked down on by families like the Barlow-Barretts. But I want you to do me a favor. Save these papers. When you're calmer, I want you to read them, particularly the commentary Seth wrote on the editorial page of *National News*. It might give you some insight into what's going on."

She gave him a wry grin. "What are you, their champion now?"

"Not at all." Mason's glance was cold and sending off definite no-trespassing signals. He picked the papers up and set them on the counter near the door. "Come on. I got a couple of guys coming over after they get their catch sold to help unload the goodies I brought you. Want to see what I've got on the truck?"

"Definitely."

When Mason opened the box truck he'd driven, Lucy laughed. "Good heavens, Mason. It looks like you cleaned out my studio. You even have the kiln in here!"

"Don't worry," he assured her. "I'll move everything again when you decide you want to go home."

She touched his cheek. "You are amazing. Why hasn't some smart female snapped you up?"

"Maybe you and I are more alike than you think, in that respect," he muttered. "Come on, we can get the lighter stuff until the strong backs show up."

"I love you, Mason," Lucy told him.

He arched a brow at her. "If that were the truth, both of us would have a lot fewer problems."

* * * *

"Your mother is on line one, Mr. Barrett," his secretary told him via the intercom.

"Great."

"Excuse me, sir?"

"I said I can't wait…to speak to her." Brandon made a face, feeling a little like he had as a boy when he'd been called to her sitting room. His mother wasn't the spanker. That had been his father. No, Patricia Barlow-Barrett dressed him down without ever raising her voice, but making it crystal clear how very disappointed she was in him. In some ways, that had always been much worse than a smack on the ass.

"Good morning, Mother."

"Good morning, Brandon. Your father and I would like you to join us for dinner this evening."

Yup. He was in for the adult version of being called to her sitting room. This was no invitation, it was a command performance. "Of course, Mother. What time shall I be there?"

"Six will be fine. That will give us time for a before-dinner drink and some catching up."

More like time for either interrogation or remonstration, or a combination of both. "I look forward to it." Like he would look forward to a root canal or a visit to a proctologist.

He pulled the stack of papers in front of him, beginning with *National News*. He couldn't fault Seth on the article he'd written. It was fair and factual, but as he read it, he knew Lucy would have a tough time seeing it that way. Damn. He wished he'd had a chance to talk to her beforehand. He'd gone by her house again this morning. There were fewer news vehicles there, but still one or two unmarked ones he'd spotted. The house appeared deserted other than her car, which still sat in the same location. Where was she?

He turned to Seth's commentary: *Heroes Come From All Walks of Life*. The gist of his message was judging a person by their character, not their occupation. He used Lucy for one example, but brought up others too. Brandon could have added commentary about crossing the line between good journalism and simply being intrusive. The profession had lost something vital—its humanity. He recalled the framed plaque on Seth's wall. *The Journalists' Creed*, written by Walter Williams, the first dean of the University of Missouri School of Journalism. One line had always stood out for him: "*I believe that no one should write as a journalist what he would not say as a gentleman...*"

Lucy had become the victim of a reporter who didn't follow Williams's creed. Brandon looked out over the city around him, wondering if she was out there somewhere hating him for what had happened. He had been angry and hurt, but he'd never intended to throw her life into such complete chaos. He tried calling Mason Hatch again later in the day, but was told the man was out of town.

The havoc he'd wreaked on Lucy's life preyed on him that evening when he drove down the long, manicured drive to his parents' estate. There was no other way to describe the massive Barlow-Barrett home. Sure, it had needed to be large enough to contain six active children, but this went way beyond, complete with a very stiff-upper-lip English butler. That gentleman greeted Brandon at the door with an impassive smile.

"Mr. and Mrs. Barlow-Barrett are in the living room, Mr. Brandon."

"Thanks, Forbes. I can find my own way."

"Of course, sir."

Brandon stopped outside the doorway, took a deep breath and checked to be sure his tie was straight. After smoothing a hand over his hair, he pasted a smile on his lips and stepped through. His mother was seated in a chair near the window, so he knew she must have observed his arrival. His father stood nearby, his hands behind his back.

He crossed the room, leaned down and kissed his mother's proffered cheek. "Good evening, Mother."

"Brandon." Not a good sign.

He turned to his father and stuck out his hand. Alexander squeezed his hand a bit when he shook it. "Son." Brandon met his father's steady regard. Was it his imagination, or was there a glimmer of feeling there?

"Dad." He was the only one of his brothers who addressed their father as anything other than *Father*. "You're looking much better."

"Feeling that way too. I understand you've gone ahead with your proposal to head into e-publications."

Brandon smiled. He'd swear he saw a twinkle in the old man's eye. "We are pursuing the research, but I'm waiting for your return to implement." There was no mistaking it. Somewhere deep inside the old curmudgeon, something had changed.

His mother cleared her throat. All it took was a raised brow, and his father shifted. "Your mother and I wished to discuss this unfortunate incident with the stripper."

Brandon's mother made a pained sound. Apparently, the word was enough to overwhelm her sense of propriety.

Through stiff lips he muttered, "Her name is Lucy. While it might be true she danced at a strip club, she is also the woman who saved me after the crash in Colorado." He turned to stare at his parents with narrowed eyes. "I realize the purpose in calling me here is to rake me over the coals, but I would like to know one thing."

"What is that, Brandon?" His mother's voice was cool.

"Did either one of you make any attempt to find out about Lucy following the plane crash, to find out if she was even hurt?"

Silence greeted his question.

"You were so injured, Brandon," his mother responded. "We needed to get you to a competent surgeon without any undue delay."

He glared at her. "I'll take that as a no." His stomach hurt like hell.

His father cleared his throat. "When I learned her name, I did try to contact her, but she had already left the resort. I didn't pursue it."

Brandon nodded. "Well, that's honest at least."

"Brandon, we must be concerned about how all of this reflects on our family…"

"Spin it any way you like, Mother, but any reflection on our family is your concern. Not mine. Because I was angry, I did something stupid, and in the process I may well have destroyed Lucy's life."

"Don't be melodramatic," his mother snapped. "The woman is a stripper."

"The woman is a potter with a master's degree in fine arts…from Georgetown. She danced to pay for her education and to support herself while she pursued her art. She had just gotten her break…and my actions may have screwed that up."

"She will survive," his mother commented. "Her kind always do."

Brandon's eyes narrowed. "Like Tessa?"

Her chin lifted a notch and he knew he'd scored a hit. His mother had taken to Tessa the moment Seth showed up with her because Tessa had possessed the requisite family background. Although she had cooled after the trouble between Seth and Tessa, they were still cordial, which said a lot about how his mother regarded Seth's wife.

"Tessa has nothing in common with your stripper."

"Really? Perhaps you don't know your family quite like you think you do, Mother."

"That will be enough, son," his father cut in. "I think we can agree we owe Lucy. Can we help her find employment? Write her a check?"

Brandon almost choked on the bourbon he'd poured. "You have no idea how ludicrous that is. If you knew her—no, you can't find her a job or write her a check. She'd be as apt to take your head off if you tried."

"Then what can we do?" his dad asked.

Brandon rubbed his forehead. "Something that will be infinitely harder, I'm afraid. You can accept her."

"What do you mean, Brandon?" Now his mother sounded appalled.

"She was much more than a passenger in the plane," Brandon admitted. "We fell in love. I'm not sure I can ever get that back, but I'm damn well going to try, if I can find her."

"You cannot be serious!" his mother snapped.

Jamming his hands in his pockets and looking more than a little uncomfortable, his father said, "Tricia, leave it."

Brandon didn't know for a moment who was more shocked—him or his mother. Alexander might have ruled the board room, but Patricia was the one in control at home.

Before she could respond, Forbes stepped into the room. "Dinner is served, madam."

His father took his mother's arm and preceded Brandon into the dining room. After seating her to his left, he waved Brandon to the chair on his right. Just an intimate little family gathering.

Once the first course was served, his father looked over at him. "Does Miss Cameron have any family around the area?"

Brandon shook his head. "Her parents died when she was young. She was raised by a grandmother, also a potter, somewhere along the bay I believe. Lucy mentioned sailing when she was a child." As he anticipated, both his parents' interest picked up. Sailing was a Barlow-Barrett tradition.

"That must have been pleasant, being so close to the water." Brandon had to give his mother credit, she was making an effort.

"I believe she has fond memories of those days. Unfortunately, her grandmother suffered a stroke when Lucy was twelve. She was shuttled around to various foster homes and schools."

"Well, some of them must have been okay," her mother remarked, "if she had good enough grades to get into Georgetown."

"I think her success was a function of Lucy, not her foster placements. She told me she realized if she was ever going to have a decent life, she had to be an excellent student." Brandon pushed his plate away. "Look, I'm not trying to get your sympathy, but you need to understand where she came from. She had to switch homes so often because she was a very pretty teenager. There were problems not only with foster brothers, but also with foster fathers. I think there's more she didn't tell me. We didn't have a lot of time together when it comes right down to it."

"I was told she was treated and released after the plane crash," his father said, "but no one would explain what had happened to her."

"Bruises. Physically that was the extent of it."

"Physically?"

"I think she's seeing a psychologist…something that's started just since the crash."

Forbes cleared their salads and a maid delivered their main course. Once the door had closed again, his father inquired, "So are you saying she's having some sort of stress reaction?"

Brandon nodded. "She's thinner than she was in Colorado. Look, I don't know if you read the crash report or not but, Dad, she went through the aftermath all alone. I might have been alive, but I wasn't functioning… and Tom didn't make it. She had to see that, had to deal with it, and then had no one to talk to about it. I didn't even remember her."

He set his knife and fork on his plate and stared at his food for a minute while he tried to control the sudden rush of emotion that threatened to choke him. When his father reached over and squeezed his forearm, Brandon put his hand over his eyes.

"I keep thinking how she must have felt, what she'd been through." His voice was tight. "And all I've done since then is make it worse for her. Look, give me a minute. I'll be right back."

He stood and left the table. He needed to pull himself together. He'd been straddling a fine edge ever since the crash, and remembering everything had made it more difficult.

"Son?" Brandon turned away from the window in his father's study to see Alexander standing a few feet away. "I haven't told you how proud I am of the job you've done since Seth left, how proud I am of the way you've stepped up to the plate during my illness."

Brandon's mouth twisted. "Yeah. I'm not seeing that right now, Dad."

"I know you aren't. You and Seth have both done a great job handling the story with Lucy. I read the papers and I think the company will come through this just fine. As far as the family is concerned." Alexander paused. "Well, I'm discovering I can't orchestrate my children's lives. I nearly lost Anna because of that. I'm still on shaky ground with Seth. I don't want to be in the same spot with you."

Brandon nodded, his lips tight.

"If Lucy is who you want, then you need to go get her."

"I don't know where to find her."

His father raised his brows. "Really. You're smart enough to run a multi-billion dollar corporation, I think you can figure out how to find one woman. I want you to take the time to do what you must. Seth and I can hold the fort for a while, and maybe I can even convince him to come into the fold while we do."

"Are you serious?"

"As a heart attack, pun intended. I'd like to live long enough to enjoy my grandchildren. I'd also like to learn how to quit alienating my children so they'll give me access to the next generation."

"Thanks, Dad."

Alexander smiled. "Let's finish dinner before your mother quits speaking to me."

Chapter 16

The dreams were back. Lucy wasn't sure what had triggered them, but every night she relived the crash, only Brandon was the fatality. She would wake up gasping for breath, still seeing his gorgeous eyes possessed of a vacant, dull stare. She knew she should call Angelina, but wasn't that wimping out? She should have been past this. Brandon was past the crash and her, so she would push her way through too.

She drove herself hard during the day, hoping to exhaust herself to the point where she either wouldn't dream or wouldn't be able to remember. So now as the weekend approached, she was returning from an early morning run. Leaning on the porch railing, Lucy sucked in air, staggering a bit when a wave of dizziness washed through her. She wondered if part of her problem was no longer having the release of her dancing. Sure, she was working out, but she hadn't danced. After all, it wasn't like Mason had a pole set up in his basement. She smiled at the thought and trudged up the steps. The smell of coffee greeted her, followed by the sound of her cellphone ringing. While she poured a mug with one hand, she flipped open the phone with the other.

"Hello."

"Good morning. You up for a visitor?"

"Hi, Mason. I guess. Company would be nice."

"Sound a little less enthusiastic, I might get a big head."

"Sorry. I just came in from a run. It's your house and God knows there's plenty of room. However, I'm guessing you have an ulterior motive."

"I want to see how you're getting along, and if you have anything for me to bring to the gallery, I can take it with me and save you the trip."

She laughed. "That's so thoughtful of you."

"More than you know," he muttered.

"What's that mean?" Lucy pounced.

"Brandon has been by here every day."

"You haven't told him where I am, have you?"

"No, but honestly, the guy looks desperate. I think you should take pity on him."

"Don't go to the dark side, Mason. You're supposed to be my friend."

"Yeah. I'll be down this evening in time for dinner. You like oysters?"

"Love 'em."

"Great. We'll grab some, maybe some crab cakes too."

After hanging up, Lucy forced herself to eat a couple slices of toast and finish her coffee. She would work until lunchtime, then pack a sandwich and take the dinghy out. She'd already inspected it and had even taken it for a short sail to get her sea legs under her. Sailing was something she had missed since she'd left the coast.

With something to look forward to, the work flowed. She removed a load of dishes from the kiln and began setting it up for another batch of cups and bowls she had finished glazing. There wouldn't be enough to fire until tomorrow. Once she finished glazing what was ready, she turned her attention to the wheel for a while. For now at least, the fine art projects were on hold because she needed the rhythm and the routine of working with the wheel. There was no thinking, simply the memories of tasks she'd learned at her grandmother's side.

She would be able to send plenty with Mason, even a couple pots he would be able to put into his fine art section. Those were pieces all she'd needed to do was glaze and fire. When the clock showed noon, Lucy removed the bat with a finished bowl on it and set it on the drying rack before cleaning the wheel and her other materials. Only after everything was spic and span did she shower and change clothes.

Although the weather on shore was warm enough for shorts, once she got out into the wind on the bay, it would be cooler. Wearing jeans and a lightweight windbreaker, her long braid pulled through a Nationals cap, she grabbed her sandwich and a bottle of water and all but jogged the length of the deck. She was looking forward to this. Maybe she'd hit on the thing that would keep her mind off Brandon and the crash.

Mason's dinghy was a newer, shallower-hulled style than what she'd sailed as a kid. She'd always joked with her grandmother that the little boat was like the wooden shoe in the nursery rhyme and they would both laugh.

"*She's an oldie, but she's a goody*," her grandmother would tell her. "*I don't worry when you're out in her that you'll tip over.*"

Well, that had been a fact. The little boat had barely tilted in even the stiffest wind. She hadn't been fast, but she'd done everything Lucy wanted. Mason's boat would be a bit more of a challenge in the brisk wind out on the bay today. But it would be fun, and maybe getting her adrenaline going was what she needed.

* * * *

Brandon wasn't keen on Stacey's boat, but she seemed happy with her. The sailboat had been a gift from her husband of six months. Being the annoying brother he was, he started to ask her why her husband wasn't the one out sailing with her, but decided against it. Something in his sister's expression had made him slam his mouth shut before the question popped out.

Stacey had known her husband for most of her life. They'd run together in the same circles through high school and college. He could remember them hanging out together around the pool at the country club and then at the yacht club once they got a little older. It seemed to him, though, ever since their marriage last fall, Jason Winchester had all but disappeared except when it came to any functions involving their parents.

Now, here it was a beautiful weekend for sailing and he was crewing for his sister while her husband was God knew where. Sticking his cap on backward, Brandon slapped on his reflective wraparound sunglasses and zipped his lifejacket.

"Ready when you are, sis," he called. "Where are we going, Captain?"

"South."

In truth, there wasn't much to be done on the boat and Stacey could've sailed her by herself, but she wanted company, that was obvious. Plus, she wasn't as confident as he and his brothers, so he knew she did like to have someone else aboard with her. Since he was making no inroads wearing down Mason Hatch into telling him where he could find Lucy, Brandon had decided he might as well go with her.

"Take the helm, Brandon," Stacey told him once they were out on the bay and the wind was pushing them along. "You play captain, and I'll sit here with a beer. You've always been a better sailor than me anyway."

"Don't underestimate yourself. You used to do pretty well with those racing dinghies."

"Whatever." She disappeared into the cabin and returned with two beers. "You want one?"

"One. With it being the weekend, I'm not about to get boarded and given a ticket. In case it's escaped your notice, I don't have a track record for making great decisions in recent months."

Stacey pushed her sunglasses on top of her head. "I don't know, looks to me like you made the decision to go after what you want. That takes some guts."

Brandon smirked. "Dad suggested it."

Stacey's eyes widened. "Father suggested you take time away from work to find Lucy? Yeah. Right. We are talking about Alexander Barlow-Barrett, aren't we?"

"I know, I know, but it's true. Swear." He took one hand off the wheel and crossed his chest. "Mother wasn't thrilled, but I guess she'll figure out how to deal with it. Dad actually told her to back off when I got called over to their house for the big lecture dinner."

Stacey took a long pull on her beer. "Can I touch you? Maybe some of your current favorite son status will rub off."

Brandon angled them along the shoreline, his gaze focused on the sails. "Don't think you'll need it. I think this heart thing's shaken Dad. He even said so." He narrowed his gaze on his sister. "So why would you need any luck? Anything you want to talk to your older brother about?"

Stacey opened her mouth, then clamped it shut and shook her head. She took another swig of beer and gave him the fake little society smile he'd always hated. "Everything's great, silly. What could be wrong? I've married my lifelong sweetheart. He's given me a beautiful sailboat. I have a great house and enough decorating clients to keep me busy. Life's good."

"Right." He handed her the beer. "Here, take this. I want to see what kind of speed I can get out of your little boat since we have such a great wind going today."

"Not a racing yacht, bro," Stacey reminded him. "She's a weekender, designed more for comfort than speed."

Brandon just grinned.

* * * *

It had taken Lucy a little while to get comfortable with the differences in Mason's dinghy. Its sleeker hull made it much easier to pick up speed. It had more of a tendency to heel, so she'd adjusted her position in the boat to help balance it. After finding a quiet cove, she'd lowered her sail and bobbed along while she ate her sandwich and drank about half of her water. Lucy rested against the stern and propped her feet up on the gunwale, letting the sun warm her face behind her sunglasses.

She remembered Brandon mentioning his family sailed, but she doubted any of them would be caught dead in a dinghy. No, she could envision him captaining a sleek racing yacht. God knew he was fit enough, but racing could be time consuming if someone was serious about it. Somehow she couldn't picture the head of Barrett Newspapers getting enough free time to be that devoted to a sport. Kind of the way he'd been about skiing, she supposed. Maybe there was some security in always knowing what he would be doing with his life, but it must have been confining too.

As hard as growing up had been for her at times, she at least had never had anyone breathing down her neck expecting her to follow in their footsteps. She glanced at her watch. Three o'clock. She should head back so she'd have plenty of time to clean before Mason arrived. When she pulled out of her quiet cove, the first thing that struck her was how much busier it was. Well, it was the weekend. Lucy kept a careful eye out because it wasn't just sailboats out on the water. Plenty of motorized boats raced along the waves this close to Annapolis. They were supposed to yield the right of way to a sailing vessel, but it was foolish to press her rights when she was sailing a dinghy with a motorized cabin cruiser bearing down on her, like now.

Lucy reduced sail, struggling for balance after the other boat failed to slow and she caught its wake. "Damn it. Stupid weekend boaters."

The dinghy bobbled a bit, but she got it balanced and began working again to set the right trim.

* * * *

"Jesus!" Brandon swore, watching the water ahead of him. "That cabin cruiser almost capsized the dinghy off our port bow."

Stacey stepped to his side and shaded her eyes. "Brandon! There's another guy coming up on her starboard side and I don't think he even sees her." Stacey's comment ended with a gasp as the speeding boat veered off to the right at the last moment, narrowly missing the small boat, but disaster was already in the works. The sharp turn sent up a wake the sailboat couldn't withstand. They watched while the steep wave sent the boat onto its side and the unfortunate sailor flying into the air in a tangle of rigging.

"Here!" Brandon slapped her hands onto the wheel. "Take over and bring us alongside while I start reducing sail. Turn on the motor. Jesus, whoever it is doesn't seem to be moving." His temper simmered while his sister maneuvered them near the capsized dinghy. The guilty boater had taken off. "I'm going in. Looks like our sailor's tangled."

Brandon pulled his knife from his pocket, opened the blade and jumped overboard when they drew alongside. In the water nearby, he saw a Nationals cap floating amid the debris.

"Hey! Are you okay?"

All he got in response was a moan. Sticking the knife between his teeth, he stroked closer, his heart beating faster when he saw a long blond braid floating out from the lifejacket, which had puffed up enough in the water to obscure the face of the injured sailor. As he closed the distance, he reached feet tangled in rigging first. Grasping the knife in his hand, he sliced through the rope and tugged.

"Jesus, Mary and Joseph! *Lucy?* Lucy!" Frantic now from her lack of response and not even questioning yet how she'd come to be sailing a dinghy in the bay, he pulled, but her wrist was caught. Rope burns marred her skin and the angle of her arm looked odd. "Lucy? Oh, baby. Come on, let me get you out of here."

He turned his head over his shoulder, his gaze meeting his sister's. "Throw me a line, Stacey. It's Lucy. She's hurt. Help me get her on board. I'll secure the dinghy to the rear of your boat." Between the two of them, they boosted Lucy's deadweight over the gunwale. Brandon didn't want to leave her, but he needed to secure the damaged craft. They should file a report with the Coast Guard, but it could be like finding a needle in a haystack unless Lucy had gotten a registration number from the cruiser that nearly ran her over.

Working as fast as he could, it was still several minutes before he pulled himself up the ladder on the stern. Stacey dried Lucy's ashen face. When he approached, he breathed a small sigh of relief to see her eyes were open. Her gaze darted from Stacey to him and her eyes widened.

"Brandon?" She coughed. "Oh God, I'm going to be sick."

Not the words he'd hoped to hear.

Stacey turned Lucy's head sideways. "It's okay," she murmured. "You swallowed water." She turned to Brandon, who was still rooted to the spot he'd been in. "Bran! She's hurt. I think her arm or her wrist or something is broken."

"Let me see." He squatted at her side, taking the raw skin of her wrist in his hand. Being as gentle as he could, he turned it, noting the swelling and bruising in addition to the rope burns. Lucy had turned to watch him with such a wary expression it made his throat ache. "We need to get you to a hospital, baby."

"I'm fine," she muttered. When she struggled to sit, Brandon reached out to help her, not surprised that she tried to avoid his touch. Cradling her wrist to her stomach, she brushed her soggy hair off her face. "What about Mason's boat?"

Brandon stiffened. He couldn't help it. *Mason's* boat? "It's got a broken mast and the daggerboard is missing, but it looks like the dinghy itself is okay." Everything he was saying came through stiff lips. "Lucy, you need to go to a hospital. I'm concerned you've got a fracture."

She was huddled on the deck, shivering from cold or shock, he wasn't sure which. "Okay."

That one word told him more than anything she was hurt and in pain. The Lucy he knew would never give in if she felt all right. He looked at his sister. "Stacey, you have extra clothes?"

"Yeah."

Though he didn't want to let Lucy out of his sight, he suggested, "Why don't you let me take the helm while you take Lucy below deck to help her into dry clothes."

"What about you?" Stacey asked. "You're shivering."

"I'll be okay. Take care of her first, okay?"

He might piss Lucy off, but he was taking her to the marina where Stacey kept her boat moored. After ensuring the dinghy would tow behind them okay, Brandon set their course and trimmed sail. He was freezing but kept his jaw clenched so his teeth wouldn't chatter. Amid his worry over how hurt Lucy might be was complete and utter amazement. He had spent the week cruising past her house, haunting Mason's gallery and lurking around Flamingo Road at night but had never caught a glimpse of her. Had she been here all week? And where was she staying that she'd been out in Mason's dinghy? Most people kept a dinghy right at their houses. Was she staying with *him*?

He blinked away the moisture in his eyes that he tried to tell himself was from the wind. Grabbing his wraparounds off the shelf near the wheel, he stuck them back on. No sense for his sister or Lucy to see how unmanned he was at the moment.

"She's in the main cabin, lying down. I've given her ice for the wrist and wrapped it the best I could." Stacey put her hand on his arm. "Why don't you change?"

"I don't have…"

"Use Jason's clothes. He's not as tall as you, but I found a pair of shorts that should work. There's a polo shirt and a jacket too. Can't help you with shoes. Your feet are too big."

Brandon glanced at his canvas deck shoes. "They'll dry soon enough. Do you… You think I should check on her?"

Stacey arched a brow. "I think you'd be a fool not to. She's a captive audience until we make it to the marina, although she did ask about a cellphone." Stacey paused and her expression tightened. "She wants to call Mason Hatch."

He reached inside his jacket and pulled out his Droid. Having learned from experience, the phone was in a waterproof case on a lanyard around his neck. Stacey shook her head. "You know I can't be without my phone, Stacey, come on."

"Well, I guess that's a good thing because I left mine in my car. Why don't you get changed and then help our guest make her phone call."

Brandon nodded. After stripping in the guest cabin where Stacey had set out clothes for him, he realized he would either have to leave on soaked boxers or go commando. Not much of a choice. He put his bare ass in the shorts that were a bit large. They hung on his hips, but the polo shirt was long enough to cover the sag. Leaving his deck shoes to dry, he knocked on Lucy's cabin door. Upon hearing her muffled *come in*, he opened the door, his throat tight with anxiety. Lucy turned her face toward him. For a moment, her expression was unguarded.

"Lucy…" he whispered.

Her jaw tightened and the fleeting glimpse of vulnerability disappeared. "I need to call Mason." She stared at him with an expression that revealed nothing.

"Give me his number. I'll enter it since you're one-handed at the moment."

She recited the number. From memory. Fuck. He handed her the phone, then moved to the door. "I'll give you some privacy."

"Don't go," she said. "I don't know where we're headed."

"Right." Idiot. Of course she needed to know where to tell Mason to find them. Jealousy surged so he wanted to refuse to tell her, refuse any information that would allow Hatch to get anywhere near her.

"Mason?" she murmured. "I took your dinghy out. A cabin cruiser nearly mowed me down."

Pause.

"I'm okay, I guess. Your…your boat's not. I'm sorry."

Pause.

"I'm on a boat. Brandon…" Pause. "Yes, him."

Another pause. Brandon saw her try to lift her injured hand. She was going to tuck hair behind her ear. She did it whenever she was nervous or upset. He looked away, staring out the small porthole.

"I don't know." She sighed. "Where are we going, Brandon?"

"We're headed to Mac's Marina outside Annapolis. ETA's about twenty minutes."

She relayed the information and listened for a minute. Was that disappointment on her face? "No, I don't mind. I'll see you a little later then." She handed the phone to Brandon. "Thanks."

He slipped it in his pocket. Spurred by the jealousy eating at him, he asked. "So, is Mason going to meet you at the marina?"

"No. He's running late."

Brandon's hands fisted in his pockets. "I want to take you to the hospital, Lucy. Your arm is injured."

"It'll be okay."

He frowned. "You should have it checked. It's your livelihood."

"Like you give—"

"Don't," he interrupted, his tone hot. "Don't even finish that!" He sat on the edge of the bed. "Lucy, I've spent this past week trying to find you. I've driven past your house, past Flamingo Road and I've haunted Mason Hatch's gallery so often I thought the guy was going to call the cops and have me arrested as a stalker. So don't even hint I don't care."

"Why?" she whispered.

He swallowed. "Why what?"

"Why were you trying to find me?"

"Because..." He couldn't tell her he loved her, couldn't lay himself out there like that. "I was worried. When you left Monday..." He stopped, took a deep breath. "Look, there's a lot we need to discuss, but now is maybe not the best time to do it. Please let me take you to the hospital, baby. I know you're hurting."

"Okay."

She looked tired and miserable. He wanted to hold her, tell her everything would be all right, but there was still too much distance between them, too many things needing to be talked out before they could move forward. But he needed to touch her. Reaching out, he took her uninjured hand in his and stroked the back of it. He couldn't look at her, was afraid he would see rejection there.

"Can I get you anything?" he asked after a few seconds. "Something to drink or eat?"

"No," she whispered. Now the silence stretched a couple of minutes. "Brandon, could you just sit with me?"

"For a few minutes. I'll need to help Stacey once we get to the marina." Taking a chance, he moved next to her, stretching his arm along the shelf behind the head of the bed. "I've missed you, Lucy," he said at last.

"Me too."

He took her hand again, clasping it where it rested on the firm muscles of his thigh.

* * * *

Lucy stared at his profile, etching his sharp features into her brain so she wouldn't forget him. He looked tired and thinner, something she could relate to. Her glance dropped to where he held her hand against his thigh and she swallowed at the surge of emotion threatening to choke her. Biting down on her lower lip, she shifted her face to the porthole.

Her arm ached, and she feared Brandon might be right. She might have broken it. God in heaven, what was the saying she used to hear? *If I didn't have bad luck, I'd have no luck at all.* That was it, and exactly how she felt of late. Since meeting Brandon her life had become a series of peaks and valleys, not the placid plain on which she had existed until a few months ago.

She wanted to cry, between the pain and the embarrassment, but damn it, she couldn't do it. Not in front of Brandon.

"Thank you," she whispered.

The stroking of his thumb paused before continuing once again to soothe and relax her. "No thanks necessary, Lucy."

She swallowed. "Are you okay?"

"Me?"

"You were shivering…on deck. And I know your leg… Well, it's not quite where it should be, is it?"

He tugged at her damp braid. "You don't worry about me. I'm good. It's you we need to get checked out."

"I don't have any of my ID or anything with me." Lucy knew how sticky hospitals could be. Would they even treat her?

"I'll take care of it," he assured her.

She wanted him to hold her. She wanted to be able to lean on him and know everything would be all right. The minute the thought occurred to her, she closed her eyes. They were as awkward as near strangers.

"What is it? What's wrong?" At Brandon's urgent questions, she realized she must have made some sort of noise.

"I…" Oh hell, she would go for it. What was one more slapdown in the grander scheme of things? "Could you hold me for a minute?"

He groaned. "Oh God, Lucy. That you would even have to ask…" He pulled her to him, careful to avoid jostling her injured arm, and nestled her head against his shoulder. She leaned her cheek on the solid, reassuring warmth of him. When his hand stroked her hair, she sucked in a shaky breath. "Don't cry, baby," he whispered. "We'll get you to the hospital. Everything will be okay."

Yeah. They could heal her arm, bandage her cuts and bruises, but who would stitch up the heart he'd broken?

Chapter 17

Brandon hated leaving Lucy to help Stacey bring her boat in and tie up, but he'd return in a few minutes. "I have to go," he whispered, "just for a bit. Stacey needs help. Then I'll get you taken care of."

When he came on deck, Stacey looked at him. "How's she doing?" His sister was already lowering sail and switching over to the boat's motor so she could maneuver into the slip.

"She's tired. Worried."

"Did you talk?" Stacey asked in a casual tone, but he noted the guarded look on her face.

"Not really. There's too much to discuss for the few minutes we had."

"Hmm. So is she staying at Mason's place?"

Brandon's gaze narrowed. "Curious, aren't you?"

Stacey shrugged. "He has a reputation."

"To answer your question…I don't know. I'll get to that once I've gotten her arm tended." His phone rang. Brandon pulled it out, saw it was Mason calling.

"Yeah?" He couldn't help the *fuck you* that came through in the one word, but that's what he was feeling.

"You'd better treat her right, asshole," Mason barked.

Brandon turned away from Stacey. "You know, you don't need to worry about that. I think I can handle it. After all, I'm here. Where are you?"

There was silence on the other end. "I'm about to make your day, although God knows I should have my fucking head examined because I have no idea why."

"What's that supposed to mean?"

"Give the phone to Lucy, 'cause I sure as shit ain't talking to you about this."

Brandon started to hit the End button, but he couldn't do that to her. No matter how much he might want to cram his fist down Mason Hatch's throat—and that was the understated response—the guy meant something to Lucy. "Call back in five. I'm helping Stacey bring her boat in to dock."

More silence. "Your sister?" There was something in Mason's tone Brandon didn't even want to go into.

"Yeah, dude. My *married* sister."

"Whatever. I'll call."

In a few minutes, Brandon was leaping off the boat onto the dock, then tying up. Once he was satisfied Stacey's boat was secure, he untied the dinghy and towed it around to the empty slip next door, hauling it out of the water with Stacey's help.

"Find Mac," he told his sister. "He can find a spot for it until Mason decides what to do with it." His phone buzzed. "This will be Mason again. Let me return and give it to Lucy."

Back on board, he handed her the phone before going to stand near the porthole while he watched Mac and Stacey discuss the dinghy. He didn't want to see Lucy's face while she talked to Mason, but he couldn't help but hear her end of the conversation. There was a stretch of silence, so Mason must have been telling her something.

"You can't? Mason, I..." Pause. "He said he'd take me to the hospital." She lowered her voice, making it harder for him to hear.

Another pause. Brandon snuck a glance at her and saw her cradling the phone between her head and her shoulder while she tucked a strand of hair behind her ear.

"I don't know... I'm not sure I can..." Pause. She sighed. "That hasn't worked well for me." This time when he glanced at her, she was biting her lower lip while she listened. "I guess it will have to be. I'll see you then, Mason."

She held the phone out to him. "Everything okay?" Brandon asked.

She shook her head. "Mason can't make it here tonight. Do you think you could wait for me at the hospital, then take me to his house?"

Anger flared. She thought he would drop her and leave her? Swallowing the sharp retort that threatened, he sucked in a deep breath. "I'm not going to desert you, Lucy. I'll be happy to take you."

She glanced out the window. "What about your sister?"

"She came in her own car. I was staying the weekend at the family's house, but Stacey planned to go to the city. So no worries there."

"Oh."

"We should go," Brandon murmured. "The sooner we get someone to look at your arm, the better."

* * * *

She hated hospitals. Nothing had changed about that. Brandon didn't look much happier. Although he'd gotten everything arranged so the bills would come to him, they were standing their ground when it came to allowing him into the treatment area with her. Lucy looked at the doctor while she clutched Brandon's hand.

"Please. He's my fiance." She didn't dare look at Brandon and just hoped he kept a poker face, but she did not want to be on her own while they examined her arm or did anything else. When the doctor started to waffle, Lucy added, "I get panic attacks." She breathed a little heavier.

Now the young doctor looked nervous. "All right."

Once they were in the glassed in cubicle and the curtains were drawn, she dared a glance at Brandon.

He had one brow arched. "Panic attacks?"

She stuck her chin up. "I don't like hospitals. It was either that or I was walking."

"Oh no, Lucy. Not happening."

"See. That's why you should be here, to make sure I don't."

She lay on the bed and closed her eyes. From across the room, the scrape of the chair moved closer to the bed, then stopped. After a faint rustling, the upholstery creaked as Brandon settled his big frame in the seat. The silence stretched for a minute, so she opened her eyes and found him staring at her with a thoughtful expression.

"What did you do at the hospital in Colorado?"

She closed her eyes again. "They didn't need to do much. I was out of there pretty fast. Matt gave me a ride."

Brandon took her hand. She felt calluses on his fingers. Must have been from sailing because being a hotshot executive didn't give anyone calluses. "Lucy, I'm sorry I couldn't be there for you."

She swallowed. "Don't! I can't do this right now. I wasn't telling a total lie about how I feel about hospitals. I just…need…"

He squeezed her hand. "It's all right. You want me to see if I can light a fire under them?"

She nodded. "I don't like it here. It's where my grandmother…"

"Oh shit! God, baby, I'm so sorry."

She forced herself to look at him. "You couldn't know. But if you can influence them, I would appreciate it."

He touched her cheek. Instant warmth where his fingers made contact with her skin eased her.

She caught his hand and pressed it close to her for a moment. "Thanks, Brandon."

It seemed to her he was gone for only a minute, but when he returned, the head of the ER department was with him. A tall, older woman, she got down to business without delay, unwrapping Lucy's arm and examining not only the bruising and burns but also the swelling. After pursing her lips, she said, "I'll need an x-ray, but I'm inclined to agree with your assessment, Mr. Barrett."

"You think it's *broken*?" Lucy was horrified. How the hell could she work with one arm incapacitated?

"A fracture. It is probably pretty small, but we'll get some pictures so we can be sure. The tech will be here in a minute to take you to radiology." She patted Lucy's good hand and departed.

"I didn't want to believe you," she whispered, glancing at Brandon and then looking away. Her stomach knotted and her throat tightened. The panic attack she'd fibbed about earlier to get Brandon permission to stay with her was more of a reality now. "I won't be able to work."

He took her hand and squeezed. "Don't borrow trouble. Wait until you know for sure, baby. Once you do, then we'll figure it out."

We. The two of them would figure it out. It seemed he meant it. He stayed with her while they went to radiology. Once the ER doc looked at the pictures and discovered what Lucy did for a living, she called in an orthopedist. It was a small fracture, but they wanted to make sure it wouldn't require surgery since she would need full use of the wrist.

After looking at the x-rays, the arm and wrist and Lucy's general physical condition, he said, "This is your left wrist. Tell me what you do with your left hand?"

She explained both the process of working on the wheel and also what she did with coils and slabs. He listened, nodding every now and then.

"The fracture is very small, and the bone is still in position, so we won't need to do any reduction. However, the abrasions you suffered complicate the situation. I can't very well put you in a cast until those are healed. We can immobilize with a brace, which will fit over the bandages. Once the abrasions are healed, we'll take more x-rays and make a determination then."

"How soon will you need to make a decision about surgery?" Brandon asked.

"We have about a two week window. I'd like to see her again in a week."

Lucy closed her eyes, willing herself to be calm. "What type of recovery time are we talking about before I can be fully functional again?"

"That depends on the course of treatment."

A non-answer.

When Brandon helped her into his Porsche and even buckled her seatbelt, Lucy stared at him. "I have to be able to work, Brandon."

His gaze was sympathetic. With a gentle touch to her cheek, he murmured, "We'll get it figured out. Let's get the prescription for the painkillers and get you home."

* * * *

When Lucy gave him the address for Mason's house, he ground his teeth in frustration. She'd been here almost a week, less than five miles from his family's summer home. He pulled up in front of the house, which stood dark and still in the night. There were no nearby neighbors.

"Do you have keys?" he asked her, switching off the Porsche's engine.

"No, but I left the kitchen door unlocked. It's around back."

Brandon grabbed the prescription from behind her seat, hopped out and came around to help her out. "Can you walk?"

Lucy sighed. "It's a fractured wrist, Brandon, not an ankle."

He grinned in the dark at her exasperated tone. "Lead on, then. You know where you're going."

"You don't have to stay," she said over her shoulder. "I'll be all right."

He touched her arm, holding gently until she stopped and turned. It was difficult to read her expression in the dark. "I'm not leaving, Lucy. Not this time."

"Suit yourself." A world of weariness lay in those two words, and he sensed it was more than the accident today, but then he'd seen that in her face earlier and Monday when she'd stormed into his office. Neither one of them had fared well in the wake of the plane crash.

She climbed the stairs to the deck and from there opened the door into the kitchen. He reached in, found the light switch and then followed her into the airy room.

"Have a seat, Lucy," he told her. "I'll get you some water so you can take these pain pills. Are you hungry?"

She shrugged. "Thirsty."

He located a glass, ran water in it then shook a couple pills into her hand before handing her the water. After she'd swallowed them, he touched her shoulder. "If you'd like to lie down, I can scramble you some eggs or make an omelet. I'm afraid that's about how far my cooking skills extend."

She smiled, and some of the tension eased from his shoulders. "That would be nice. Just scrambled eggs."

He watched her leave the kitchen, and for the first time in a couple months, hope surged. They were under the same roof. They were talking. Damn, if he could keep Mason away… He left thoughts of the other man alone for the time being and opened the refrigerator. Good Lord, other than yogurt and fruits and vegetables, there was nothing inside. He did manage to find some eggs.

While he heated the pan and mixed the eggs, Brandon decided a cook would be the first thing in order if he could ever convince Lucy to marry him. He paused for an instant. The word didn't make him break out in hives or wince…even a little. He did want her in his life for good. Now he had to convince her.

Brandon plated the eggs, added some sliced fruit and grabbed a bottle of Pellegrino. Following where he'd seen Lucy go, he discovered her curled on a loveseat, her head leaning into the corner and her eyes shut. She looked…defeated.

"Lucy? I have your food."

Those dark gray eyes of hers opened, focused on him. "Thanks, Brandon."

He brought in his own food, watched her while she ate and cleared the plates away when she was done. When he came into the room, she was sitting with her feet on the floor, her right hand brushing hair off her face. She glanced at him, then away.

Uneasiness ate at him. "Can I get you anything else?"

"No, thanks." She tucked a strand of hair behind her ear. "You've already done so much. I don't want to keep you any longer—"

"I'm not going anywhere." He cut into her rehearsed speech.

She focused on him and held his gaze. "I'm here. Home, such as it is, and not going anywhere. I'll be fine. You don't need to stay."

He held her gaze. "Yeah. I do. We both need it."

"I don't want to rehash the past," she whispered, but no conviction lay behind her words.

He squatted in front of her. "But it's lying there between us and not going away."

She closed her eyes for a moment. When she opened them again, tears glistened there. "I can't do this."

He caught her right hand, felt the fine tremble in it. "I'm not asking you to do anything right now other than let me stay with you tonight. God, Lucy." He stopped, swallowed then forced himself to go on, hearing the tightness in his voice. "When I saw you in the water… I'll sleep out here, but I need to make sure you're okay." So much pain lay behind those stormy irises of hers. "Come on. I'll help you get settled, get changed. Where do you sleep?"

She pressed her lips together as if she was trying to collect her emotions. "I'm using the room at the end of the hall, but I can do this on my own. I'm not a baby." Her cheeks were flushed.

With a touch to her chin, he turned her attention back to him. "This isn't about sex. You're one-handed right now. This is about preventing you any more pain."

A nervous giggle slipped out of her mouth. "I don't think I'm feeling any pain right now."

The tension between them eased. Brandon grinned. "Come on, kiddo. Up you go." After pulling her to her feet, he put his arm around her waist and guided her along the hallway. "Which room?"

"That one." She pointed, lurching at the same time. "Damn. I should have told you to give me one. I'm kind of a lightweight when it comes to painkillers."

He propped her against the doorjamb while he reached inside and found the light switch. "Fortunately, you'll be able to sleep it off."

Brandon tried to turn off his imagination and his emotions so he could help her get ready for bed. Since she could use only one arm, he ended up undressing her, finding her an oversized t-shirt, then tucking her into bed once she'd used the bathroom.

She grinned at him. "You'd make a good daddy," she whispered.

His hand hovered for an instant, then he tucked a wisp of hair behind her ear. Not what he was feeling at the moment. "Yeah. Go to sleep, baby, before you end up saying stuff you'll regret."

She caught his hand, her expression serious. He thought she was going to say something, but she shook her head and dropped her gaze. "'Night, Brandon."

His fingers trailed across her cheek. "Sleep, baby. I'll be here if you need me."

She smiled, but her eyes were already drifting closed. He turned off the lights and leaned on the doorframe for a few minutes. He told himself it was to make sure she was okay, but the reality was he didn't want to leave her, would have given just about anything to lie next to her and feel her snuggled close to him. When her breathing altered, letting him know she'd slipped into sleep, Brandon returned to the kitchen and cleaned the dishes they'd used.

At loose ends, he wandered, found her makeshift studio and examined what was there. This was the Lucy he knew. She had talked about working in clay and pottery while they were together in Colorado. Here he could be closer to her, the Lucy he loved. The woman he'd seen on the stage at Flamingo Road was a persona, but not her. After running his fingers along the edge of a beautifully glazed and fired bowl, he acknowledged how much it had hurt to realize she hadn't felt she could share that part of herself with him, that she had to hide it.

But hadn't they both hidden from each other?

Brandon returned to the living room and sat in an overstuffed chair, stretching his long legs in front of him while he fought off the urge to check on her again. How pathetic was that? He couldn't even leave her alone for five minutes without needing to see her. Forcing himself to use some restraint, he pulled his phone out and began checking messages. When he saw one from Mason Hatch, he frowned. The last thing he wanted to do was talk to him, but damn it, he was in the guy's house, sitting on his furniture. *Taking care of his woman?* Brandon wasn't even going there. That just opened a whole lot of shit he couldn't deal with tonight.

Brandon listened to Mason's message two times, then hit erase. Mason was at the marina onboard his own boat. He'd be here midday tomorrow so Brandon had better make use of the time he had. *What. The. Fuck?* He shoved the phone into his brother-in-law's shorts and leaned back, staring down the darkened hallway. First his father, then Stacey, now Mason. With everyone pushing him at Lucy, why did he hesitate?

* * * *

He must have fallen asleep. When Brandon awoke sometime later, his neck was stiff. After he sat up, he rubbed the crick in it and struggled to alertness. A minute passed before he remembered where he was. Mason Hatch's house. With Lucy. The sailing accident came to mind, seeing her flying into the air and then how still she'd been when he'd reached her. It was almost worse to relive it because now he knew who it was, knew how easily the boat could have plowed right over her.

He shook his head to clear those thoughts, becoming aware of sounds drifting down the hallway. Brandon sprang to his feet. Lucy? Something must be wrong. She was crying. Had she hurt her wrist by accident while she slept? God, he hoped not. Hurrying down the hall, he raked his fingers through his hair and blinked several times to rid himself of the last vestiges of sleepiness.

"Lucy?" he called, hurrying over to her in the darkness. She flailed on the bed, twisting in the covers. "Wake up. You're dreaming."

"Not you!" she cried. "Not you!"

Brandon's gut clenched. Was it Mason she wanted? He caught her arms, felt her shaking and heard her sobs. She cried with a hoarse weariness that made his throat tighten, as though she had cried this way night after night. When she continued to sob, he sat on the edge of the bed and took her into his arms, careful to keep from jarring her.

"Hush, Lucy. It's okay." He smoothed a hand over her hair.

"You were dead," she choked. "In my dream, it's always you I find dead when I dig you out." She twisted, reaching toward the night table. "Turn the light on. Please. Turn the *light on*."

Her tone bordered on hysteria, and Brandon hastened to comply. As soon as the lamp glowed, Lucy stared at her hands, breathing like she'd run a mile. "What is it? Are you in pain?"

She shook her head. "It's always so real. I can't make it go away until I see there isn't any blood." The *this time* was implicit. Brandon let his eyes close while he rested his cheek alongside her head. She trembled again. "And then I feel so guilty because I'm always so relieved. A man died and all I can feel is relief."

He pulled her across his lap, careful of her wrist, and tilted her chin so she had to meet his gaze. "There was nothing you could have done."

She twisted her face away. "I dug you out first, got you out. Only then did I try to help Hanson."

He cupped her chin in his hand. "Listen to me," he ordered. "There was nothing you could do."

"You don't know…"

"Yes," he interrupted. "I do. You had your head between your ankles. I didn't. When my memory returned, Lucy, it wasn't just the memories of you. I also regained my memories of what happened that afternoon. I saw him die." Brandon stopped, touched his forehead to hers. "There was nothing you could do. He was dead before the plane stopped moving." She clutched his shirt with her good hand. Silence stretched for another instant, then it was broken by her harsh sob. "That's it, baby," he coaxed. "Get it out. You did everything you could, more than many people would have, and thank God or I wouldn't be here."

"I've felt so guilty," she whispered.

"As I have. Even before I remembered, I knew there'd been something between us, had seen firsthand what you'd had to do." He stopped, struggling to get his emotions under control. "To know I failed you, when you needed me..." He couldn't continue, pressing her face to his body instead. When her arms crept up to hold him, he shuddered.

"I've missed you so, so much," she murmured.

"Then let me hold you now like I've longed to." He couldn't breathe as he waited for her response. If she turned him away this time, he would have to accept it was over.

Chapter 18

Could she accept what he offered? Was it that simple? Lucy let her head fall back so she could study his face. His blond hair was tousled, his cheeks rough with beard stubble and his eyes… His eyes were a little wary, a little vulnerable. In fact, they reflected what she felt. She touched his full lower lip with her fingertips, saw the heat blaze in his light hazel irises.

He needed to know what she felt, what she feared. She needed to tell him before they could move forward. He captured her hand, touched his lips to her fingertips, once again holding her gaze with his. His expression took her breath away.

"Lucy," he whispered. "God, baby, don't leave me hanging."

"I'm scared," she admitted, not even attempting to hide the way her voice shook.

He stroked his hand across her cheek. "Why?"

"All my life I've been alone, even when Gram was alive. Then I met you and we clicked. In a few days, I felt closer to you than I had to anyone…ever. When I pulled you out of that plane, Brandon, my only thought was I couldn't lose you. I would do anything…anything to keep you alive, keep you with me." She paused, closing her eyes for an instant and continuing in a voice choked with emotion she couldn't control. "Then when you looked at me and asked who I was…my world fell apart. I can't do that again."

Tears rolled down her cheeks. Brandon brushed them away with his thumbs and she watched his Adam's apple bob a couple of times. "I'm not going anywhere, Lucy. I can't change what's already happened. If there was any way I could, I would have been there to support you. Don't shut me out because you're afraid. Is that why you left?"

She shook her head, her mind going to their arrival at the hospital. "I didn't know who you were," she whispered. "Then it all blew up. You were this really rich, really powerful person. It was everywhere on the news. Your parents were there, looking so...so..."

He leaned his forehead against hers. "You don't have to explain. Strangely enough, I get that part. I should have told you. I'm sorry."

Lucy clutched at his shirt. She needed him to understand. "I didn't leave just because of me, because I was scared and hurt. Part of it was because of who you are...and what I am."

"Because you're a stripper, you mean?"

She nodded. "And my instincts were right. Look what happened. You can't be with me, Brandon. It will ruin your career."

"Bullshit," he growled. His arms tightened around her. "Look, we don't have to go over all this right now. You look exhausted, and I know I am. We should both get some rest."

Lucy stroked her fingers over his chest. "Would you stay with me? Hold me?"

"I can do that. And we'll talk in the morning. Really talk."

* * * *

Brandon woke with Lucy nestled in his arms. God, it felt good. It felt right. He pulled her tight, his hips—and the erection he sported—shoved flush with her round bottom. He groaned. Lucy shifted, her butt brushing him and making him ache even more.

"Brandon?"

"Right here, baby." She sighed and snuggled. Brandon swallowed. She needed comfort, not sex. He tried to remind himself, but part of his anatomy wasn't listening to his noble self-talk.

"You stayed." There was wonder in her voice, but instead of bringing him comfort, it brought him pain. She'd doubted it. His arms tightened.

"For however long you want me, however long you need me."

She rolled over to face him, careful to protect her injured wrist. "Would you kiss me?"

Would the sun rise? Would he be able to stop? "Yes."

He tilted her chin and lowered his mouth to hers. Need shuddered through him, but he kept tight control over it. He had a second chance and didn't want to blow it. With his lips, he teased hers until she opened to him like a flower blooming. A hoarse moan escaped as he forced himself to go easy when what he wanted to do was plunge inside her—her mouth, her body—marking her, making her his. Her hand pulled him closer, her tongue touched his lips and he was lost. He needed to stop. She was hurt. With monumental effort, he eased away from her mouth, leaned his forehead on hers. They both panted for breath.

"Please," Lucy whispered. "I need to be with you."

"You're hurt."

She brought one of his hands to her chest. "Here. Inside, I hurt. Heal this, Brandon. Heal us both."

His breath caught and then he caressed her cheek, slipping the hand to the back of her head so he could fuse their mouths once more. His hands moved over her restlessly, touching and relearning her body. He scooted away, slid his hands beneath her t-shirt and removed it, paying careful attention to her injured wrist.

When his hands slid beneath her panties, she stopped him. "I want to touch you."

He smiled. "Next time. This time is for you. I need to do this." He slid the silk down, tossed it aside and let his eyes feast on her nude body. She was his alone. And, though he had minded at the time, Brandon found the fact she had danced nearly nude in front of countless men didn't matter one iota to him. She was his, would always be his. Now he would convince her of the same thing, leave her in no doubt she needed only him. When he glanced at her face, he was surprised to see a blush on her cheeks. For him.

"Let me…" He didn't finish, instead dipping his head to taste her mouth. "So sweet. Lucy, I've missed this, missed you."

"I need you." The need was in her voice and her words, making his desire soar.

He returned to kissing her, letting his mouth slide along her throat and over her chest until his lips covered her puckered nipple and sucked it into his mouth. His rhythmic pull made her gasp and quiver. Brandon's cock throbbed, but he ignored it. He would do this for her. With restless movements, he slid his hands over her hips, cupped her buttocks and kneaded the firm globes. Even though it was tempting to unzip and enter, there had been too much haste in their relationship already. It seemed to him their lovemaking in Colorado had always had a frantic edge to it, and hurried wasn't the message he wanted her to get now. He wanted her to know how much he cherished her, how he would never again let her go.

With lips and tongue, he moved lower, across her belly to the dip between hip and thigh. She whimpered, twisting in his hands.

"Easy, baby."

The moment he touched her with his tongue, Lucy cried out and arched up into him. Brandon felt like a man who'd been lost in the desert and had found his oasis. The sounds of her passion urged him on so nothing but her complete capitulation to the pleasure he brought her would satisfy him. And when she arched up to him in climax, he trembled, unsure if he could control his own orgasm. When her body quivered in the aftermath, he wrapped her in his arms and held her.

"You…" she began.

"Don't worry about me. I'm good." Oh, and wasn't that the biggest lie. He ached with the need to come. "It's still early. Sleep, baby."

* * * *

The sun's rays shimmered through the blinds on the windows when Lucy at last awoke. She was alone, and a feel of the space next to her told her some time had passed since Brandon had left her side. Her satiety told her what happened earlier had not been just a dream. He had made love to her with his hands and his mouth, taking no pleasure for himself. She rolled over and stretched, the persistent throb in her wrist reminding her of her injury. The smell of coffee on the air stirred her appetite.

Would he still be the tender, passionate man who'd lain with her last night and this morning? Lucy trembled as she pushed up from the bed and padded into the adjoining bathroom. One damp towel was already hanging on a peg near the shower. She would clean up too before she went to find him.

Yes, it was a chicken way out, but she wasn't ready to face him yet. It wasn't until she started to get into the shower she realized she had another dilemma. While she could remove the soft cast on her wrist, the bandages were another matter. She'd figure it out, she always did. With her arm braced out of the way of the shower spray, Lucy managed to accomplish the task one-handed, then discovered drying was also difficult. Worse was getting dressed. In disgust, she called down the hall for Brandon.

He appeared at the end of the hall, his face pale until he saw she was all right. "What is it? What do you need?"

She sighed. "I can't get my bra on." When he grinned, then started to laugh, she stomped her foot. "Don't laugh. It is not funny."

He ambled down the hall. "Well, I have to admit, I have a lot more practice taking bras off than putting them on, but I'll be happy to help."

Lucy turned her back to him, her breath hitching when his fingers brushed her skin, followed by the snugness as he fastened the clasps of her bra.

"Looks like I'll have to move in with you so you'll be able to get dressed."

Her throat tightened. "Don't joke, Bran…"

"I'm not joking. Can you manage everything else? Because we need to sit and talk."

* * * *

He had to make her see they could be together. The stiff set of her shoulders right now was a good indication she wouldn't be easy to convince. The last thing Brandon wanted was her martyring herself and their relationship under the mistaken idea it mattered one bit that she'd been a stripper.

She pulled away from him. "I think I can handle the rest of it."

He dropped his hands. "All right, then. I'm making omelets for breakfast, with toast. After that, we've pretty much exhausted my culinary abilities."

"I'll be there in a couple of minutes."

He waited a heartbeat, hoping she would turn, but she kept her back to him. With a sigh, Brandon returned to the kitchen. It was already nine. Hatch had said he'd be here midday, and if Brandon knew the man, that meant right on the dot of noon. The real question was how to convince Lucy they needed to be together.

He waited until she'd eaten, although when he tasted his somewhat rubbery omelet, he thought he might have made a miscalculation. Brandon cleared the dishes off the table, topped off her coffee and sat.

"So I think it's time we hashed this thing out between us. I'm not much good at this shit, so I'm going to rely on what I do know and that's negotiating business deals." He shifted. "What's it going to take to get you in my life?"

Lucy stared at him open-mouthed. "Are we seriously having this conversation? Discussing out relationship like it's a business merger?"

"Well, fuck. I don't know how else to go about this. Damn it, Lucy, I love you. I want to marry you, have babies with you and grow old with you. I don't want to end up in any more plane crashes, but I would like to take you to Colorado, and I'd like to take you sailing far, far away on my sailboat, not necessarily in that order. There. My cards are on the table."

"I won't be the factor that causes a rift between you and your family," she stated. "You and I both saw the media feeding frenzy the moment they found out Jasmine LeFleur, Flamingo Road stripper, was the woman who'd saved you in Colorado. I won't go through that. I won't put your family through that."

"Do you love me, Lucy? Even a little?" He'd take any morsel he could get but, God, he wanted the whole pie.

"Of course I do, idiot," she snapped. "Why the hell do you think I've been avoiding you?"

"Okay. Time out. That doesn't even make sense. If you love me, wouldn't you want to spend time *with* me instead of *avoiding* me?" Brandon blew his breath out. "You keep bringing up this whole family thing, so let's get it out in the open. My mother has already thrown her fit, but trust me, she'll love you the minute she gets to know you because, Lucy, you've got guts and you've got class. My father's the one who told her to zip it, and told me to get the hell out of the office and come find you. So this whole scenario you've built about our relationship causing a rift in the fabric of the Barlow-Barrett family doesn't hold up." He shifted her coffee mug aside and grabbed her uninjured hand. "If you won't give me a chance because you don't love me enough or trust me enough, then say so. Put us both out of our misery."

Her eyes widened. "I do love you, Brandon. I love you so much it hurts when I'm not with you, but..."

He kissed her hand. "No buts. Mason, that asshole who I am now indebted to, fuck me very much, will be here at any moment. He arrived last night and went to his sailboat to give us time alone. So I guess we're both going to have to thank him—that is, if you'll agree to marry me."

"I will."

"Thank you, Jesus, Mary and Joseph." Brandon smiled. "I do have one request."

"What's that?"

"If I put a pole in my place, could you do a private dance for me—after you're healed, of course?"

Lucy laughed. "It's a deal. Invite the family. I'm sure it would be an eye-opening experience."

Brandon's laughter filled the house. "I don't think the majority of the Barlow-Barrett clan is anywhere near ready for that."

Epilogue

They kept their engagement quiet until the night of her showing. Right in the middle of it, Brandon got down on one knee in front of everyone gathered there and handed her the tiny pot he'd bought in Colorado. Every person inside Mason's went silent.

"Lucy," he said in a voice loud enough for everyone to hear, but also one with a faint tremor in it, "would you do me the very great honor of becoming my wife?"

She stared at the pot, remembering the afternoon he'd bought it, and had to blink the moisture from her eyes.

"It's beautiful," she whispered.

"Turn it over in your palm."

When she did, a sparkling diamond pendant trickled into her hand.

"I know you don't like to wear rings because of your pottery, so I hoped this would do instead. May I put it on you?"

"Yes! Oh yes. Stand up, Brandon, people are staring!"

As he settled the diamond and chain around her neck, his hands shaking ever so slightly while he fastened the clasp, everyone in the gallery applauded—including Alexander and Patricia Barlow-Barrett.

Meet the Author

From the moment Rhett walked out on Scarlett, Laura's been hooked on romance. Deciding truth really is stranger than fiction, she chose a career path in journalism. Laura now teaches English and has returned to her first love--writing fiction.

She lives with her husband and son in central North Carolina along with a menagerie of animals that includes five rowdy terriers and a gentle white mare named Tweed. When she's not reading or writing, Laura enjoys riding, photography, and baking the best darned cakes you've ever tasted.

Turn the page for a special excerpt of Laura Browning's

Broken Heart

Perfection isn't all it's cracked up to be.

Stacey Barlow-Barrett has the perfect life–or, at least, the illusion of one. She's married to the man her parents approved, and she's making it work. But keeping up appearances is wearing her down. Her husband, Jace, wants to start a family. Her former lover, Mason, is a business associate she can't cut off, and he twists the knife at every opportunity. Trying to make everyone happy–everyone except herself–has her on the verge of a breakdown.

When Jace's best friend moves in, everything that seemed tenuously tolerable is now completely unbearable, and Stacey realizes something is very wrong in her marriage. Jace is keeping up appearances too, and it's at Stacey's expense.

Mason is the only one she can turn to for help…if he can forgive her for marrying Jace while the sheets were still warm from their last encounter. And even if he does forgive her, and she does dig her way out of the mess her marriage has become, Stacey may not be ready for what he needs in return: love.

On sale now!

Chapter 1

Avoiding him was nearly impossible. Wherever Stacey looked, Mason Hatch was in her line of sight. Since she was attending her brother Brandon's wedding, she couldn't leave, but she sure wished Jace would stick by her side this once. She scanned the room, but her husband was nowhere to be seen.

"Hubby MIA again?" Mason's voice was as smooth as silk in her ear. The fact he simply echoed her thoughts didn't make his intrusion into them any more palatable. "I could tell you where to look, but I don't think you'd like what you'd find."

"Stop it!" Stacey hissed between clenched teeth. Every time she encountered Mason, he made some cryptic remark about her husband. Stacey was tired of it, in part because she had enough doubts concerning her marriage. But not today. She refused to have them today. Today was supposed to be perfect. Jason had made love to her last night, had tried once again to talk her into starting a family. She wanted children. She did, but something always held her back. She couldn't stall too much longer, doing so wasn't fair to either of them, yet the mere thought of a divorce in her oh-so-Catholic family made her shudder. God, was she really contemplating divorce? Her mother would flip.

"Just trying to make conversation among these Virginia purebreds," Mason purred, once again barging into her brain. Why was there always a hint of amusement in his voice, as if he were actually laughing at her? Yes, she had been unfair to him, but had his contempt been there all along? Had he always regarded her with a smirk?

She sneaked a glance, finding her heels brought her nearly eye-to-eye with him. He was not short by any means, she'd simply inherited every bit of the Barlow-Barrett height and her mother's slenderness to boot. How often she had wished for even a touch of her younger sister Preston's curviness and her infinitely more diminutive height.

"Why can't you single out someone else to talk to?" she demanded, knowing she sounded as petulant as she felt. "Don't you have a date?"

He arched one dark brow, his eyes glittering like obsidian. "Perhaps I'm conducting a scientific experiment."

"Oh? And what would your experiment be?" She didn't want to continue this conversation, but she had no defense against his goading, had never been able to resist it, and that was what had gotten them in trouble to begin with. He was the match. She was the kindling.

"To see if there's actually a living, breathing woman still left under your high-class brittleness, or has the rarified air of your married life already drained it away?"

It shouldn't hurt. Not anymore, but it seemed she could still bleed if pricked. And Mason was stabbing deep with his verbal needling. She stared into his still cynically amused expression. "Fuck you," she whispered, her lips barely moving because she felt so frozen.

"The F-bomb, baby? In public?" He laughed, letting his gaze drop along her body. "Been there, done that."

Before she could think of any response, he had walked away, leaving behind only the deep contempt with which he'd stared at her. Stacey stood at the edge of the laughter and the crowd, feeling more isolated than if she'd been standing alone on the deck of her sailboat somewhere in the middle of the ocean. She swallowed and stuck her chin up.

A Barlow-Barrett must always stand straight and hold her head high. It had been one of the hardest of her mother's lessons for Stacey to learn as a gawky teenager. Taller than her peers, what she'd wanted to do was slump. As she did now, right before she slunk away into some dark corner where she could lick her wounds in private. But there was never any privacy in her family. They were in the spotlight whether they liked it or not.

Stacey needed to move. If she continued to stand here on her own, she would draw attention, something her mother would never forgive. Feeling some disgust at how tied she still was to pleasing her parents, Stacey moved back among the guests. No one would be able to fault her for not circulating, not making people feel welcome. The entire time she nodded, smiled and made appropriate comments, one part of her brain was detached. Nearly a half hour passed before she saw Jason return to the ballroom in the company of a man she had seen once or twice at various functions she'd attended recently with her husband. They were both tall, attractive men--perfect foils for one another. Jace's dark hair appeared slightly ruffled, but his companion's short blond locks were in perfect order. Even as she looked at them, she saw the two men laugh before they gripped hands and parted company. Her husband looked more relaxed than he ever seemed to be with her.

Jace headed her way, a smile curving his generous mouth as he saw her. Cupping her elbow a moment later, he leaned in and kissed her lightly on the cheek. "You look lovely, Stacey, as always." His compliment sounded impersonal as his gaze skated over the gathering. "Everything going all right? No outbreak of pole dancing by the bride or her guests?"

"Jason!" Stacey admonished. "Lucy is a wonderful person. You know the dancing was only to support herself until her art career got going."

He grimaced. "Still, darling, a stripper, no matter how noble the cause, is not exactly our kind of people."

"You pay too much attention to what other people think," she shot back, then realized the same applied to her.

Stacey remembered the day she and Brandon had plucked Lucy from the bay after her dinghy capsized. She'd been prepared to think badly of the woman until then, but after meeting her and getting to know her, Stacey had realized how lucky Brandon was. She opened her mouth to defend her brother's bride, then shut it. She didn't want to create any dissension with her husband, not when it seemed things might be going better between the two of them. Besides, her defense would do nothing to change what was so ingrained as to be second nature to him. Anything or anyone different was hushed, hidden or looked down upon.

"People like us have to, darling. Have you thought any more about what we discussed last night?" Jason's hand rubbed the small of her back, his head bent solicitously to her.

Her stomach fluttered with nerves rather than desire. "I don't know, Jace. I… Can you give me a little more time?"

Displeasure flitted across his aristocratic features before he once again assumed the urbane smile he wore at all social functions. "We're Catholic, darling. Babies are expected. You'll turn thirty next month, so you're not getting any younger."

She wasn't getting any younger? As if her eggs were any older than his sperm? But Stacey didn't say anything. Once again she heard her mother's voice, like a metronome of patrician aphorisms. As a Barlow-Barrett, you must support your husband. Lord, she was trying, but it seemed more and more that she was the only one in this marriage with a legitimate career, and getting damn little support of her own.

"I'll think it over," she finally muttered. It would be an easier decision if you'd ever give me an orgasm or even look me in the eye while we make love. It might be on the tip of her tongue to tell him so, but it would never actually leave her mouth. She wouldn't dare. Not with Jace. Not like she had with Mason. She'd been able to say anything to him. She glanced nervously again and found the man in her thoughts still watched her, this time from across the room, and he still wore an expression of cynical amusement.

Tilting her chin, she pasted a smile on her face and turned to her husband. "I don't know why I said that, darling. Of course I want to have children. I had just thought we could wait until the excitement of the wedding was over with. You know, so it would be easier to change my lifestyle--more exercise, less alcohol, maybe cutting back on my client list."

Jason was smiling again. This time he leaned down to kiss her lingeringly on the lips. Sometimes he seemed more demonstrative in public than he was at home. Stacey relaxed a bit, noticing for the first time the tanginess of his aftershave. She sniffed. "Is that a new cologne?"

Her husband laughed. "Mmm. Yes. Do you like it?"

She shrugged. "It just seems different."

He glanced around the room once more, almost as though he were searching for someone. "I hope a lot of things will be different, Stacey, better."

She looked at him in some confusion, but the approach of an old friend of the family prevented her from questioning what he meant.

* * * *

Mason ground his teeth as he watched Winchester laughing with his wife. If what he suspected was true, Stacey Barlow-Barrett--oops, Winchester--was in for some serious disillusionment, but he wouldn't be the one to burst her bubble of domestic bliss. In fact, he'd already dropped too many hints over the last couple months on those occasions when running into her at the gallery had been unavoidable. It would be better all the way around if he put her where she belonged--in the past-- and moved on with his life. So why was it so damn hard to do?

When his date, an aide for a senator he counted among his clients, stepped off the dance floor, he handed her a fresh glass of champagne and set his arm around her waist. If the gesture was more intimate than their first date called for, he wasn't ready to apologize for it now. That could come later when he dropped her safe and sound at her door with a peck on the cheek and returned to his penthouse alone.

There was only one woman in this room he'd had the urge to make a commitment to, and she was taken. Mason sneaked one last look at

Stacey. How many people were truly aware what passion lurked beneath her cool, blond exterior? He seriously doubted her husband was one of them.

Mason turned his gaze to the bride. Lucy Cameron danced, a bit stiffly, in the arms of her father-in-law, Alexander Barlow-Barrett. Only the elder Barrett could make a professional dancer appear ill at ease. The guy was the poster child for puritanical American capitalistic dynasties. It amazed Mason that already three of Barrett's children had found their own ways to rebel. Brandon had just married Lucy, a former exotic dancer. The eldest Barlow-Barrett, Seth, had quit the family's newspaper empire to run his own small town paper on the Delaware coast, and the sister, a couple years younger than Stacey, had beaten them all--bearing a child out of wedlock, becoming a veterinarian and finally settling down with a horse-trainer husband. Mason discounted the two youngest siblings. Phillip was too focused on his legal career and the girl apparently wasn't old enough to instigate her own rebellions yet, so only Stacey remained--the dutiful daughter. God damn her.

Mason could still feel her hips arching against his and hear her crying out in passion. Fuck. He set his drink aside and nabbed his date's, setting it aside too. "Let's dance," he growled. It was a fast number, which suited the hell out of him. Maybe if he worked up a sweat, he could work out the lust he still felt for the eldest Barlow-Barrett daughter, lust he no longer had a right to feel.

"Are you having a good time?" he asked his date.

She nodded, her glance darting around the room. "This is like being at a who's-who of Washington powerbrokers. God, Mason, how did you get to be friends with people like the Barlow-Barretts?"

Mason laughed. "Trust me. I'm no friend of theirs. Lucy Cameron, the bride, is one of the artists my gallery represents. Most of the time her husband is torn between punching me in the face or thanking heaven for me."

His date's only reaction was a slightly puzzled smile. Just as well. He didn't want to go into explanations of his not-so-willing role as cupid. He still kicked himself for that, but then anyone could look at Lucy and Brandon and see there would never be anyone else for either of them. When the song ended, another male guest claimed his date. He glanced around the dance floor and saw Winchester escort his wife onto the floor. Mason felt only relief, but when he saw Winchester's friend take over on the next song, a slow number, the only thing he could think was fuck no.

* * * *

Stacey had hoped to dance the slow song with Jace. She needed to feel him next to her, needed reassurance that everything was all right with their world. Now she was in the arms of Justin Worthington, one of Jace's closest friends. She hadn't realized who it was when she'd seen them together earlier. Jace had mentioned Justin a lot, but it had always seemed to her there was an edge of tension to him when he did and, until today, she had never met him.

"I'm so happy to meet you," Justin told her now. "Jace talks of you constantly."

Stacey gave him a look she was sure must be slightly puzzled. "Really? He's mentioned you too. I can't believe we haven't met before now."

His grip on her hand tightened slightly. "I've been working out of the country until recently."

She nodded. "I hate you missed our wedding. I know Jace wanted you there. It must have been a disappointment not to be able to share the celebration."

Justin smiled, his green eyes twinkling. "Now I'm in the area, maybe we'll be able to remedy that."

Was it her imagination, or had he pulled her slightly closer? As he turned her in time with the music, his thigh brushed against hers. Now she was uncomfortable. By no means did she consider herself a prude, but she could have sworn more than his thigh had touched her. Just about to open her mouth to ask him to hold her less closely, the sight of Mason tapping her partner on the shoulder had her clamping her mouth shut. She wouldn't mind a rescue, but exchanging Justin for Mason was like jumping from a campfire into a forest fire.

"May I cut in?"

Justin smiled graciously, but something in the way the two men eyed one another made Stacey catch her breath for an instant.

"Certainly." Justin smiled at her and said, "I'm sure we'll be seeing a lot more of each other, Stacey."

It was only when Mason spun her back into the crowd on the dance floor, and she caught a whiff of the spicy bite of Justin's cologne, that she realized Justin wore the same scent her husband did. Stacey shook her head slightly. Maybe that was how Jace had discovered it. After all, it was obvious the two men had re-established their long-standing friendship.

"Are you all right?" Mason's rumbled inquiry caught her off guard so she nearly stumbled. He caught her, his hand on her hip where, to her chagrin, he left it. The tingling it sent along her nerve endings filled her with guilt.

"Yes. Get your hand off my ass."

He moved it to the small of her back, his thumb stroking her spine through the silk of her evening dress. "So exactly why I love you. You appear to be such a lady, but you have a mouth like a sailor."

"Mason," she muttered. "Please don't. This one night, can't we have a ceasefire?"

"I didn't start this war, Blondie, but I'm willing to negotiate terms." His expression was inscrutable.

"There are no terms, Mason. I'm married. I won't be unfaithful to my husband."

"How old-fashioned of you. I hope your spouse is equally reciprocative."

"Stop it." Stacey felt as though he took her heart and twisted it in his grasp. "I'm sorry things didn't work out between us."

Mason put his mouth next to her ear. "Don't be sorry, baby. You were one of the best fucks I've ever had…and had…and had."

She couldn't control the gasp, the hurt stabbing through her, nor could she control the way she jerked away from him. Aware their sudden cessation of dancing would attract attention, Stacey put a hand to her mouth. "Excuse me," she said loud enough so the other couples dancing could hear. "I feel ill."

Without giving him a chance to grab hold of her again, she rushed from the dance floor and out of the ballroom in search of the sanctuary of the women's lounge. She longed to simply break down, but she knew her mother, knew her family. Someone would be in here in a moment, and she needed to have a believable story to cover behavior that had drawn unwanted attention. Rushing into one of the stalls, she slammed the door behind her, stared at the toilet and let out a defeated sigh. From years of practice, she leaned over, stuck a finger down her throat and gagged before she brought up the contents of her stomach.

"Stacey, darling?" It was her mother's voice. "Are you ill?"

She leaned one hand against the marble wall then grabbed a wad of tissue. "It's nothing, Mother."

"You're not pregnant, are you?"

There was such a wealth of hope in her mother's voice, but all Stacey felt were manacles tightening another notch around her wrists and throat.

* * * *

Mason had endured all he could. Even for Brandon and Lucy's sake, he couldn't stay here any longer. He was making himself miserable, and he'd made Stacey quite literally sick. He watched the doorway through which she'd fled, had seen her mother follow her, and waited now to see them return. As much as he wanted to get the hell out of there, he wouldn't until he was sure she would be fine.

What the fuck had he been thinking? How could he have said that to her? It would be better all the way around if he made sure to avoid any contact with her. She had made her bed the moment she'd accepted Jason Winchester's engagement ring. If her marriage now turned out to be something other than what she'd hoped, it was none of his concern. As soon as he saw her return to the ballroom with her mother, he located his date, making the excuse he had plans to sail early the next morning.

After dropping off the senator's aide, Mason drove past the house where he and Stacey had met. It was nearly two years ago now. And how pathetic was that? He was still lusting after a woman who'd dumped him so long ago. As the Porsche idled outside the brownstone, Mason remembered seeing her for the first time. Tall and willowy, dressed in a conservative suit with her hair pulled back into a neat bun, she'd turned her Barlow-Barrett haughtiness on him, thinking he was nothing more than a delivery boy. He'd set her straight in pretty short order, right before he'd eased her tight skirt up, shoved her lacy underwear to one side and taken her on the dining room table. Even remembering it now, so long after the fact, his cock swelled and his balls throbbed.

That was what pissed him off more than anything. He knew, given half a chance, he'd do the same thing again, married or not. But no matter how bitter he was, he wouldn't be the one to disillusion her about her husband. That was a journey she'd have to make on her own.

* * * *

They were going home. Finally. While Jace drove the Jaguar, Stacey leaned her aching head against the rest and stared out the passenger window. She wanted nothing more than to be able to take off the fancy clothes, let down her hair and soak in her tub with a glass of seltzer water in hand. Instead, in the side mirror, she saw the headlights of Justin Worthington's car. Jace had invited him for a drink. Stacey sighed. Her husband caught her hand.

"Are you feeling better, darling?"

"Yes." Did she have a choice? Without even asking, he had invited his friend to their home, so no matter how she actually felt, she would still need to play hostess for their guest.

But of course, she was positive none of what was going through her mind showed on her face when she smiled and welcomed Justin inside. It would go against everything she'd been taught to be less than gracious to a guest. When she started to remove the silk shawl from around her shoulders, it was Justin who took it from her. His grin was charming. "Allow me."

"Thank you." Stacey watched as he folded it carefully and laid it across the arm of the chair near the steps. It helped redeem him a bit in her eyes. Jace was never so careful with her things. Stacey hated disorder. Justin was obviously a man who did as well. Perhaps she had only imagined his penis brushing against her thigh while they danced, but even so, she supposed she could excuse him. After all, it wasn't necessarily something a man could control, was it?

"Sherry, darling?" Jason asked. At her nod, his glance moved to Justin. "And you, Justin? Still drinking Remy Martin?" At the other man's nod, Stacey watched her husband splash some of the cognac in two snifters. After handing her the glass of sherry, he delivered one of the snifters to Justin. Stacey settled herself on one end of the couch, a bit unsettled when Justin seated himself in the chair nearby, close enough his knee nearly brushed hers.

After a sip from her sherry, she steeled herself. "So, do you also know Brandon?" She was trying to figure out how Justin had become one of the guests at the wedding, although she couldn't remember seeing him at the church.

He laughed. "The groom? No, I don't know either your brother or his lovely bride. I happened to show up at the club, thinking I might get a decent, quiet meal there, when I ran into Jace. He invited me in to join the festivities."

She smiled and darted a glance at her husband, who seemed to be watching them both with unusual intensity. When she raised a brow at him, he shook himself and smiled. "You know, it's uncanny, darling. There is an amazing resemblance between the two of you."

Justin laughed. "Coincidence, Jace, I can assure you. I don't believe any of the Worthingtons, other than me, have ever traveled east of the Mississippi. That would certainly preclude any chance of our actually being related."

Stacey laughed, but she had to admit, Jace was somewhat accurate. Both she and Justin had blond hair of a similar color, though his was closely cropped while hers was confined in a sleek French twist, the way her husband liked it. They were of a similar height, particularly when she wore heels, and even his build was slender, though she had a feeling from having danced with him he was a lot stronger than he might initially appear. "You are too funny, darling. To even imagine Alexander Barlow-Barrett might have strayed…"

Her father was far too uptight and upright. She had spent a lifetime trying to live up to his strict ideas of what was right and wrong. And even though she had done everything she'd ever been asked, had gone to the right schools, participated in the right sports and married the right man, she sometimes couldn't help but feel she was more of a disappointment to him than the children who had thrown everything back in his face.

Jason laughed. "You're right. How absurd. So, tell me Justin, how are the renovations going on your condo?"

The other man grimaced. "None too well, I'm afraid. Everything is torn up. The contractors have mentioned having me relocate for a month or so until they get the heaviest work out of the way."

Before she realized it, Stacey impetuously invited, "You must stay here, Justin. We have plenty of room, and I know the staff get bored with only Jace and me rattling around in this big house. We bought it with plans for the future…"

He touched her hand. "I wouldn't want to intrude. You two haven't even been married a year."

Jace set his glass aside. "It wouldn't be any intrusion. We'd love to have you, wouldn't we, Stacey?"

She had regretted the impulse as soon as the invitation had left her mouth, but she could hardly take it back now. What had she been thinking, particularly when Jason had made it plain he wanted to get busy starting a family? But the invitation had been made, so she smiled and nodded. "Of course you must move in here while the work on your place is finished. I won't hear of anything else."

His hand stroked her forearm. "That's very generous of you, Stacey." His gaze shifted to Jason, though his hand remained on her arm. "Thanks, man. You're a real friend to share your home with me. I should get home, leave you two to get to bed."

* * * *

Jason prowled his study long after Stacey had gone to bed. After tossing back another brandy, he slumped into the chair behind his desk, rubbing his aching temples. He couldn't believe Justin had actually come. He'd emailed him just two days ago, knowing he was on yet another business trip, but too upset over the news he'd gotten to consider the consequences of contacting him.

And Justin had come back. Jace's throat tightened. He'd surprised him by appearing at the wedding. As soon as Jace had seen him, he'd dragged him into the deserted men's locker room where Justin had wrapped him in his arms. They'd always been so careful, so discreet. Would they be able to continue if Justin was under the same roof?

Restless, Jace popped out of his chair again. He pulled shut the door to his study so Stacey wouldn't overhear and called Justin--his best friend and the man he loved more than life itself.

www.ingramcontent.com/pod-product-compliance
Lightning Source LLC
Chambersburg PA
CBHW020446270626
47155CB00022B/1706